Bridie's Choice

Karly Lane lives on the mid north coast of New South Wales. Proud mum to four beautiful children and wife of one very patient mechanic, she is lucky enough to get to spend her day doing the two things she loves most—being a mum and writing stories set in beautiful rural Australia.

Also by Karly Lane
North Star
Morgan's Law
Poppy's Dilemma

Karly
LANE

Bridie's Choice

ARENA
ALLEN&UNWIN

This edition published in 2013
First published in 2012

Arena Books, an imprint of
Allen & Unwin
83 Alexander Street
Crows Nest NSW 2065
Australia
Phone: (61 2) 8425 0100
Email: info@allenandunwin.com
Web: www.allenandunwin.com

Cataloguing-in-Publication details are available
from the National Library of Australia
www.trove.nla.gov.au

ISBN 978 1 74331 757 0

Set in Sabon by Midland Typesetters, Australia
Printed in Australia by McPherson's Printing Group

15 14 13

To the women of my family:
thank you for your inspiration, wisdom and love.

Bridie Farrell watched in the rear-view mirror as the *Welcome to Tooncanny* sign faded from sight.

With the town finally behind her and infinite possibilities ahead, her heart should have leapt with excitement, but something was holding her back. As always.

The horizon blurred as heat weaved its shimmering dance, seeming to lure her with its promise of adventure.

Luke.

An image of his face flashed through her mind and she slammed on the brakes, sending a slew of gravel up beneath the dusty old Holden. She dropped her forehead against the steering wheel in defeat. Squeezed her eyes shut.

She was never going to escape.

She reluctantly lifted her head and stared at the worn old picture tucked into the sun visor. The face of the bright-eyed smiling woman in the photo was almost identical to her own. She shoved the ute into gear and did a U-turn, heading back to town. There were too many ties binding her to this place.

They were *never* going to allow her to leave.

One

Shaun Broderick muttered a curse as he pulled up in his custom-ordered Holden Maloo R8 ute. His father was striding out of the house towards him. The engine had barely stopped, the dust wasn't yet settled, and already the old man was on the warpath.

'I wanted those fences in the bottom paddock fixed this morning. What the hell time do you call this?' Douglas Broderick demanded as Shaun shut the driver's door.

Shaun saw the scowl Douglas sent his fancy sports ute and secretly enjoyed the fact that his shiny, impractical vehicle annoyed his father so much. He whistled Mick, his black and tan kelpie, out of the back.

'I had to go in and see the bank first thing this morning, I told you that last night. I have a few phone calls to make now, and then I'll get to the fencing,' Shaun said, readying himself for his father's next outburst.

'And I told *you* to forget about that stupid notion. You don't mess with something that's working, son.'

'I've leased that bottom fifty acres off you, Dad, just like we agreed, and I'm going to plant canola. I'll prove what I've been trying to tell you for the last five years.'

'I'm not sinking any of Jinjulu's money in this stupid venture,' Douglas warned.

Shaun bit down hard on his anger. 'I know that, Dad, that's why I went in to see Larry Jenkins. I'm doing this on my own.'

'It's a waste of time and money. Canola's too expensive. We've always grown wheat, that's where the steady money is.'

'Broadleaf crops are more expensive initially, yes, but if you'd just look at the printout I've been trying to get you to read, you'd see that in the long term they're more profitable. It's been researched, Dad; proven.'

'Proven!' Douglas spat. 'By a bunch of university know-it-alls who've never even set foot on a property in their lives.'

Shaun closed his eyes and silently counted to ten, trying to control his temper. Why was it so hard to get the old man to hear him out? Why did he continue to make things so difficult?

He couldn't help it. 'Do you think I'd be wasting my breath trying to get you to change your mind if I didn't know it worked? What do you think I've been doing all these years?'

'Wasting your bloody time working on other people's

properties instead of here where you belong—that's what,' Douglas snapped.

'Yeah, well, now I'm back.' Shaun leaned into the cab to grab his akubra. He slammed it on his head, moving around his father to head inside and make his calls.

'I want those fences finished today,' he heard as he walked up the stairs to the timber verandah that ran the length of the old homestead.

'Yes, Dad.' Pulling open the french doors, he breathed a sigh of relief. Everything was always a battle with the old man.

His plan was simple: he'd lease the land off his father, since the old bastard wouldn't make it easy, and put his years of study to use. He believed in this new approach. He also understood his father's reluctance—Douglas wasn't alone in his opposition, the majority of older farmers had the same reaction.

Change was always slow to make it out here. His father's generation hadn't had the privileges his generation had. University had been a thing alien and out of reach for most of his father's peers. And when were they supposed to find the time to update their knowledge? If it wasn't sowing time, there was drenching or harvesting or a thousand other things to be done. It was easy to understand his father's reluctance, but what Shaun couldn't fathom was why the hell Douglas had allowed him to go away to study if he didn't intend to let him implement the things he'd spent all those years learning.

Today's meeting at the bank had been the first step in his plan to drag Jinjulu Station into the new millennium—with or without his father's backing.

That evening the mouth-watering smell of roast beef greeted Shaun as he hung his hat on the peg inside the back door. It had been a long day out in the paddocks fixing fences. The short, stout woman standing at the stove, stirring the gravy, turned and smiled at him.

'That smells good, Daisy,' he said. 'Hope you cooked enough to feed an army. I could eat a horse and chase the rider.'

'It's almost ready, so go wash up and get to the table. The others are already in there waiting.'

Shaun snagged a piece of meat on his way past, and scooted away as a wooden spoon swung around, only just missing him. 'Go on with ya, ya cheeky devil,' Daisy called after him. It was a nightly ritual that had been going on for as long as Shaun could remember. He thought the world of Jinjulu's resident housekeeper-cum-cook-cum-first-aid officer, stand-in roustabout and general dogsbody. The woman was ageless. She looked the same as she had when Shaun was a kid—God only knew how old she really was.

After he'd washed his hands and face he made his way through to the dining room where the family was required to gather each night for the evening meal. It was important to his mother to keep up the appearance that theirs was a normal loving family. He had no idea why; it wasn't as though there was anyone around to witness it. Still, it kept his mother happy, and his father was happy if his wife was happy, so it was paramount to ensure Constance Broderick got her own way.

His parents sat at each end of the dining table, an heirloom passed down through the generations. His family history humbled him; the original Brodericks had carved

Jinjulu out from nothing but a vast scrubby wilderness to the impressive business it was today. The weight of all that history was a heavy burden, but he was prepared to carry it. He'd always loved this property; it was part of him and he felt a deep kinship with the land. Jinjulu was in his blood.

Suddenly an image flashed through his mind—a memory of his own hands covered in blood—and he glanced across at the empty place setting. Once he would have sent Jared a brief glance to gauge the general atmosphere around the table, but those days were gone.

Shaun had left Jinjulu seven years ago, grieving and ridden with guilt. He'd come home to find that his mother still set a place for Jared at the dining table. His bedroom was untouched—magazines, wallet and keys still on the bedside table, clothes still in the cupboard. Each time he'd tried to bring it up with Constance, to suggest that it was perhaps time to pack away Jared's things, she'd steadfastly refused to discuss it—subject closed. He'd been home almost twelve months now and he still wasn't used to it.

Shaun thought it best to keep his head down and mouth shut tonight and escape as soon after the meal as he could.

'Nice of you to join us, Shaun.' His mother's tone irritated him. It was starting early tonight: he'd barely even sat down.

'Sorry, Mum, but someone has to work around here,' he said, striving for a cheerful tone.

'Some of us started work at the proper time this morning. We didn't skip off into town and waste half the day without telling anyone where we were,' his father muttered from the end of the table.

A mock 'tsk' drew his father's gaze from Shaun to his

sister Phoebe. 'And I don't know why you're being such a smart arse; at least he was out of bed before noon.'

If Shaun got too much of his father's attention, then Phoebe suffered from the complete opposite. When doing her best got her nowhere, she had tried a different angle and started getting into as much trouble as she could away at boarding school. But no matter what she did, it seemed the old man would barely give her the time of day. Shaun had given up trying to convince her she was really better off not having him breathing down her neck all the time. Her latest stunt must surely have caught Douglas's attention, though. She'd been suspended from school for having drugs in her room and sent to counselling.

Shaun had been shocked when Phoebe first arrived home. Gone was the fresh-faced girl he remembered; in her place was this broody shell of a young woman who dressed in black and rarely smiled. His parents, it seemed, were just as bemused by their new sullen daughter as he was. Once, Phoebe had worshipped the ground he'd walked on, always following him and Jared around. The three of them had been inseparable . . . until Jared's death.

'Well, it's all good now, I got the last of the fencing finished, and I even stayed back on my own time to do it.' Shaun couldn't resist taking a jab at the so-called wage his father paid him just to remind him who he worked for.

'If you'd started on time, you'd—' Douglas began.

'Can we all please just eat without bickering for once?' Constance cut in from her end of the table.

Suitably chastised, the family concentrated on their meal. Shaun's stomach was growling and he was happy to turn his attention to the delicious spread of roast beef, veggies and gravy. Thank goodness for Daisy; sometimes Shaun thought she was the only good thing about Jinjulu these days.

'Have you read through the information I left on your desk, Dad?' Phoebe asked eventually, breaking the silence.

'You seriously think I'm going to change my mind about sending you overseas on some paid holiday?'

'It's not a holiday—I'll be studying. It's a chance to study art at one of the most prestigious art schools in the world. It's what I want to do, Dad. I want to apply for this course in France.'

'Have you ever noticed the only famous artists are dead ones?' Douglas said, popping his fork into his mouth.

'That's rubbish,' Phoebe said irritably.

'Hanging around those artsy-fartsy types in Sydney was what got you into trouble in the first place.'

'No, Dad, I didn't take up drugs because of my *friends*.'

'If we can't trust you to behave yourself here, why on earth would we trust you on the other side of the world?'

'This is important to me,' she said in a brittle tone.

Shaun listened to the exchange in silence. He felt bad for his sister—there was no way their father was going to pay for a semester of art school in France. He'd been on the end of this kind of plea bargain himself many times and knew it was pointless.

'I suggest you find something *useful* to apply for right here in Australia. And hurry up about it.'

Phoebe gave a small snort.

'I'm sure we can find you something to keep you occupied around here,' Douglas went on.

'I'll move into the flat in Sydney.'

'And do what?'

'More than I'd be doing out here,' she mumbled, poking at her food. 'I don't even know why I had to come back out here. I'd rather stay in the city.'

'Because Jinjulu is your home,' Douglas declared, settling back in his chair. 'Besides, we all know what kind of trouble you get into when you're left unsupervised. Clearly you can't be trusted on your own.'

'I'm not a child, Dad.' Phoebe jumped to her feet. 'I don't need supervision! This place gives me the creeps and it hasn't been a *home* for a long time, not since . . .'

She didn't need to say any more; they all knew what she meant. And she was right, Shaun thought, dropping his gaze to the table top. Jinjulu hadn't been a home since Jared died.

Two

Bridie sat in the principal's office and for a minute felt disoriented. It was almost as if time had stood still and she had been summoned into this very room as an angry, disillusioned teenager. She'd matured since then . . . into an angry, disillusioned *adult*, but other than the brand-spanking-new computer on the desk, little else seemed to have changed in the last decade.

'I really don't know what you expect me to say here, Miss Farrell. Your brother understood that he was on his last warning, after the exploding watermelon incident . . .'

Bridie heard her younger brother's unrepentant chuckle beside her and kicked his foot in warning. 'It was a stupid prank, and it was *wrong*,' she said, sending her brother a glare before returning her attention to the pompous man across the desk. She forced herself to sound calm as she went on, 'But he wants to get into the army at the end of the year and that's dependent on his grades. He can't afford to be expelled now.'

'He should have thought about that before he threatened a member of my staff.' The principal leaned back in his chair and nonchalantly linked his hands behind his head.

Bridie felt her jaw clench at the familiar gesture. Puddin' Guts Shaffer had always been under the misguided impression that he was some kind of tough-guy principal, in touch with the younger generation. How he had come by this impression was a mystery to Bridie. The red tufts of what remained of his hair, and his thick-rimmed glasses perched on his too-large nose, made him look as though he should have been put out to pasture years ago.

From behind his desk, he liked to look down upon the summoned as though he were some kind of presiding judge. It made Bridie sick. Thankfully, you didn't work in the town's only drinking establishment without hearing a few titbits of gossip along the way. She'd heard rumours about the good Principal Shaffer and his habit of travelling three hours out of town to visit some unknown woman for the weekend . . . seeming to forget his long-suffering wife at home, and their pale, unfortunate-looking children with bright orange hair. She'd lost any respect she might have had for the man after she'd heard that.

'I agree that it's unacceptable to swear at a teacher, and he *should* be punished for that, but to suspend him would be counterproductive. Surely we can work out a suitable punishment and still allow him to stay in school?'

'I take the wellbeing of my staff members very seriously, Miss Farrell. I will not tolerate threats to their welfare.'

Luke gave a snort of contempt. 'I was only joking. As if it's even humanly possible for someone to shove their head up their own arse, sir.'

Bridie shut her eyes and bit back a groan of dismay before turning another glare upon her petulant younger brother.

'That is *exactly* the sort of disrespect I'm talking about,' put in Principal Shaffer. 'I don't know why I was expecting anything other than trouble from a Farrell.'

Bridie felt the familiar rise of indignation inside her chest. 'Excuse me?'

'Look, I realise your . . . family circumstances are less than ideal; however, that is no excuse for unruly behaviour.'

'And what family circumstances would those be?' she asked icily.

'Surely you don't want to go into all that now,' he said, easing back further in his chair and eyeing her with a self-righteous expression.

'I think we *should* go into it. Exactly what are you trying to imply? That because in the past there have been other Farrells who have caused trouble here, Luke's now being discriminated against for it? Or are you referring to the fact our father's in prison? Or maybe it's because Luke's being brought up by his older sister? Exactly which family circumstance would you be referring to?'

'All I'm saying is, despite . . . all the things you've mentioned, they still don't give Luke the right to be disruptive. I have plenty of other students to consider. Students with very bright futures, who are not here to waste my time.'

Bridie held the man's smug gaze as she got to her feet, hitching her head at Luke to indicate they were leaving. 'Unlike my brother, I don't like to believe that anything in this world is impossible, so I think you *should* give shoving your head up your arse a really good try. And while you're at it, maybe you should look around for your morals—it appears you've lost them as well.'

Bridie hurried her brother out of the office, ignoring the fact that he chortled the whole way back to the car.

Bridie pulled the door of the ute shut with a bang and shot Luke a thunderous look. That wiped the smirk from his face, and he wisely shut his mouth. She tried to force herself to concentrate on the drive home, but the truth was she was so angry that when she pulled into the driveway she could barely remember the trip.

'He's right, you know,' Luke said as she switched off the engine. 'What difference is it going to make? I don't even like school. I'm going to leave at the end of the year anyway.'

'What about the army? They told you, providing you stayed in school and kept passing, you could join up as soon as you turned seventeen. I thought that's what you wanted to do?' Bridie demanded.

'I don't want to do that any more.'

'Since when?'

'Since ... I don't know.' He shrugged irritably and looked out the window.

'Luke.' She forced him to look at her. 'Since when?'

'Since a few months ago. It was just a stupid kid thing. I'm not a kid any more.'

'It's because of Jacko and Spider, isn't it?' Bridie said, slumping in her seat.

'I told you, I've just changed my mind. Would you get off my back about it? It's no big deal.'

'It's your future, Luke. It *is* a big deal. The army was your ticket out of this place.'

'You're the one who wants to get out of here so bad—why don't *you* join the army?'

'If I had a choice, trust me I'd take it. Tomorrow I'm calling the Department of Education. Everyone knows Puddin' Guts is a tosser. I'm sure they can work out some way to keep you in school.'

'No.'

'Excuse me?'

Luke lifted his dark eyes, so much like their father's, to her face and held her gaze. 'I'm not going back to school. I'm done.'

'You're *done*?' Her voice rose an octave in disbelief at what she was hearing.

'I'm not going back to school. Spider's dad said he'd get me some work.' He got out of the car and slammed his door shut, leaving Bridie staring after him in stunned silence.

She quickly recovered her wits. Shoving open her door, she stormed inside, following her brother into the kitchen, where he was examining the contents of the fridge. 'What the hell are you talking about?' she said, pushing the fridge door shut.

Luke yelped and withdrew his head seconds before the door slammed on it.

'Spider's dad is a crook and you damn well know it,' she went on. 'There's no way you're going to work for that man, do you hear me?'

'You can't tell me what to do, Bridie. I'm sick of it.'

'I'm your legal guardian, mate. I can tell you exactly what to do.'

'If I have a job to go to, I can leave school. I'm telling you, I'm not going back there, whether you like it or not.'

'Luke, you're making a huge mistake. What about all the things you wanted to do? You wanted to travel, to buy a decent car. You're never going to be able to do that if you leave school now. Do your exams, apply for the army, and afterwards you can do anything you want to.'

'Maybe I want to stay here. I can buy a decent car and make money here. Spider and Jacko make twelve hundred a week. How much do you make?'

'Spider and Jacko are going to end up in jail very soon— you know damn well they're mixed up in all sorts of nasty crap. Shearers as young as them don't make that kind of money around here *legally*.' A shiver went through Bridie as she thought of her little brother caught up in the shady world of drug manufacturing that Spider and his father were into, or so rumour had it. 'Is that what you want? To end up in jail like Dad? How much of the world has Dad seen, Luke? Where's Dad's cool car? Oh, that's right, he doesn't have one, and his prison cell is the furthest he's ever been outside of Tooncanny.'

'Yeah, well, at least he isn't stuck here with you, the lucky bastard!'

Bridie caught her breath; Luke's words hit her like a slap across the face. She watched as he stomped out of the kitchen, then heard the slam of the ancient screen door in his wake.

Bridie crossed to the weathered timber dining table and pulled out a chair, sinking into it and feeling a hundred years old. She squeezed her eyes shut and willed away the threatening tears. Why was it so hard? Why did she always have to fight so hard to break the hold this miserable bloody town had on her family? Was it really too much to ask that they let just *one* Farrell try to make something of himself? Luke had only had to last till the end of the year and then he could have enlisted in the army and got out of here. One lousy year . . . that was all it would have taken.

Three

Lee Kernaghan's 'Boys from the Bush' belted out of the ancient-looking jukebox. Conversations grew louder as people tried to talk above the music.

The loudest of these came from the table in the far corner where Cheryl Farrell, Bridie's cousin, was holding court with three young shearers Bridie knew only vaguely. Cheryl's high-pitched squeals caused the other patrons to send the occasional irritable glance her way.

'What are you having, Jack?' Bridie asked the old farmer who'd just walked up to the bar.

'Just a middy today, thanks Bridie.'

Bridie selected a small beer glass from the row below the bar and pulled the beer with the ease of experience. 'Only a middy, Jack. You got a hot date or something?'

'I wish.' Jack gave her a toothless grin. 'Nah, I've got

a meeting with the bank tomorrow morning. Better not turn up with a hangover while I try and grovel for an overdraft.'

'Probably a good idea,' Bridie agreed. 'I'll be thinking positive thoughts for you tomorrow.'

'Thanks, but I think it's going to take more than that to put a smile on my bank manager's face.'

'Things that bad?' she asked as she collected the empty glasses left on the bar.

'They aren't great. If I don't catch a break soon, I might just end up in that retirement home up the coast that my daughter's been pestering me to look at.'

Bridie knew farmers were doing it tough out here; Jack was just one of them. It broke her heart to see them so despondent. Since the mines out Parkes and Orange way had opened, it was harder for both farmers and local businesses to keep workers. No one could compete with mining wages. Added to that was the high Australian dollar and a hike in costs of fuel and fertiliser—it was not a great time to be a farmer.

Someone caught her eye over Jack's shoulder. *Some* farmers were doing it tough, she amended. She watched the man move towards the bar and felt something shift way down low in her stomach.

Shaun Broderick.

Ever since she'd heard he was back in town she'd battled this silly reaction. She had no business feeling like some nervous schoolgirl even at the thought of him, and yet that was exactly how she felt. This wasn't the first time she'd seen him, of course—he'd been back now for close to a year, but she'd managed to avoid anything more than simply taking his order the few times he'd come into the pub. She really should be over this reaction by now! It wasn't as though they'd ever been close acquaintances or anything. She scoffed at herself. *One conversation seven years ago hardly counts as a shared past.* Besides, he'd barely spoken a word to her either, so it was unlikely he thought much about that night so long ago . . . They'd been kids, for goodness sake.

Still, it wasn't fair that one family got such a large share of the good looks genes. As cold as Douglas Broderick was, he was a good-looking man, and his son was no less blessed in the looks department. Even the women of the family were stunning—in a haughty kind of way.

She knew from local gossip that the Brodericks had a place in the city, and that Constance Broderick liked to spend a large portion of her time there. Bridie rarely saw them around town, but whenever she did they managed to make her feel as out of place and underdressed as a stripper at a church dance.

Bridie looked at the man before her, taking in his broad shoulders and the dark shadow of stubble that gave him a rugged, bad-boy look, and reminded herself just how easy it was to be taken in by all that charm. She'd already been burnt once by Shaun Broderick, and the humiliation of that experience still left a bitter taste in her mouth.

'What can I get you?' Bridie asked coldly.

'A schooner, thanks,' Shaun said, holding her gaze while digging out his wallet from his back trouser pocket.

As she selected one of the schooner glasses, she could feel Shaun's eyes on her, and she had to concentrate hard on pulling the beer to make sure she didn't end up with a glass half-full of foam. Eventually, though, she had to look up, and when she met Shaun's steady gaze, she held it as calmly as possible. 'That'll be four bucks, thanks.'

He handed over a crisp twenty-dollar note and she reached out to take it from him.

'Busy night?' Shaun asked. He was leaning on the bar, as though getting ready to settle in for the evening. She wondered briefly if he was meeting up with someone tonight, and then quickly dismissed the niggly, jealous part of her that wondered what type of woman Shaun Broderick was interested in now that he was all grown up. It was none of her business, and yet it bugged her far more than it should.

'It's been steady so far.'

'Oi, Bridie, how about shakin' ya arse up here and gettin' us another round.' Tyler Jennings's shout put an end to any further conversation, and Bridie fought to control her flare of anger at his rude behaviour. Bridie couldn't stand the Jennings boys. Tyler was the older cousin of Luke's new mate, Spider. In Bridie's opinion, the Farrells were choir-boys compared to the Jennings. Gritting her teeth, she made her way to the other end of the bar. She wished Alf would hurry up and get back from his tea break. It had been a fairly slow afternoon and so far a quiet evening, but even though it was still early, things were already beginning to pick up and she was getting tired of Jennings and his mates.

The three men leaning over the counter wore lopsided, drunken grins, and they elbowed each other as they ogled Bridie in much the same way as a dog eyes a juicy bone.

Bridie took a breath then tried to speak with calm authority. 'I can't serve you any more alcohol, but I can get you a soft drink or orange juice.'

'You have *got* to be joking,' the loudest of the group hooted.

'Tyler, I don't want any trouble here tonight,' Bridie warned, her voice light but her eyes wary.

'Listen, sweetheart, we've been out bush for the last week. We've come to town to blow off some steam, so be a good girl and pour us another round,' Tyler said, loud enough to make himself heard above the other conversations in the bar.

Bridie narrowed her eyes. 'I don't care if you've been on the moon for the last week. You've been drinking all afternoon and that's your sixth round of bourbon, not to mention the four rounds of beer and two tequila shots earlier. You've had enough. I'm not serving you any more tonight.'

Just then Cheryl sauntered over and slipped her arm around Tyler Jennings's narrow hips, her low-cut singlet top barely covering her breasts. 'What's the matter, baby?'

'Your stuck-up cousin here doesn't want to serve us any more beer.'

'Who the hell are you to tell us when we've had enough to drink?' one of the other men demanded.

'I'm the bartender. It's my job to tell you that you've had enough when you're too stupid to work it out for yourself.'

'I don't think old Alf would be too impressed if he found out you were turning away customers,' the third man piped up.

'Well, I'm not losing my job over you guys. So I'd suggest that if you don't want a soft drink, you go home,' Bridie said.

She reached for an empty glass on the counter and gasped as Tyler wrapped his dirty hand around hers and squeezed. She saw his cruel smirk and her heart paused mid-beat. If he squeezed just a fraction tighter, the glass would shatter beneath his strong grip and cut her hand—badly.

'I'm not going to ask again,' he growled in a low, dangerous tone that sent a flutter of terror through her body.

'Let go of her, Jennings.'

Bridie looked up and saw that Shaun had moved quietly up behind Tyler.

With a furious glare at Shaun, Tyler swore bitterly and flung her hand away, sending the glass sliding along the bar to hit the floor in an explosion of splintering glass. All conversation stopped dead as every set of eyes in the pub fixed on the unfolding drama.

'Mind your own business, Broderick,' Jennings growled, facing the bigger man with the swaggering bravado that only a bellyful of grog could give a bloke.

Shaun didn't back down. 'When I see a man picking on a woman, I make it my business. You want to pick a fight with someone, then why don't you try it with me?'

'Because I don't have a problem with *you* ... yet.' Jennings's snarl drew his mates to stand alongside him, no doubt ready for a release brought on by long hard days shearing sheep.

'Well, don't let fear stop ya, mate,' Shaun said simply.

As she cautiously edged away, Bridie switched her gaze between the two men, wondering where the hell Bulldog was. Bulldog Jones was the security for the pub, as well as cleaner and glass washer, and right now nowhere in sight.

'Listen, Broderick, you might be the big man around the district, but in here you're no one special. So just stay out of it. I got no bone to pick with you, and I don't work for ya, so bugger off.'

'Okay, enough. Jennings, out,' Bridie snapped, thinking that the longer this went on, the closer these two might come to destroying the pub.

Tyler gave a snort. 'You gonna make me, darlin'?'

'No. He is,' she said, jerking her head in the direction of the approaching brick wall affectionately known as Bulldog, who was storming across the room towards them.

'You three. Out!' Bulldog roared.

The young shearers didn't even bother to argue. Everyone knew Bulldog Jones had once gone to jail after crushing the head of a man with his bare hands. At least, that's how the story went—nobody really knew if it was true or not, and no one had ever been brave enough to ask him.

'You're nothin' but a bitch on a power trip. You'll keep,' Tyler shouted before jumping out of the way as Bulldog slammed the front door in his face.

Cheryl shoved at Bulldog to let her outside and left a torrent of unsavoury language in her wake.

Conversation resumed, picking up where it had left off as though nothing had happened, and Bridie released a shaky breath as she took out the small dustpan and began sweeping up the broken glass on the floor behind the bar.

'You okay, Bridie?' Bulldog asked as she emptied the shards of glass into the bin.

'I'm fine, but what took you so long?'

'Had me hands full outside in the car park. Must be a full moon or something.'

'Great. Going to be one of those nights then,' she muttered. All she wanted was for this shift to end so she could go home and snuggle into her nice warm bed.

'Did he hurt you?'

Bridie turned, thrown for a moment by Shaun's concern. 'No. I'm fine. Thanks,' she said. 'Do you want another drink?' She nodded towards his empty glass.

'Sure. Same again, thanks.'

Bridie tried to keep her hands steady under the weight of his gaze. Congratulating herself on not spilling a drop, she met his eyes and was thankful she'd waited until she finished pouring the beer. Time sure had been kind to him. He'd been good-looking at nineteen, but now, seven years later, he was downright dangerous, with those chocolate-brown eyes, sinful enough to make your mouth water. He'd always been the clean-cut rich boy growing up. Not that she'd seen him close up often—the Farrells and the Brodericks rarely crossed paths.

Since Shaun had returned to the district to take his rightful place in the Broderick kingdom, she'd noticed he seemed tougher, world-weary somehow, and she wondered where he'd been in the years between going away to university and coming back home. Her eyes fell once more onto that dark shadow of beard on his face, and goosebumps rose along her arms as she thought of him rubbing it against the sensitive skin of her neck. A rush of humiliation washed over her as she realised she'd been staring. Blushing, she began gathering empty glasses and stacking them in the dishwasher beneath the bar.

'You forgot to charge me for the beer,' he said in a slow drawl.

The thought that he'd guessed the lurid nature of her thoughts was too mortifying to consider. She told herself firmly that there was no way the sexy grin on his face had

KARLY LANE

anything to do with the fact that he'd just caught her staring at him and quite possibly drooling.

'Consider it a thankyou for trying to play the hero before,' she said.

'Gee, thanks, way to completely castrate a guy,' he chuckled. '*Trying* to play the hero?'

'I work in a pub six days a week—do you honestly think testosterone-flexing impresses me?'

He flashed a charming grin and she quickly lowered her eyes to the bench, sweeping the cloth across the gleaming surface and refusing to acknowledge the tug of desire his smile created inside her.

'I guess not. So what *does* impress you, Bridie Farrell?' he asked softly.

'Not much nowadays,' she admitted, slowly looking up to meet his watchful gaze. 'There's very little in this town that holds anything other than bad memories.' She saw something flash across his face: guilt, shame, or could it be regret? For a split second, she almost felt sorry for him, but what had happened that night still stung and the humiliation hardened her heart once more.

'Bridie—'

'Is there anything else you need?' she asked, holding his gaze for a few moments before turning away to check on her other customers.

For the rest of the night she tried her best to ignore his silent, brooding presence at the end of the bar, but that was an impossible task—he was imprinted onto her mind like a brand. A deep, permanent wound.

Four

Bridie waved goodbye to Bulldog and stepped out into the fresh night air. The coarse gravel crunched loudly in the stillness of the car park. The white stones seemed to glow brightly in the moonlight against the dark shadows.

Her trusty old ute, which she'd saved and scraped together the money to buy after leaving school, had become a treasured friend. A small smile touched her lips when she saw it, strong and sturdy, parked next to a few of the flashier, modern utes, left overnight by owners who had obviously thought better of driving home after too many drinks.

As she reached out to open the door, a shadow detached itself from the wall at the rear of the pub. A flash of fear raced through her when she realised who it was.

'Well, look who's here. It's the beer nazi,' Tyler Jennings crowed. Two other shapes materialised from the shadows to join him, and Bridie knew she was in trouble. Judging by the slightly off-centre swagger, and the slur in Jennings's words, they'd obviously found somewhere else to get hold of more alcohol.

Backed against her vehicle, she had nowhere to run. Briefly she thought about screaming for Bulldog, but she knew he wouldn't hear her. Bridie forced back the panic she felt clawing up her throat and made herself think rationally.

She was sober, they were drunk. That was something in her favour. Their reaction times would be slow, so all she had to do was stall them until an opportunity to run presented itself.

'Not so tough now you're out from behind your bar, are ya, sweetheart,' Jennings crooned, moving closer until she could smell the alcohol on his breath. His mates giggled behind him in anticipation.

'I was just doing my job. Get over it.'

She saw his mouth twist into a smile. 'You know what's always puzzled me about you, Bridie?'

'I can't begin to imagine,' Bridie drawled, but beneath her bravado was a rising dread.

Tyler ignored her sarcasm. 'How you think you're above everyone else around here, considering you're a Farrell—scum of the district. See why I'm confused?'

'I see why you're a *moron*,' she snapped. It hit a particularly raw nerve that he'd brought up her family reputation. All her life she'd fought against her name, trying to distance herself from all its shameful connotations. She should have known better—no one around here was about to let her escape the mould that her family had cast a long time ago. Once a Farrell, always a Farrell. That was why she'd been dreaming about leaving this place for most of her life.

Tyler moved quickly, quicker than she'd expected, and she found herself pinned against the side of her ute, Tyler's hard, sinewy length pressed into her from thigh to shoulder. Struggling only made him laugh at her attempts to escape.

'Come on, you don't have to keep pretending, Bridie. We know what you are. All Farrell women know the score—they put out to anyone, ain't that right?'

'Get off me.' Bridie's primal urge to fight back surged through her. She lashed out at his face, aiming for his eyes. He swore and wiped at the blood she'd managed to draw, before capturing her hands to stop her.

'It's time someone knocked you off your high horse and reminded you where you come from, girl. You're a nothin'. *A nobody.* You hear me? You're just like the rest of your family. The only thing you're good for is putting out. A quick lay, ain't that right, boys?' He held her wrists in a painful grasp and wedged one filthy denim-covered leg between her own.

The excited cheering-on from his mates behind him and the smell of his sour sweat-stained shirt against her face momentarily made her freeze in horror at the realisation she was about to be raped by this pack of drunk morons.

She let out a roar of frustration and hopelessness before a brutal mouth clamped down on hers, smothering her cries of outrage and pain.

⟳

Shaun lay in his bed above the pub and stared at the ceiling. In the hope of attracting Bridie's attention for a bit longer, he'd ordered more beers than usual, only to realise that he'd drunk too much to drive home to Jinjulu. He was acting like a lovesick teenager. Since coming back he'd been trying to work up the courage to talk to her, but it seemed he still couldn't do more than order a freaking beer. What was bloody wrong with him?

After the run-in with Jennings he'd decided to keep an eye on Bridie in case the lowlife came back. Much to his disappointment, there'd been no further opportunity to talk to her as the evening went on—the crowd grew steadily and kept her and Alf busy. When it got late he'd had to cut his losses and take a room upstairs for the night.

Now, frustrated and wide awake, he lay on the saggy double mattress, hands behind his head as he stared up at the dark spot on the ceiling that Alf obviously hadn't got around to fixing since last rainy season, judging by the size of the spreading damp stain.

A noise outside like someone kicking an empty tin made him sit upright. Remembering he was in town and not at home on the property, his thoughts suddenly went to his beloved ute that he'd bought on special order and driven all the way back from Sydney just last month. While Tooncanny was a relatively safe town, it wasn't crime-free and cars did get stolen or vandalised occasionally. The issue of teenage boredom and their need to make trouble seemed to be a problem in every town, big or small, right across the country. *Did I lock the ute?* He couldn't remember. He never usually needed to during the day, and for the life of him he couldn't recall if he'd done it tonight before going into the pub.

'Bugger,' he muttered, reaching for his shirt. He'd never get to sleep until he went downstairs and checked.

The pub was quiet, having long since closed. He let himself out the back door reserved for the hotel's overnight guests and used the bright moonlight to help find his way through the car park towards his vehicle.

The scream made him freeze in surprise for a moment before he sprang into action and ran towards the huddle of jeering men around an old Holden ute.

Blindly pulling bodies away, shoving the unsuspecting men back, he grabbed a fistful of shirt and spun a shocked Tyler Jennings around to face him.

Shaun knew who he was going to find pinned against the car even before he caught sight of her. Then, the terror in her eyes was all the reason he needed to start swinging punches.

The first punch didn't even register, and it wasn't until he felt her hand on his arm that he realised Bridie was yelling at him to stop.

He looked down at the man pinned beneath his knee on the cold, hard gravel of the car park and suddenly realised the damage he'd done. Tyler's face was a mess of blood and swollen flesh. Slowly Shaun stood up and staggered backwards.

The two other men, who'd been unable or unwilling to do more than watch as Tyler received the full brunt of Shaun's rage, now edged over to drag their mate to his feet and hustle him away.

'Are you all right?' Shaun asked as he caught his breath, searching her frightened face in the moonlight. He saw her nod but noticed her hands were shaking as she tucked a few stray tendrils of hair behind her ear. She was obviously trying to hold it together in front of him.

'Did he hurt you?' Shaun realised his voice sounded more like a snarl, but he couldn't help it—the thought of that bastard touching her made his blood boil.

'No. I'm fine,' she said, and although her voice was barely louder than a whisper, she managed to look at him.

Shaun dropped his head and closed his eyes as he fought to gain control over his shaking body. Looking down at his knuckles he saw they were grazed and bleeding.

'You're hurt. You better let me clean you up. We can't stay out here; they might come back,' Bridie said.

Together they walked back inside the pub, but when Bridie went to turn on a light in the main bar area, Shaun stopped her, pointing towards the staircase. 'I'm staying up there tonight. Don't wake up everyone else by turning on the lights down here.'

Bridie glanced towards the staircase, then back at Shaun's battered hands. 'Just let me get the first-aid box from the storeroom.' She returned after a few minutes and they made their way slowly up the wide staircase.

Once in his room, Bridie sat him down at the small table and went to the handbasin to wet a washcloth. When she turned back around he saw that she wasn't as composed as she'd said.

'He *did* hurt you,' Shaun said, immediately searching for injuries, before she turned away, wiping angrily at the tears that had begun to fall.

'I said I'm fine,' she snapped, then turned back to face him. 'I'm sorry—it's just shock or something. I don't really know why I'm crying.'

'Being attacked would probably do it,' he said wryly.

'Oh yeah? I don't see you bawling like a baby.'

'I wasn't the one being attacked. I was just trying to play the hero again.'

He saw her give a small grin, but he sensed she was uncomfortable displaying her emotions and so he said nothing else, giving her time to get herself under control.

She took a while running the washcloth under the tap before crossing the small room to sit down beside him and clean his wounds. 'I didn't thank you before. I'm glad you turned up when you did.'

Shaun watched as she gently wiped the blood from his injured hand, a frown of concentration on her face. 'No worries. Glad I decided to check I'd locked the car. Damn it—I still didn't do that.' He began to stand up.

'Sit down. I'll send Bulldog out to make sure they aren't lurking around and get him to check your car.'

'What happened?' he asked cautiously as he settled back in his seat and allowed her to resume cleaning his wounds.

'They were waiting in the car park when I finished work. I guess Jennings thought he had something to prove after I kicked him out earlier.'

'We need to report this to Tim Stanley.'

Bridie seemed to hesitate, then reached for the antiseptic cream. 'There's no need to get the police involved. I think Jennings got his just deserts tonight. Besides, you might end up in more trouble than they do.'

'Doubt it. He was about to—' Shaun stopped, unwilling to actually say the word aloud, and his anger reignited at the thought.

'But he didn't. So there's no point making a big deal of it.'

'What if he thinks he can get away with this again?' Shaun growled. Not report it? Was she crazy?

'Leave it alone.'

'For God's sake, Bridie, you have to report him.'

Bridie threw the antiseptic tube back in the box and stood up abruptly. 'And what do you think they're going to say? He'll tell them I led them on and they'll believe him. I'm not reporting it.'

'I was there. I'll testify that he was *attacking* you.' He saw the bitter twist of a smile as she shook her head and snatched up a small packet of gauze to cover the abrasion on his knuckles.

'I'm a Farrell, remember. It's *always* our fault.' She taped his hand quickly and stepped away. 'Thank you for coming to my rescue. You might want to get that checked out by a doctor. You can get a nasty infection from wounds that come in contact with someone's mouth—I think I saw a few teeth marks.'

'Wait up. You're not going out there alone,' he said, getting back on his feet.

'I'll go and wake Bulldog and let him know what's going on.'

'I'm coming with you.'

'No, don't. I don't want any more fuss tonight. Just go to bed and get some rest.'

'Would you just wait a minute?' Man, this woman was frustrating the hell out of him. 'How are you getting home? Let me drive you.'

'No, that's not necessary—I'm fine.' She closed the door on him before he had a chance to argue any more, leaving him wondering what the heck was going on with her.

He reached out to open the door, but paused. She was adamant she didn't want to report Jennings to the police, and without her making the report there wasn't much he could do. It rubbed him the wrong way to let the slimy bastard walk away scot-free.

He heard her knock softly on a door further down the hallway and then the low murmur of voices. At least she was keeping her word about filling Bulldog in on the incident. He knew Bulldog wouldn't take the matter lightly and he felt a little bit better.

Fatigue hit him fast as he sat down on the edge of his bed. The after-effects of his adrenalin rush were now taking hold and he gave in to the temptation to lie back against the big white pillows. Later he'd get up and check on his car, make sure he'd locked the damn thing, but he'd just close his eyes for a few minutes first . . .

Five

Bright sunshine flooded through the window and Shaun blinked rapidly to clear his sleepy mind and remember where he was. The pain in his hand brought him back to reality It throbbed like a bastard, and he swore under his breath as he swung his legs over the side of the bed and stood up.

He splashed water on his face with his good hand, then braced his arm against the edge of the sink as he stared at his reflection in the mirror.

The face staring back at him was a stranger's. He couldn't remember the last time he'd stopped and had a good hard look at himself. His once clean-shaven jaw was now a permanent dark shadow of stubble, which he wore to irk his mother, tired of her constant nagging to find a wife and start producing heirs. He had enough problems without adding a woman and a tribe of kids to the equation.

His dream of introducing a better way of cropping to Jinjulu was just about all he thought about nowadays. He wanted to be taken seriously by his father, to be able to put to use what he'd researched and studied. He wanted to use the experience he'd gained working with other farmers to turn his beloved Jinjulu into a state-of-the-art property.

Seven years ago he'd fled Jinjulu. He hadn't been able to stay after Jared's death; he'd needed to escape for a while. He hadn't known where he was headed or what he was going to do but he suddenly hadn't wanted to return to finish uni. Instead, he'd gone interstate and worked on the mines—much to his old man's ire. In the back of his mind he had a plan, and over the next few years he worked long hours to get some money of his own behind him and finish his degree. The fire that had always burned in the pit of his belly to run Jinjulu had well and truly reignited over the years he'd spent away. He'd made connections with farmers down south who were using innovative techniques with crops and livestock management to create environmentally sustainable farms, and he'd worked alongside them, often for free, in order to learn first-hand how to transform Jinjulu. Fat lot of good that'd done him. His father was simply not interested in making any changes.

It frustrated the hell out of him that his old man was so stuck in his ways. His father had made no bones about wanting him to return to Jinjulu—but Douglas still wasn't ready to let him make any genuine contribution to the place. He was the hired help—nothing more. Douglas's word was law, and God help anyone who dared challenge him.

Shaun's attention returned to his sullen reflection in the mirror. Twenty-six and still taking orders from his parents.

He'd missed Jinjulu over the years—too much to think about at times. The wide-open paddocks, the smell of freshly turned dirt, the gentle wave of crops in the breeze; the images he saw when he closed his eyes had been both a blessing and a curse. The place where he belonged also held too many memories he would give anything to go back and change.

With one last frown at the stranger in the mirror, he pushed away from the basin and collected his belongings, shoving his wallet into his pocket and leaving the room without a backwards glance.

He was halfway down the stairs when he met Bulldog coming up. 'I was on my way up to get you. You might want a stiff drink before you go out there, mate,' the older man said, slapping Shaun's shoulder and almost sending him flying down the stairs in the process.

Shaun forced himself not to run out to the car park, taking a deep breath as he pushed open the back door. Even with some warning, the sight of his prize possession with its windows smashed and paintwork scratched was enough to almost drop him to his knees.

'I followed Bridie home last night after she woke me up. I wanted to keep an eye on her house in case the mongrels decided to pay her another visit. The bastards must have snuck back here while I was at her place. I've called the coppers, they'll be here shortly. Sorry, mate.'

Shaun couldn't drag his eyes from the wreck before him to acknowledge Bulldog's explanation. He just stared at his pride and joy in stunned disbelief.

A few minutes later the town's only police officer, Tim Stanley, walked around the smashed car, shaking his head. 'Not a panel unmarked.'

Shaun's scowl deepened. 'Something I've already established, thanks, Tim.'

The tall policeman turned to look Shaun in the eye. 'So run it by me again, how this all started.'

Shaun dug the toe of his boot into the white gravel. 'I had an altercation with Tyler Jennings and his sidekicks earlier in the evening, and when I came out at about midnight to check I'd locked the car, I found them out here in the car park and we got into a scuffle. They ran off and I went back inside. This morning I came out to discover this.'

'Bulldog said he was out all night and you were the only guest staying in the pub. They must have really laid into it,' the policeman said. 'You didn't hear anything?'

'You think I wouldn't have come down and stopped it if I had?' Shaun snapped.

'Yeah, fair point. So what caused the altercation when you came out at midnight?'

Shaun paused. It was obvious Bulldog hadn't mentioned anything about Bridie, so he decided it would be best to keep his mouth shut too. 'Jennings is a cocky prick—he was asking for a fight all night. Guess he was waiting around for me to come out.'

'Well, it's a bit early to find anyone who might have seen anything, but I'll come by later and ask around. I'll get back to you if I find something.'

'Yeah, righto, Tim.' Shaun kicked at the gravel as the police officer walked away, then he pulled his mobile from the belt clip on his jeans. Jabbing in the station's number, he waited impatiently for someone to pick up.

'Hi Daisy, it's me. Can you get Pete to drive into town and pick me up? My ute's out of action for a while.' He said a hasty goodbye before she could start asking questions; he really wasn't in the mood to rehash it all right now. It was just lucky it had been Daisy and not his father who'd answered the phone.

Shaun headed back inside and ordered a hot breakfast. In spite of his urge to get his hands on Tyler Jennings and inflict a whole lot more pain than he already had, he was starving. He wondered what Bridie Farrell was doing this morning and felt a small leap of something suspiciously like excitement stir in his groin. He pushed the thought away and concentrated on his breakfast. He had enough to worry about without adding Bridie to his problems.

༄

Bridie stared at her arms. She turned them to catch the light and grimaced at the ugly red and purple marks that stood out starkly on her skin. But other than the bruises on her arms, a sore hip that must have caught the brunt of being slammed against her car, and a few muscles that protested when she moved, she was relatively unscathed from the night's events.

The sunrise made a spectacular backdrop as she sat in the garden behind the small house she'd been scrimping and scraping to pay off for the last five years or so. She sipped at her hot coffee and let her gaze drift out over the lush green of the paddocks beyond. The little cottage backed onto crown land, which farmers leased to fatten their livestock. It was the best of both worlds, Bridie thought. She had the convenience of living close to town but still had cattle and sheep grazing beyond her back fence. She loved cattle. There was just something about their big, gentle, nonjudge-mental eyes that made her feel at ease.

There was no sign of movement from Luke's bedroom, which was a good thing. She wasn't ready to face a surly teenager just yet. Bridie shook her head. Where had that cute five year old with the big brown eyes and chubby legs gone?

A car pulled up out the front of the house. Bridie heard its engine turn off and she made her way to the door to see who it was. As she reached the hallway her steps faltered and that old familiar sense of foreboding settled in her stomach at the sight of the police car parked in her driveway.

'Bridie.' Tim nodded a brisk welcome. Being the only cop in Tooncanny, he knew a lot about everyone. The fact that he was aware of her family connections had always made Bridie feel uncomfortable, even though he'd never used it against her. He'd only been in Tooncanny three years and he'd already made a positive impact on the town. He was the driving force behind the setting up of a police youth group and he helped run a small gym, with basket-ball games, indoor cricket and boxing. It was something the whole town had supported with fundraising raffles and ongoing cake stalls. Luke had, up until recently, been a regular there and Bridie had appreciated the time Tim had put into her little brother.

Bridie and Tim had dated a few times, but it had made her feel awkward knowing that the policeman was familiar with all the things her family had been involved in, and it was something she hadn't been able to get past. After the first two dates, Bridie had stopped accepting them, and soon Tim had stopped asking. There didn't seem to be any hard feelings, but they had never talked about it either.

'How can I help you, Tim?'

'I have a few questions I'd like to ask about an incident at the pub last night.'

Immediately Bridie's reliable old mask slid carefully into position. If her family had given her one thing of value, it was how to hide your emotions and protect yourself from the outside world. It was the only useful thing they'd given her.

'I hear there was a bit of a stir when you stopped serving Tyler Jennings and his mates.'

Bridie held the officer's gaze steadily. 'He wasn't too happy, yelled a bit and knocked a glass off the bar, nothing serious.'

'Did you witness an altercation of any sort between Jennings and Shaun Broderick in the pub?'

This line of questioning surprised Bridie a little. She'd been waiting for something about the incident in the car park, thinking Shaun must have reported it, despite her objections. 'They had words, but they didn't fight. Jennings left when Bulldog threw him out, but he wasn't too happy.'

'Yeah, that's what I've been hearing.' Tim nodded thoughtfully.

'Why do you ask?' *A Farrell doesn't trust a copper— ever.* She heard the statement as clearly as though her father had spoken it.

'Someone smashed up Broderick's ute last night in the car park. No witnesses, unfortunately. I've been trying to work out what went on.'

She frowned. Tyler wouldn't have been in any fit condition to go back and smash up Shaun's car. It was obviously the work of his sidekicks—Tweedle Dumb and Tweedle Dopey. Tim seemed to be a decent kind of bloke, but she wasn't prepared to explain what had happened and risk everyone in town passing judgement on her over a near miss in the car park. She had enough problems to deal with. She shrugged.

'Thanks for your time, Bridie.' Tim began to turn away but then swung back as though something had just occurred to him. 'How're things going with Luke?'

She tried not to bristle at the mention of her little brother's name. 'Okay.'

'I haven't seen him down at the gym lately. Pity—he was doing well. I really appreciated his help with some of the younger kids there. Tell him it'd be great to see him come back, will you?'

'I'll let him know. Thanks, Tim.' She gave a brief smile and watched him walk back to his car. Sadness crept through her at his parting words. She couldn't let Luke blow it now. Not when she'd kept him on the straight and narrow for so long.

Damn it! He'd been doing okay at school. The kid was never going to be a rocket scientist, but he was going okay. She was proud of him for trying so hard, and then a few months ago his best mate had left town and he'd begun hanging around some new friends, friends with a nasty habit of finding trouble.

Not for the first time, Bridie felt a wave of helplessness wash over her. It didn't matter how hard she tried to be there for Luke, the fact remained that she couldn't be a mother and father to him. Especially now, at Luke's age, when he was pushing all the boundaries she'd set in place, nothing could replace a united parental front.

She ran a hand through her hair and a tired sigh escaped as she let the screen door close.

Shaun Broderick would not be a happy camper today. Everyone knew how much he loved his shiny metallic-red ute. At least he'd respected her wishes and kept her out of his statement. Surely they'd be able to catch the culprits without her input. She told herself that it wouldn't make any difference if she came forward about Jennings—without witnesses to verify who had vandalised the ute, her word didn't mean much. She'd have to go through a court case, stand up before everyone. It was her greatest fear to have people shrugging off something like this because of her name—as though being a Farrell automatically meant you deserved whatever you got.

There were good reasons behind it, of course. The Farrells walked a very fine line where the law was concerned, and yes, they had a sordid and dangerous past—two of her uncles had been mixed up in drug dealing and bikie gangs, her father was in prison, and her cousin Cheryl wasn't exactly shy about sharing her assets with any and everyone—so it was understandable that people around town looked down on them. But to assume the entire family was bad was unfair. It was a case of guilt by association around here, and that was never going to change. The only way to escape it was to leave, and that was exactly what she planned on doing. She needed to get Luke out, too, before he fell into the same trap his father and uncles had fallen into. Lack of work and shady connections just spelled disaster. Nope, Luke was getting out of Tooncanny—she'd make sure of it.

Six

Shaun sat staring out the window as Pete drove him back
to Jinjulu. His father had signed Pete on as an extra hand
when Shaun had left, and at twenty-three he was still happy
enough to be working there. Shaun liked him—he seemed
a dependable kinda guy—and the two men had clicked
immediately and worked well together.

The insurance assessor was coming to town in two days'
time to give the verdict on the ute, but Shaun didn't even
want to think about it right now. He was still too angry
to think straight. There wasn't much the police could do
without a witness and with no evidence left at the scene to
tie it to anyone.

For the next week, he threw himself into work; thankfully, even his father must have picked up on the signs
because everyone steered clear of him and left him to his
brooding silence.

Eventually he had to go back into town to pick up supplies. As he locked the farm vehicle in front of the farmers' co-op, he looked up to see Bridie crossing the road, heading for the pub. With a quick look both ways, he jogged across the wide main street and called out her name. She stopped and shaded her eyes as she watched him approach.

They stared at each other in silence for a moment before Shaun shook himself irritably. *What are you, fourteen and tongue-tied?* 'Hey.' *Real smooth, Broderick.*

'Hey.' He saw her lips give a twist of amusement and felt a blush creep up his neck. Christ, this was worse than the time he'd tried to make out with Simone Johnson at a combined schools dance and she'd laughed herself stupid as he'd fumbled his way through the whole ordeal. 'I just wanted to make sure you were all right.'

The glint of laughter disappeared from her eyes and she looked away. 'I'm fine.'

Shaun rubbed the base of his neck with his hand. This wasn't going too well. What the hell was happening to him? He'd wined and dined women before and managed to dazzle them with his wit and charm. But when it came to Bridie Farrell, he was a freaking basket case! 'I guess you heard about the ute,' he said.

He caught her slight wince. 'Yeah. Do you think they'll find out who did it?'

'We both know who did it—even the coppers know who did it—but no, they haven't got anything to go on other than speculation.'

'I'm sorry. If you hadn't come to help me, your car would still be in one piece.'

He studied her serious expression and the rage that had begun to boil again cooled. He could stare at her biting her lip like that all day and not get tired of it. 'If I hadn't gone out to help you, I can't even begin to think about what might have happened, so don't worry about it . . . You're worth more than any damn car.'

Her eyes flew to his in alarm and he held them steadily, refusing to drop her startled gaze. This time he wouldn't pretend to ignore the chemistry that had always existed between them. Truth was, he felt guilty and had no idea how to broach the subject of that brief encounter between them years before. Too many times he'd shied away from explaining it, but seeing that bastard all over her the other night had jolted him out of his cowardice. Big time.

Neither of them had spoken about the incident all those years ago. He had a fair idea she remembered it all right—she'd been giving him the cold shoulder ever since he'd arrived back in town—but he had never quite known how to bring it up. It wasn't something he was proud of and he knew he needed to apologise for it.

It had happened at a party when he was a cocky nineteen year old. A bet had been suggested and Shaun, then a testosterone-fuelled, overconfident country boy, had accepted without a moment's hesitation. The dare was simple: see how long it took to get the Farrell sheila to put out. The fact that Bridie was a Farrell was enough—it hadn't mattered that she'd never had the kind of reputation some of her cousins in town had. Her surname made her fair game. He'd been drinking, but he hadn't been drunk, so he couldn't honestly use that as an excuse, and even then, Bridie Farrell had been a stunner.

For weeks before the party he'd looked forward to catching sight of her at the small grocery store where she worked in the afternoons. He'd asked about her and found out she was still in high school, so he'd judged her to be around seventeen. He'd also heard her father had just been thrown in jail over a drug bust. There was something about Bridie that grabbed his attention the minute she walked into the crowded house with a grace he'd only ever seen at a thoroughbred sale.

As he'd walked across the room to talk to her, she had lifted her head and his confidence had faltered. Those blue eyes, the colour of deep sapphire, had pierced him with a look so intense that for a moment he'd forgotten to breathe. It was a feeling he had whenever she looked at him . . . like now.

'Well, I have to get to work,' she said finally, moving towards the pub doors.

'You start your shift this early?'

'I'm in the kitchen in the afternoon and then behind the bar at night.'

'That's a big workload.' He saw her expression harden and knew the moment was lost.

'Some of us have to work for a living. Not all of us get everything handed to us on a silver platter.'

He didn't even get the chance to open his mouth in protest at her unjust accusation before she'd turned and disappeared into the cool shadows of the pub.

He felt offended that she considered him to be some spoilt rich kid. He did seventeen- or eighteen-hour days on a regular basis. The day didn't finish once the sun went down—there was always machinery that needed fixing before the next day's work started, or late-night emergencies to be attended to. For all its history and opulence, Jinjulu was a working farm first and foremost, and the Brodericks were the main employees. His father and a long line of Brodericks before him had become rich by being tight with their money and breeding sons for their workforce.

With one last glance in the direction of the pub, he turned and crossed the road back to the co-op.

He *did* have work to do.

ЭЭ

Bridie's week hadn't improved. Luke hadn't been home when she'd finished work on Saturday night, and when she'd heard him creeping in at two in the morning she'd discovered he'd been drinking. Bright and early the next morning she'd pulled up the blinds in his bedroom and made him get out of bed so she could give him the third degree. It'd had little effect, because the next night he was out again and he hadn't bothered to return home since.

Bridie wasn't in an outright panic, though, because he wasn't missing. She knew exactly where he was.

Sunday was her day off, and she decided that enough was enough. She drove to the outskirts of town and pulled up in front of a rundown assortment of shacks. She took a deep breath and climbed out of her car.

She hated coming out here. Her uncle Tom was not her favourite person. Her father had four brothers and all of them had done time. Tom Farrell was her only uncle not in prison.

Two shaggy, half-starved dogs raced towards her, yapping as she opened the rusty front gate. Ignoring them, she pounded on the front door and waited as she heard the shuffling of slippered feet on lino.

The stale smell of fried food and cigarettes rushed out to greet her as Cheryl opened the door. 'What do you want?' she said irritably.

'I've come to pick up Luke.' Bridie didn't like her cousin. Even as a kid, Cheryl had been a bully. There was only a month between them, and more than once as they'd grown up Bridie had wished they could be closer. She would have loved to have a cousin she could count on as a friend, but for some reason Cheryl always treated her as though she was some kind of threat. Bridie suspected it might have had something to do with the close relationship between Bridie and her mum. Cheryl's mother had been a heavy drinker and the complete opposite of Beth Farrell. She'd left Tom when Cheryl turned twelve. Bridie's mum had tried to step in and fill the gap a little, but Cheryl was already on a downward spiral. By the time she was fourteen she'd been picked up for underage drinking more times than Bridie could count. At school, as teenagers, if Bridie had so much as looked at a guy twice, Cheryl would immediately start flirting with him, thus ending any hope Bridie might have had with him. It saddened her that Cheryl allowed herself to be treated so badly by the men in her life. They were all the same—Tyler Jennings clones. Wild, loud, crude drinkers.

Cheryl smiled slyly at Bridie's announcement. 'He likes it here. He's sick of you trying to make him into some sissy.'

'Just go get him, Cheryl.'

Cheryl's smile slipped slightly at the order. 'Luke! Your prison officer is here!' she yelled.

Bridie concentrated on not reacting to her cousin's sarcastic grin. You couldn't show weakness or they'd pounce like a pack of hyenas.

There was a movement at the end of the hallway. Despite the worry and stress Luke had put her through over the last few days, her heart gave a grateful leap to see him.

'Come on, mate, pack up your gear, we're going home,' she said briskly.

'I'm staying.'

'Luke, I don't have time for this. Get your stuff.'

Luke folded his arms across his chest and lifted his chin defiantly. She was about to order him out to the car when there was a deep hacking cough behind her. She turned sharply, slightly unsettled that she hadn't heard his approach.

'Well, if it isn't little Bridie.'

'Uncle Tom,' Bridie acknowledged him without enthusiasm. 'Thank you for putting Luke up here for the last few nights. I've just come to pick him up.'

Her uncle gave a raspy chuckle. Living in the same town it was hard not to run into her family, but for all intents and purposes, after her father had been sent to prison she had estranged herself from everyone except Luke. Because she wasn't eighteen at the time, Luke couldn't be placed in her care and so Tom had been given temporary custody of him. However, three months later, once she turned eighteen, Bridie was appointed Luke's guardian, something she suspected had never gone down well with her uncle.

'You know, I was only saying to Luke the other day, we miss having you around the place, Bridie. You should come over for a barbie one night, love—we can have a few drinks and catch up.'

'I work nights.' Bridie looked back at Luke and narrowed her eyes meaningfully, but he ignored her.

'That's too bad. Family's important. We're here to help both of you. I promised your dad I'd keep an eye on you two.'

'Thanks, but we're doing just fine on our own.'

'Told ya she was a stuck-up bitch, Dad,' Cheryl put in nastily. 'You always think you're so much better than the rest of us, don't ya, Bridie?'

'I just came to pick up Luke.' She was not going to get into a domestic with these people. *Just keep your cool and get out.*

'He's not a kid any more. He's too much for you to cope with. He's at the age where he needs a man around to keep him in line. Here he has all his cousins . . . and me,' said Tom.

Yeah, and you, Bridie thought with another flare of anger. *Just what he needs, a role model who thinks the world owes him and he doesn't have to work to make a living—fantastic principles.*

'For at least another year he has me—his legal guardian. So he needs to get his things and get into the car.'

'He can make up his own mind what he wants to do,' her uncle said with a shrug.

Bridie saw the flicker of discomfort that crossed her brother's face as he realised all eyes were now on him and he was being forced to make a choice between the sister who was raising him and the uncle and cousins who made him feel like a grown-up. It hurt her to make him choose, so she decided to end it quickly. 'Forget it. I'll bring back the police to help sort it out.'

She turned and walked outside, forcing herself to stay calm. Behind her, she could hear Cheryl hurling outraged insults and her uncle's low growl, no doubt telling his daughter to calm down and that Bridie was probably bluffing. She'd reached the front gate when she heard Luke yell over his shoulder as he all but ran out the front door, 'She's not bluffing. I'll go, just to shut her up. I don't want her to bring the cops around here and cause trouble. Thanks for letting me stay, Uncle Tom.'

She'd given him an excuse to leave without losing face. If he could do it and make her out to be the bad guy, all the better. It made no difference to her what the rest of her father's family thought.

The drive home was made in silence; fortunately, it wasn't a long trip. Waves of resentment and frustration washed over her from the angry teenager beside her, and once she'd pulled into her driveway it was a relief to escape the confines of the ute.

'Before you go back to your cave and hibernate, the bins need emptying, please,' she called as he headed towards the back of the house and his bedroom.

He muttered something under his breath and she decided to ignore the comment, happy that at least he was taking the bins out. She'd figured out the first rule of survival with a teenager—choose your battles. She breathed a small sigh of relief as she heard the lid of the big wheelie bin slam shut, followed soon after by the bang of the screen door.

She flicked on the jug. She'd let him blow off some steam for a while before they had a chat about this latest act of rebellion. First, though, she needed some caffeine and something to eat. Lesson number two in handling teenagers—*never* go to war on an empty stomach.

Seven

'You're not suspended. I spoke to Shaffer and he's going to let you go back to school. You will, however,' she continued as he opened his mouth to protest, 'be volunteering to weed the gardens and paint the toilet block next weekend.'

'No way!'

'Way. And be thankful that's all you get.' The fact that she had stopped just shy of blackmailing the man over his sneaky jaunts out of town didn't trouble her conscience one jot. Luke's grades were the only thing she cared about right now.

'I'm not going back.'

'Luke, you don't get a choice, mate. You're going to finish school, and if you don't try your best I will personally make your life here a living hell—and don't think I can't.'

He must have seen in her unflinching gaze that she wasn't kidding, because he dropped his glare and sulked.

Satisfied that he was at least taking her seriously, she let out a small sigh and gave him a hug.

'You'll understand one day,' she promised.

'Don't hold your breath,' he muttered and pulled away from her.

There had been a time when he'd give her spontaneous hugs—she missed those days. 'Why can't you see that I'm doing my best to get you out of this place? I don't want you to end up like Dad.'

'Why do you hate him so much?' Luke yelled.

'Because he's not the hero you keep making him out to be,' she shouted back. 'He abandoned us, Luke!' Bridie fought to control her emotions. Where the hell had that outburst come from? She never allowed herself to erupt like that. Control was the only thing she had to protect her fragile heart. She risked a swift glance at her younger brother and winced. He was staring at her as though he'd never seen her before.

'He went to prison. He didn't mean to abandon us.' Luke's hands were clenched by his sides.

'He *had* a choice—he didn't put us first. He knew what he was doing and he still went and followed his stupid brothers and got mixed up in that drug deal. If he cared about us, he would *never* have taken that risk . . . Parents who love their kids don't do that.'

'He went there for his brothers.' When she shook her head, he jumped in defensively. 'Uncle Tom sat down and told me what really happened. Dad didn't want to go along with it. He tried to warn them this deal was a set-up, but he went along with it to try and protect Uncle Mick and Uncle Wally. There was a shoot-out and the coppers turned up and everything went wrong.'

Bridie frowned, uncertain for a moment how to react to her brother's blind acceptance of the story her uncle had given him. 'Like you can believe anything Uncle Tom says.' She moved to walk away but Luke surprised her by taking a step and blocking her exit.

'He's doing time for something he didn't even want to do.'

'I don't care, Luke! He was still there and he knew what he was doing.'

'How can you not care? He's our father!'

'You don't remember what it was like when he made Mum cry. Tom's just like the others: he always twists the truth around to make it seem as though the Farrells are so hard done by—it's *never* their fault. None of them think they should have to work like everyone else, so they take the easy way out of everything. It makes me sick.'

'Tom wasn't lying about Dad. I believe he was trying to change.'

'Then you're setting yourself up for a big disappointment.'

The slam of the front door sounded loud in the quiet room. It was a constant struggle to keep going some days . . . days like this.

Bridie glanced over at the photo of her parents on their wedding day. Her mother wore a simple pale blue sundress and held a small bunch of daisies in one hand. The other hand was hooked through her new husband's arm as they smiled at the photographer on the courthouse steps. Beth had already been pregnant with Bridie, but there was no sign of a baby bump on her mother's slim figure. In her mind, Bridie could still hear her mother telling the story of how she'd met Bridie's dad. Beth had lived in Dubbo and had just finished her Year 10 certificate. She'd just got a position as an apprentice chef in a restaurant in Surfers Paradise and the night out was her final act of rebellion before she left to start her big adventure up north. Underage, she snuck into the hotel with a group of her girlfriends. There she met Brian Farrell.

There was no doubt, looking at the photo of her father when he was young, that Brian, at twenty, would have been hard to resist once he turned on the charm most of the Farrell men were famous for. One look and Beth had been lost to the tall, handsome guy at the bar who later swaggered over to her table and told her she was the woman he was going to marry.

When Bridie had heard the story as a child it had sounded like a fairy tale. Once she'd been old enough to see the fallout from their volatile relationship, however, she'd found it hard not to feel cynical towards her mother's naivety. Bridie could still remember the look on her mother's face as she talked about all the things she'd dreamed of doing before she met Bridie's father. The regret in her voice had been unmistakable, even to a child, although Bridie knew it was only after a heated argument, or when her father had gone away for days at a time with his brothers 'working', that her mum would fall into the doldrums and recall her youthful dreams. Once Bridie got older she couldn't understand why her mother didn't leave him if he made her so unhappy, but she knew the truth was she'd loved him and had nowhere else to go. She'd been a teenage bride and mother, and she had no job skills and no family to support her. Bridie vowed she would *never* be trapped in Tooncanny like her mother.

୬

She heard a shuffle on the front porch and the squeak of the screen door opening. Her hands tightened around the mug of coffee she'd made earlier and she waited for the sound of footsteps up the hall. Sitting in the dark with only the moonlight to see by, Bridie watched her brother sneaking back into the house. 'Where have you been? It's almost eleven pm.' Her voice sounded loud in the silence.

Luke jumped. 'Jesus, you gave me a fright.' Reluctantly he made his way into the kitchen and Bridie stood up and switched on the light above the stove.

'I was coming home from Wellington,' he said at last.

Bridie stared at her brother in disbelief. 'Why would you want to go to Wellington?'

'To see Dad.'

Of all the things she'd been imagining him doing while she waited up for him, this had never even entered her mind. He'd been commuting all over the central west in the dead of night! 'Hang on. There are no buses this time of night. How did you get home?'

'Uncle Tom. When I was at his place I told him I wanted to see Dad and he made the arrangements for today and took me over. Next time you should come along,' he threw at her casually, as though inviting her along to a barbecue at a mate's house. She watched him open the fridge and reach in for the milk, before brushing past her to take a box of cereal from the pantry.

'Have you lost your mind? What on earth could have possessed you to do such a thing without talking to me first?'

As his guardian, Bridie had made the decision not to allow Luke to visit their father in prison. She didn't want him anywhere near the place—she had vague memories of accompanying her mother there when she was very young, although he'd only been in for a few months that time, but the memory was not something she recalled fondly.

'I wanted to see him.' He shrugged, splashing milk on the counter top as he poured it over the contents of his bowl.

'Anything could have happened to you, Luke!' she fumed, automatically reaching for the cloth to wipe the bench as he sat down at the kitchen table to eat. 'You should have spoken to me about it.'

'You wouldn't have let me go,' he said around a mouthful of food.

'To prison? Of course I wouldn't have let you!'

'Dad told me he'd written and asked you to visit him.' He stared at her defiantly.

Bridie turned away. 'I was kinda busy trying to raise a little brother and hold down a job.'

'Stop using me as an excuse all the time,' Luke yelled, pushing away his cereal. 'I never asked you to take care of me!'

Bridie gave a bitter laugh. 'You were nine years old— where else were you going to go?'

'Uncle Tom was happy to have me.'

Bridie clenched her fingers around the edge of the sink behind her. 'You're *my* brother, you're not his responsibility.'

Luke stared at her and Bridie caught her breath at the vulnerable look in his eye. 'You won't even give them a chance.'

How was she supposed to defend her actions to a kid who was too young to remember the bad years?

'I don't care what you say, Dad's changed, and by the end of the year you won't have any say about *anything* I do. I'm going to get to know my family.' He pushed away from the table with a loud screech of the chair and headed to his bedroom.

Bridie dropped her head and stared at the cheap patterned lino she'd laid herself only a few months ago. Maybe she should just give it up as a lost cause, let Luke go and live with Tom. The idea was more than a little tempting, but her instincts were too strong. He was her baby brother. She'd been taking care of him for so long—even before their father went to jail—that it was impossible for her to ignore the protective instincts she'd developed since taking charge of his welfare so many years ago.

Ever since their mother died.

It was still painful to think of her mother, Beth, with the lovely long hair and gentle brown eyes. Sometimes, for a brief moment, after Brian had had an attack of remorse and had vowed to straighten himself out, Beth would be able to relax for a while. Bridie liked seeing her mother like that. Beth would sit and talk about better times. She'd get a faraway look in her eye as she remembered all her dreams, and for a brief moment her face would lose some of its strain. Those times never seemed to last long, though. Brian would come home drunk after losing his job, ranting that no one in this stinking town would ever give a Farrell a chance, and Bridie would watch her mother's shoulders sag and the worry lines crease her forehead once more. Then there had been the miscarriages. For a woman who'd loved being a mother as much as Beth had, it had been a cruel blow each time she'd lost a baby. It took seven years before her mother finally carried another child to term. It was a blessing and a curse, because only a few years after Luke was born her mother was diagnosed with breast cancer.

Bridie vowed never to be trapped as her mother had been. To fall in love with a man who constantly let her down. Bridie grew up watching her mother plead for her husband to break away from his brothers' influence. She'd figured out very early on that her father's loyalty to blood was stronger than his loyalty to his wife and children. Nothing and no one stood between the Farrell brothers.

'Goddamn it,' she growled under her breath as she tipped her head back and closed her eyes. It always came to this. She was the only one left to take responsibility. Well, she hadn't sacrificed all these years stuck here bringing up Luke only to have it fall apart now. She'd just have to dig a bit deeper . . . again.

Eight

Bridie pushed the shopping cart around the small super-market and tried to remember what else they needed. At least Luke's appetite hadn't been affected by the recent turmoil. He still ate her out of house and home.

After she'd paid for her purchases, she lugged the bags to her car and threw them inside. Slamming the boot shut, she looked up to see a young woman jog across the road. For a minute she couldn't place her, which was unusual in Tooncanny, and then it came to her—Phoebe Broderick.

At that precise moment, the young woman looked up and caught Bridie staring at her. Quickly dropping her gaze and pocketing the car keys, Bridie tried to remember what was next on her list of things to do. There was no time to ponder what Phoebe Broderick was doing slumming it in Tooncanny in the middle of the week.

She pushed open the door of the post office and the jaunty jingle of the bell seemed to echo in the old building. Bridie smothered a sigh as she took in the line ahead of her. There were only two people in the line, but it had to be *these* two people. Edna Sutton and Veronica Taylor—two of the biggest gossips in town. It could be half an hour before either of them were finished.

The bell rang again just as she was debating whether to come back later. Bridie looked around to see Phoebe Broderick queuing up behind her. Sending her a brief commiserating smile, Bridie turned back to wait. The musty old building and new paper smell mixed in a familiar cocktail. How many times over the years had she stood in line at the post office? Actually, not that many: she was usually too impatient to stand there for long and tried to think ahead and buy extra stamps so she didn't have to come inside. This was the first time in a long while that she'd been forced to stand still. Now that she was, it was surprising to find how many little things triggered memories.

She let her gaze travel over to the far wall where the bench ran beneath the tall windows, with its row of chained pens and bowls of wet sponges. Why the sponges were needed nowadays was a bit of a mystery, seeing as the stamps were all self-adhesive.

Edna was spouting her famous nephew's attributes to the post office staff. He was famous only because he lived in America. He worked in a steel-fabrication plant, hardly deserving notoriety, but the fact that he lived overseas— somewhere that few people in Tooncanny ever dared to venture—was enough to grant Edna Sutton's nephew celebrity status.

There was a small grunt of derision behind her. She frowned. Yes, she found Edna's preening annoying and ridiculous, too, but she'd never say it out loud—the woman had feelings, after all.

'Excuse me, but you've got customers waiting here. Any chance of moving it along a bit?' Phoebe called out impatiently.

The postmaster, Charlie Cragg, lifted droopy eyes to the line and glared a rebuke. His white whiskers and long sideburns were almost as dated as the building he'd worked in his entire adult life.

'Are they serious?' Phoebe demanded, and it took a moment for Bridie to realise the question had been directed at her.

'Well, unless you feel like driving two hours into Parkes, then you're pretty much stuck with this place.'

'Here.' Bridie turned, startled, as a pile of envelopes was thrust into her hands and a twenty-dollar note slapped on top. 'That should cover it. I don't have time to stand around here all day.'

Before Bridie could even open her mouth to protest, the door was reefed open, sending the bell into a frenzy of merriment, and she was left to stare mutely at the empty doorway.

She blinked as she looked down at the stack of envelopes in her hands. *That did not just happen*, she thought.

'Little upstart. Those Brodericks always did think they were better than the rest of us.' She heard Veronica's dry raspy voice and knew it had indeed just happened.

'Who does she think she is?' Bridie demanded as shock wore off and anger elbowed in to take its place.

'A Broderick, dear. They're all the same,' Edna added sagely.

'*She* doesn't have time!' Bridie's voice rose in outrage.

'Just bring those letters up here and I'll take care of them for you,' Charlie soothed, holding out his hand.

'Oh no, you won't. How dare she think we're all here to serve her like a bunch of . . . servants!' Bridie spluttered. 'She can bloody well come back here and post them herself!' Heading for the door, Bridie was too angry to listen to the alarmed voices behind her.

She went up and down the main street, but there was no sign of Phoebe anywhere. *She didn't waste any time hot-footing it out of town*, Bridie thought bitterly. Then she caught sight of a large four-wheel drive parked outside the pub, *Jinjulu Station* plastered across its side panels. She headed off across the road, her stride purposeful.

It took a few moments for her eyes to adjust to the dimness of the pub's interior, but when she saw Phoebe at a table across the room she pulled her shoulders back and headed over without stopping to think about it.

The three people seated at the table looked up at her as she stopped beside them. Absently she noted Shaun, and Pete Sotherby, whom she remembered had been a few years behind her in school, but her fiery glare was reserved for Phoebe.

She tossed the stack of letters onto the table and watched as they fanned out across the tabletop. 'I'm sorry, I think you must have confused me with one of your *employees*. Post your own damn mail!' She saw Shaun raise an eyebrow at his sister.

'So much for country hospitality,' Phoebe drawled.

'I don't know what planet you come from, but around here you don't treat people like second-class citizens and expect to get away with it,' Bridie snapped.

'Phoebe, what's going on?' Shaun straightened in his chair.

'I just asked her to post some letters for me—big deal.' His sister shrugged, as though bored with the conversation.

'I wouldn't be here if you'd bothered to *ask*—that's the whole point,' Bridie managed through tightly clenched teeth.

Shaun sent his sister a disbelieving glance before getting to his feet to face Bridie. 'She didn't mean anything by it.'

Too angry to reply, Bridie turned away from the table and retraced her steps across the pub, her mood none the better for the confrontation. She heard footsteps behind her but didn't pause until a large hand circled her upper arm and forced her to stop.

Bridie stared pointedly at the tanned hand on her arm, and Shaun quickly dropped his hold and gave a mumbled apology. 'She doesn't realise how she comes across to other people. I'm sorry if she offended you.'

'*If* she offended me? You think I appreciated having someone throw their mail at me because they *didn't have time* to stand in line like everyone else? You think I had nothing better to do with *my* time?'

'I know . . . *really*, I know. I'll make sure she knows she stepped way over the line today. I'm sorry.'

Bridie stared at him in disbelief.

'What?' Shaun asked hesitantly.

'She's a grown woman! How can she not know? You people are unreal—it's like you live in some alternate universe or something.'

'It's not . . .' he began. 'Look, she's going through a bit of a rough patch at the moment . . . Honestly, I don't know what's got into her. She's not usually that obnoxious.'

Bridie shook her head and gave a small grunt. 'Unbelievable.'

'Bridie, wait,' he called as she turned away. 'Let me make it up to you. I'll buy you a drink.'

'No thanks. I don't think I can take much more of your charming sister today.'

She felt him watching her as she hurried back to her ute. The rest of her jobs could wait. She'd had a gutful of the Brodericks and their high-handed ways for one day.

⁓

As they drove back towards Jinjulu, Shaun glanced across at his sister staring moodily out the passenger window. 'What's up with you anyway?'

Phoebe didn't bother looking at him. 'Nothing's up with me.'

'That's why you're such a little ray of sunshine then,' Shaun said.

'What exactly is there to be sunny about? Dad won't let me study what I want and I'm stuck out here in Woop Woop with no one to talk to.'

'Well, for starters, your attitude isn't helping win him over any.'

'Like anything I say or do will change his mind. You heard him, he thinks it's a complete waste of time—just because he doesn't have a creative bone in his body.'

Shaun took his eyes from the road briefly to shoot his sister another look. 'You've changed.'

'We've all changed,' she said, and for a moment she lost her usual sarcastic expression and just looked sad.

'I'm worried about you, Phebes.'

Then, just like that, it was back. 'Yeah, well, don't bother starting now.'

'What?'

'Worrying about me—why start now? You've never given my feelings a second thought before.'

'What are you talking about?'

'Forget it. Just go back to worrying about number one as usual.'

'What the hell do you mean by that?'

'Oh, come on, Shaun—like you've ever cared about how I'm feeling.'

'You're my kid sister—why wouldn't I care about you?'

'I don't know, why *would* you? You sure as hell didn't give me a second thought when you left Jinjulu after the funeral, did you? You have no idea how horrible it was coming back here all those years after Jared died.'

'I couldn't come back.' Shaun had to force the words out. 'I'm sorry if it felt like you were all alone, but I couldn't be here, not then.'

'You think I wanted to be back here? I didn't get a choice.'

'You were just a kid.'

'I was twelve and he was my brother too! But unlike you, I didn't get the choice to run away from it. I had to keep coming back here to walk around a big empty house and watch Mum and Dad turn into damn robots.'

Shaun flinched as he realised how lonely it must have been for his sister. But it didn't change anything. It'd been too much for him to live with back then—hell, it still was, but time and distance had helped a little. Seven years ago he hadn't understood that.

'You don't get to start acting all big brother and protective towards me now, not when you forgot about me for the last seven years.'

'That's not true. I never forgot about you.'

Phoebe just shook her head and stared out through the front windscreen.

'All I'm saying is, if you want to change Dad's mind about art, you'd better ease up on the attitude.'

'This is about today, isn't it?' Phoebe said, sending him a shrewd glance. 'Don't tell me you still have a thing for that Farrell girl?'

Shaun's hands tightened on the steering wheel. He heard a small chuckle but refused to react.

'Well,' she said, 'this should provide a bit of entertainment once the olds hear about it.'

Shaun ignored her barb, his mind going back to an almost identical conversation seven years before.

⁓

'So, you and Bridie Farrell, huh?'

Shaun looked up at his younger brother, who was grinning down at him from the huge harvester they were fixing, and shook his head.

'Come on, you know you've got a thing for her,' Jared continued.

'Do you plan on doing anything useful today, or are you just going to sit up there and prattle on?'

'I'm working—someone has to supervise,' Jared said without bothering to sound the least bit offended.

'Hand me that shifter then, will ya.' Shaun took a swig of water from the bottle by his feet as Jared dug through the toolbox.

'So what's going on between you two anyway?' Jared persisted.

'Nothing,' Shaun grunted as he struggled to loosen the bolt.

'Bull crap, you'll find any excuse to go into that supermarket just so you can see her.'

'Give it a rest.'

'You can deny it all you like, but I know what I know.' Jared reached over to take the tool Shaun held out, then handed over the next one with the practised ease of long years spent working together. 'You could have picked someone with a bit less baggage to lug around, though. Isn't her old man in prison or something? Still, it should be entertaining to see Mum and Dad's reaction,' he chuckled.

'Shut up, will ya.'

Jared looked at him with a gleam in his eye. 'I reckon you've got the hots for little Bridie—big time.'

'Jared, I swear if you don't shut up I'm going to have to teach you who your better is, boy,' he threatened as he tossed his brother a rag to wipe his hands on, even though he'd barely done more than hand over tools most of the afternoon. Lazy sod.

Jared gave a snort. 'I hope you aren't under the misguided impression that you would be my better,' he said with a straight face. ''Cause I distinctly remember that last time I flogged your arse.'

Shaun didn't wait for him to finish his sentence before he swooped and tackled Jared around the knees. Wrestling as adults was a lot different to their playful romping as kids. When Jared landed a jab to Shaun's ribs that momentarily took his breath away, the game turned serious.

Shaun felt it, the moment their light-hearted games turned into something more. They'd been down this track before. The building frustration that always seemed to be lingering just below the surface came rushing out. Suddenly, he no longer saw his brother rumbling with him, instead he saw the source of his rage and frustration. The person he wanted to beat the crap out of, to make him feel as worthless as Shaun had been made to feel lately . . . He was seeing his father, and that only made him want to flog Jared harder.

The old man had never made a secret of the fact that Jinjulu would be passed down to Jared—and it hurt. All his life Shaun had tried to prove to his father he could work the property just as well as his older brother, that the two of them could run the place together. There was no way their old man would agree to that, though—according to him, you couldn't have two top dogs on the place; it made for too many complications.

The cold splash of water in his face made Shaun gasp and splutter as he twisted out of his brother's steel-like grip.

'What'd you do that for, you little brat!' Shaun yelled as Phoebe scampered back from her two dripping brothers.

'Daisy sent me to tell you dinner was ready.' She hid behind Jared for protection. Jared always stuck up for her since he was the eldest and she was the baby of the family.

'Tell Daisy we're on our way,' Jared told Phoebe. 'Good thing she came out when she did, bro,' he added, gingerly feeling his jaw.

'Yeah, sure saved your arse, mate,' Shaun shot back with a lopsided grin. His grin faded slightly as he followed his brother into the laundry to clean up. One day all that rage inside him was going to do some real damage. He hated that the one person in this world he could depend on usually took the brunt of his temper.

⌇

The memory of the wrestling match prompted Shaun to take a long hard look at his family as they sat around the table that night. When had they become a family of strangers?

He looked across at Phoebe, who pushed her food from one side of her plate to the other. It was hard to see any trace of the happy young girl he remembered. He knew she was rebelling—he'd been exactly the same at her age. His father's hard-hand parenting had made him rebel too. Although experimenting with drugs had been a pretty drastic leap on her part.

His mind went back to their conversation in the car and he bit back a sigh. She was right—he had wallowed in his own misery a long time, and in all honesty he'd never really thought about what she'd been going through. He had to make an effort to connect with her again. He owed his sister that much.

Then there was his mother.

Constance Broderick had always been a mystery to him. Everything was about appearances to their mother. From the professionally decorated homestead to the farce of a family meal each evening, it was all part of some fixed notion of what the perfect family was supposed to look like. It hadn't always been like this. When Shaun was growing up she'd had a busy social life and left Daisy to handle the house and children, but she'd become isolated and distant over the last few years . . . harder. Shaun didn't have to wonder when she'd changed—it was the same time they'd all had to change who they were and how they saw the world.

Shaun's wandering mind was snagged by his father's droll tone at the end of the table. 'I went down to look at the fire break I asked you to clear yesterday.'

Shaun hid a sigh.

'What the hell do you call that mess?'

'It's just a fire break, Dad. I cleared the scrub away from the bottom paddock like you wanted.'

'It looks like a bloody dog's breakfast. Tomorrow I want you back down there to clean up the mess.'

'It's just a fire break,' Shaun argued. As if there weren't a million other more important things he had to do than worry about how tidy a bloody fire break was!

'I don't want it left like that. It's an eyesore.'

'Who's going to see it? The sheep don't seem to care.'

'I want it cleaned up!' Douglas yelled and slammed his fist on the table, making the cutlery jump.

'Yes, Dad,' Shaun answered with exaggerated calm.

'And you better not fall behind in any of your jobs, messing about with your little hobby farm down the back. The minute you can't keep up with the first priority, which is this place, the deal's off. Understand?'

Shaun bristled at his father's patronising tone. What was he, four years old?

'So, Shaun, I hear you have a girlfriend?' Phoebe's remark was delivered with all the subtlety of a freight train roaring through the house.

'Oh?' Instantly his mother's ears pricked up. 'Do we know her?'

Shaun groaned silently; this was the last thing he needed—his mother's interest in his love life. He glanced across at his sister and frowned at the smug little grin she wore. It seemed she had some kind of score to settle after this afternoon's run-in with Bridie. 'It's early days,' he said, realising that no matter what he said he was in trouble here.

'Well, you must invite her out for lunch. What about this weekend? I'll let Daisy know,' his mother decided with a nod of her head.

'Ah, Mum, I don't think that's—'

'What's wrong, Shaun? You're not ashamed of your new girlfriend, are you?' Phoebe asked with wide-eyed innocence.

'It's a bit early to call her a girlfriend. We're just friends.' Christ! He'd only just got brave enough to *speak* to the woman, let alone ask her out.

'Really?' Phoebe said. 'Then why did you spend the night at the pub last weekend?'

'I drank too much to drive home,' he answered tightly.

'Hmm. A little birdie told me there's a certain barmaid who works there that gets you all hot under the collar,' she said casually.

Shaun glared at her, wishing she'd get her kicks some other way.

'A barmaid?' his mother asked, sounding incredulous.

'She works behind a bar, not on a street corner,' he said dryly.

'You sure about that, big brother? She's a Farrell, and all

the Farrells around here are either in prison or living in the caravan park, or so I've heard.'

'Shaun, for God's sake.' His mother frowned.

'Give it a rest, Phoebe. You don't know a damn thing about her.'

His sister smiled. 'I know about the Farrells. I've been asking around. Did you know her father is in prison and she's got a kid in high school?'

Shaun leaned across the table to glare at his sister. 'Who the hell cares what her father did? You can't choose your relatives, can you—God knows, around here that would be a bonus sometimes. And it's not her kid, it's her younger brother. At least get your facts straight before you start running off your mouth.'

'Well,' Constance cleared her throat delicately as she put down her knife and fork, 'it's settled then. You'll invite her.'

'Mum, she's not—'

'Not what, Shaun?' Constance arched one eyebrow expectantly.

He'd been about to say, not ready to deal with *them* yet, but now that Phoebe had opened her big mouth his mother would be on his case until she finally got her way. He was under no illusions—his mother was not thrilled by the news her son was interested in a barmaid with a criminal father. He knew she wanted to inspect this woman who had caught his eye—and more than likely try to find a way to end the relationship at the earliest opportunity. Well, she could try. Shaun wasn't about to let his mother interfere with whatever this thing was between him and Bridie . . . and there was a *thing*. He just needed to wait until Bridie acknowledged it as well, and she would, he was certain.

'I'll get back to you, Mum,' he said.

His appetite was gone now. The last thing he wanted was his family ruining any chance he might have with Bridie. Dinner around this table with his family would be more than enough to put any woman off him.

Nine

The loudspeaker echoed in the distance and Bridie felt a warm glow expand inside her chest at the familiar smells of cow dung and sweaty horses.

The Tooncanny Show. It was *the* social event of the year.

As a kid, Bridie would save madly in the weeks leading up to the show. She'd spend afternoons dragging a hessian sack around, collecting empty cans and then taking them down to the scrap yard to cash in for pocket money. She loved the noise and the lights, even the smell of Dagwood Dogs in the air. There was always such a buzz around town at showtime. Held before it turned too cold to enjoy being outside, the show marked the end of autumn and the beginning of winter.

Bridie paid her money at the gate and looked about as she decided which way to go first. She'd worked the lunch shift and had the evening off. She and Alf had an understanding—she didn't work show day. Most of the businesses in town closed up for the day, it was a tradition—no school, no work, not on show day. Nervous excitement bubbled inside her and she was a little embarrassed at the stupidity of it. She was an adult, for goodness sake, and here she was feeling like a kid again, fighting the urge to run through the gates and go in search of friends from school and suss out what daredevil ride to make herself sick on first.

Those days were long gone. The only kids from school she still saw were wives of a few of the regulars; now and again their husbands would make an effort to bring them along for a counter meal or a drink to celebrate an anniversary.

Bridie often wondered if any of them wished their lives had turned out differently. Gone were the happy, carefree girls she'd gone to school with; in their place were tired faces and overweight bodies. Years of childbearing and worrying about money had sucked the life out of them. It was almost cruel at Christmastime when the ones who'd been lucky enough to leave town for university or to seek adventure outside of Tooncanny came home to visit family. They'd usually drop in to the Drovers to catch up with the locals and Bridie would see the stark differences between the two groups. These girls had pursued careers and travelled. They frequented beauty salons and hairdressers on a regular basis. They shopped at boutiques and accessorised their outfits. The Tooncanny girls usually stayed away from the Drovers at Christmastime.

The smell of Dagwood Dogs and toffee apples floated on the breeze and Bridie's stomach grumbled loudly in appreciation. The noise of sideshow alley was almost deafening. There was the hiss of compressed air as rides threw people into the heavens on arms of steel, and the screams of both terror and delight carried through the late afternoon air. Games booths overflowed with stuffed animals and gaudy prizes. Groups of teenagers laughed and yelled over the impossible noise, jostling their way through the people streaming along the narrow alleyway made up of show workers heckling them to 'come and try ya luck'. Music blared and terrifying screams came from the haunted house as Bridie followed the crowd heading for the pavilions where the judging of arts, crafts and animals took place.

As she reached the last of the rides, she found herself looking down at the show ring where the judging of Miss Showgirl had just finished. The girls were still lined up along the small stage in front of a stack of hay bales, hugging each other with all the tears and drama of a full-blown Miss Universe pageant.

Bridie found a place on the fence to climb up on and watch. She wasn't sure why she was even bothering. It was a stupid outdated institution that was as ridiculous to watch as it was to try to justify. *Then why was it the one thing you always dreamed of doing as a kid?* The truth was she had always longed to be in a Miss Showgirl pageant. When she turned eighteen, she'd even got up the courage to go into the show committee office in town and ask for an application form. Unfortunately, the day she'd chosen to go in was the day the committee had been holding their regular meeting and the whispers that followed her request had quickly changed her mind. They'd been right—what the hell had she been thinking? The Miss Showgirl winner was supposed to be a paragon of the community, not a member of the most notorious family in Tooncanny.

She was about to get down off the fence again when she caught sight of Shaun Broderick at the edge of the crowd. Curiosity made her linger, and as he walked up on stage to escort the newly crowned Miss Showgirl he looked up and caught her eye. He rolled his eyes in exasperation and she grinned, then he turned his attention back to his partner and Bridie felt her heart sink.

Climbing back down off the fence, she wasn't sure why she felt like a deflated balloon. It wasn't as though Shaun Broderick had ever been anything to her. So what if he had a girlfriend? He'd saved her from a volatile situation back in the car park, but that didn't mean he fancied her. Of course he'd have a girlfriend, and of *course* she'd be a Miss Showgirl winner—you couldn't expect anything less of a Broderick.

Better to face it and realise her silly schoolgirl crush belonged in the past with all the other crap she continued to drag around.

֍

He was getting a headache from all the hairspray fumes and expensive perfume. He removed the red talons from his arm and backed away from the matching red lips of this year's Miss Tooncanny Showgirl. The girl was barely out of high school and she'd been whispering things in his ear that almost made him blush. What the hell were kids learning at school these days?

He made his excuses and tried not to run from the show ring. He'd kept his mother happy and provided an escort for the winner—done his duty as son and unattached prime side of beef—and now he was outta here. Reaching sideshow alley he scoured the sea of faces for the only face he truly wanted to see. He took a gamble and headed for the animal pavilion. If he had to, he was prepared to undertake a grid search for Bridie Farrell.

The squealing of pigs and bleating of sheep mixed with the excited chatter of children as they ran from one enclosure to another to see all the animals on display. The judging had already been done and ribbons awarded to each category, so now the general public could meander through the big sheds and admire the winners to their hearts' content.

Shaun finally spotted her at the rails of the ram enclosure. He took his time before he approached her, letting his eyes roam over her long dark hair, hanging loose instead of pulled back for work. Her jeans and T-shirt were clean and neatly pressed. He loved that she always looked and smelled so . . . fresh. Even over the stench of manure and wool, he managed to catch a trace of her light perfume, which reminded him of sunshine and flowers— unlike the cloying sultry scent of the women he'd been around earlier.

Easing up beside her, he crossed his arms along the top rail of the pen. She glanced over at him in surprise before turning back to face the big ram in front of them.

'I wasn't sure I was going to find you, it's a fair crowd this year,' he murmured, watching her face.

'I wasn't aware you were looking for me.' She turned to face him, taking his breath away. For a minute, he lost his train of thought as he took in her full red mouth and deep blue eyes. He snapped himself out of it and forced himself to concentrate before he made a bigger fool of himself than he already had.

'I see Jinjulu won again this year. Congratulations,' she said, nodding towards the ram.

'Thanks. That's Dad's department.'

His eyes dropped to the expanse of smooth skin along her neck as she tilted her head slightly. 'You don't like sheep?' she asked.

He chuckled down at her and saw her smile. 'Nah, if I had my way we'd be scaling down the sheep side of the business and getting more into crops.'

'And your dad doesn't agree?'

He felt his grin slip slightly. 'Dad and I rarely agree about anything.'

'It must be hard to work with family.'

He wasn't going to waste the precious few minutes he had with Bridie talking about his father. 'Have you eaten yet?'

She shook her head, those penetrating eyes still focused on him intently. 'I just got here.'

'Can I buy you dinner?'

'I was planning on having a steak sandwich and a toffee apple,' she told him doubtfully, as though the concept of show food were beneath him somehow.

'Actually, I was only going to buy you a Dagwood Dog, but I suppose I could lash out on a steak sandwich if I have to make a good impression.'

'Wow, you sure know how to spoil a girl,' she said, turning to lean her back against the rails. 'Okay, why not, I'm starving.'

'I can take care of that—come this way,' he said, thinking that had been easier than he'd expected. Now, if he could only stop his heart slamming around inside his chest like a bloody jackhammer, he'd be fine.

~

The carnival music swirled around them as they threaded their way through the crowd to the food pavilion. The tantalising smell of barbecued meat and onions was thick in the air, and the sizzle and pop of the hot plate almost drowned out the screams from the hurricane ride nearby.

Shaun waved to a few men in hats but didn't stop to chat. His hand settled on the small of her back and she stiffened in surprise, but she didn't have time to think about it as the crush of the hungry masses pushed her against him. Besides, she had more . . . pressing things on her mind than his hand on her back.

She'd lived in this rural community all her life and thought she'd become immune to the country-boy look— the akubras and moleskins, the whole rugged heart-throb image familiar from romance novels with cowboys on the covers. But Shaun Broderick in a pair of jeans and a wide-brimmed hat did something to her that no other man could do.

By the time they neared the front of the queue, Bridie was a quivering bundle of nerves. The heat of his body, combined with the heady smell of his expensive cologne and the faint hint of smoke and leather, made her light-headed with desire.

'How do you want it?'

Bridie gave a guilty jump. 'S . . . sorry?' She saw his slow smile and felt like an idiot.

'Your steak—how do you want it cooked?'

'Well done, thanks,' she managed, striving for a cool reply and smiling at the man in the blue apron.

Carrying their food and a beer each, they weaved their way through the pavilion to find a place to sit. Bridie was used to the overt staring and ready whispers of some of the town's more vicious gossips, but today she was unusually sensitive to the curious glances she and Shaun were receiving as they searched for a spot to sit down and eat. Naturally all the tables were taken so they were left standing in the middle of the pavilion.

'I know a place we can sit. Follow me,' Shaun said, and she wondered if he, too, had picked up on the interest surrounding them. He turned to head out the back of the pavilion and they circled around to the white grandstand set up near the wood chopping.

'Where are we going?' she asked when he didn't climb into the grandstand.

'Just up here a bit. I've got something I want to show you.'

'Like I haven't heard that one before,' she muttered and he chuckled.

'Ta da,' he announced, coming to a stop behind a row of horse floats and old stables.

Ready to send him a scathing glare for bringing her all the way across the showground for nothing, she stopped when she turned and saw what he was looking at. Before them was a magnificent view of the sinking sun framed by the burning red trunks of distant gum trees.

'Wow.'

'See, I know how to impress a lady.'

'You certainly know how to pick a dining spot,' she agreed.

They ate in silence, with the show noise in the background and the glorious sunset before them. It wasn't until Shaun had finished his second sandwich that he asked about her life. She'd known it was coming, of course—it was natural to ask someone you didn't know that well about their life, their family, and how long they'd been in town and how come they hadn't left yet. It was just unfortunate these were the things she hated talking about the most.

'So tell me about your family. You have a younger brother, don't you?'

She sent him a sharp glance but saw that there was only genuine interest on his face, not the sarcasm she'd half-expected. She nodded. 'My brother, Luke. He lives with me. I'm sure you've heard quite a bit about my family already,' she added wryly.

'Not that much really.'

'My mother died about seven years ago, I guess,' she said. 'And my father . . . doesn't live with us,' she added succinctly. There was no way he couldn't already know exactly where her father was. Not when he'd lived in Tooncanny most of his life. 'I was getting ready to leave town but I stayed on to take care of Luke. He was only little at the time.'

'That must be tough, taking on your brother all by yourself.'

She thought back to previous show days when Luke had wanted to hang around with her, when she'd watch him on the dodgem cars and having fun on the rides. This time she'd caught sight of him only briefly when she'd first arrived. Her jaw clenched as she recalled the boys he'd been with—Spider Jennings, who was Tyler's younger cousin, and a few other troublemakers she knew by reputation only. She was hoping to catch Luke before she left just to remind him he had a curfew, although she was pretty sure he'd be doing his best to avoid running into her while he was with his mates.

Shrugging off these thoughts, Bridie looked back out at the sunset. 'He's family. You do what you have to do, don't you.'

His silence made her sneak a look over at him. He seemed to be considering her answer.

'What about you?' she asked. 'What's your family like—do you all get on?'

'We're like most families, I guess. We don't always get along.'

'You never wanted to do anything other than farming?' she prodded. She wondered whether the children of farming families like the Brodericks were expected to follow in their parents' footsteps or if they were encouraged to go out and do other things with their lives.

'I worked in the mines and on other properties after uni, but I've always wanted to be a farmer.'

'It must be nice to carry on a tradition like yours, I guess.'

He crumpled the paper from around his sandwich in his large fist. 'Sometimes it's a lot to live up to,' he said and she watched his expression tighten slightly as he added, 'Trust me, it comes with a price.'

'What do you mean?'

For a minute he stared out towards the horizon and she thought he wasn't going to answer her. 'I always wanted to run Jinjulu—the place is in my blood. I could never imagine doing anything else when I was a kid. It was all I ever wanted.'

'But you didn't come back here after you finished university?' she questioned.

'No. There was a time when I couldn't face being here. Too many memories.'

'When your brother died?' she asked quietly, remembering the accident and the talk that had followed.

'Yeah.'

Bridie studied him compassionately; she knew the grief of losing a loved one. She moved her hand until her fingers touched his on the ground between them.

'So, Bridie Farrell, tell me more about you.'

'There's not much to tell. I grew up here. I'd always planned on leaving as soon as I finished school, but then Mum got sick. Then, after Dad . . . well, all that happened with him, I put off leaving again to take care of Luke.' She shrugged. 'And here I am . . . still.'

'So how come you don't have a boyfriend?'

Bridie looked across at him. 'And how do you know I don't have a boyfriend?'

Shaun gave a smirk. 'Because I doubt I'd be sitting here with my head still attached to my shoulders if you did.'

'Maybe I have an understanding boyfriend.'

'He'd have to be an idiot if he was.'

'The pickings are pretty slim around Tooncanny,' she said. 'I'm related to half the town, and the other half are too scared to even think about getting mixed up with the daughter of Brian Farrell, convicted criminal.'

'So, no boyfriend. Well, that's a bit of good news.'

'Oh yeah, it's great news!' she said, shaking her head at him.

'Well, good news for me.'

Bridie's smile faltered slightly at his matter-of-fact statement, and she tried to control the rush of pleasure his words evoked.

'But there must have been someone, at some time? You're what, twenty-three or so?'

'Twenty-four. And actually, there haven't been all that many boyfriends—unheard-of for a Farrell, right?'

'I wasn't implying anything, Bridie,' he said, watching her with a small frown.

'Well, implied or not, I'm just telling you the facts. I've dated a few people on and off, but I don't have a very interesting social life.'

Other than being completely humiliated by you when I was seventeen, she added silently.

She'd lost her virginity to a kid in her rollcall class one night after a school disco. His name was Ron. He wasn't like the other boys in her class—he didn't call her names or pick on her, and he wasn't good-looking enough to draw Cheryl's attention. There was nothing she'd found particularly attractive about him, but her pride had been hurt by Shaun and his stupid mates at the party a few weeks earlier and she wanted to prove to herself she was desired by someone . . . someone she got to pick. Bridie brushed the thought away. Ron had left town after high school, gone away to uni somewhere, and she'd never heard from him since.

'I made a few rash decisions when I was younger, like most kids, but I was conscious of the way people looked at me around town and I knew I was never going to give anyone reason to put me down because of my family's reputation.'

'I don't think anyone could think anything bad about you, Bridie. You're a strong, beautiful woman doing a tough job raising a younger brother. I think most people would consider that pretty damn impressive.'

Bridie held his gaze for a moment, surprised and a little thrown by his words. She was relieved when he glanced at his watch.

'Listen, I have to do something for a bit, can we meet up again later?' He must have read the hesitation in her face because he added quickly, 'I promised you dinner and we haven't had dessert yet. You can't disappear before the meal's over—it's just not done.'

How could she refuse that sexy grin and those pleading eyes like a damn puppy dog? She pretended nonchalance. 'I suppose so. I wanted to watch some of the events in the centre ring anyway.'

'Great.'

He took her hand and led her back towards the hustle and bustle of show day. As they reached the edge of the crowd, he slowly let her hand go, but he left with a wink and a promise to meet her back near the wood chopping in an hour. She watched him disappear into the throng of hats, jeans and checked shirts.

On her way to find a seat in the grandstand, Bridie stopped to chat to a few locals from the pub, then she spotted an empty space on the end of a row of weathered timber seats.

The announcer was calling the next competitor for the camp-drafting event and she craned her neck to get a look at the rider working the steer in the cut-out yard just off the main arena. Once he'd shown the judges he had the beast under control, he called for the gate to be opened and out thundered steer, horse and rider.

Music blared from the speakers and excitement spread through the audience as they watched the competitor manoeuvre the beast through pegs in a figure-eight pattern. A loud cheer broke out and they clapped as the competitor chased the steer back through another two pegs, at which point the timer stopped, signalling the end of the run.

The next rider came out and Bridie did a double take as she realised it was Shaun seated in the saddle of the most magnificent animal she'd ever laid eyes on. The big chestnut horse threw back its head in an arrogant display of power and beauty. Shaun seemed to flow with the animal as horse and rider made their way around the ring. From her position close to the ring, Bridie could see the fierce determination etched on Shaun's face as all his movements were concentrated on the steer he was manoeuvring. It was a beautiful thing to watch and Bridie was transfixed.

She imagined the strong thigh muscles beneath the denim of his jeans bunching and flexing as he moved with the horse, skidding to a halt one minute only to lunge forward and block the steer's retreat a few seconds later. As he came to a stop after the run finished, it was almost as though he felt her presence and she saw him lift his head to find her.

Bridie joined in with the applause and felt a smile creep into place as she held his gaze, those dark eyes watching her from beneath the rim of his akubra.

She sat through the last two competitors but her attention kept drifting towards Shaun, who stood by his horse outside the ring. She saw three or four young women in short denim skirts and high-heeled boots fluttering around him; he chatted to them but his focus remained on his fellow competitors out in the ring. After the event had concluded and the trophies had been handed out, the crowd began to disperse from the grandstand. Shaun and his horse had come in second place; she wondered how the judges could have given first place to someone else—had they been watching a different event? The man had been pure poetry in motion.

She shook herself. What was she doing? It was madness to even consider there could be anything between them. How on earth could she expect anyone, let alone a Broderick, to even begin to understand her mixed-up family? Why would he risk getting involved with a woman whose family was always in trouble with the law and whose father was in jail over a drug deal gone wrong? Even if he could get past the associated baggage, what would be the point? She was leaving town as soon as Luke finished school.

She supposed he could be interested in a casual fling, and her spirits sank at the thought. She didn't do casual flings—she'd grown up with the heavy weight of people's expectations that she'd slip up and prove that all Farrells were the same . . . Well, she wasn't going to give them that satisfaction. He was probably just bored and she presented a challenge to entertain him until something better came along. She hadn't forgotten that bet either. What if this was just a grown-up prank? Was she prepared to risk that kind of humiliation again? The thought doused the beginnings of excitement inside her and she stood up to make her way to the car. She'd had enough escapism for one afternoon—time to get back to reality.

Now that the sun had set, there was a definite nip of winter in the air. Carefully negotiating the dried ruts of tractor tyres as she picked her way across the paddock that served as the public car park, she realised how tricky it was to find her way without the bright lights of the show to guide her. She fumbled with her keys, muttering beneath her breath as they dropped from her fingers and disappeared into the long whiskey-coloured grass beneath her feet. Gingerly scratching around in the dark, she had just felt the cold metallic shape of her keys when a deep voice behind her, followed by a gentle touch on her arm, made her let out a startled scream.

'It's okay, it's me.' Shaun's amused tone caught her slightly off guard.

'You scared me,' she breathed.

'Sorry. I thought you heard me coming. What happened? We were supposed to meet for dessert.'

Bridie kept her eyes on his chin, not daring to look into his eyes. 'I thought you'd be busy with your adoring fans. Why didn't you tell me you were riding in an event?'

He shrugged. 'I didn't want you to think I was big-noting myself.'

'It was pretty impressive,' she said, noting with surprise that he was genuinely embarrassed. 'I've never watched a live camp draft before.'

'Glad you liked it. So why were you leaving without saying goodbye?'

The keys bit into her soft hand as she tightened her grip around them. Straightening, she tipped her head back and searched the silver-rimmed clouds over the moon. 'What is it you want from me, Shaun?' she said with a long sigh.

'Because I don't understand why you're suddenly . . . everywhere.'

'I'm not a stalker, if that's what you're thinking. It's kinda hard to live in a place like Tooncanny and not keep bumping into the same people all the time.'

'That's not what I mean.'

'Why is it so hard to believe I might just want to get to know you better?'

'Because last time you paid all this attention to me it was for a bet—remember?' she said dryly.

'That was a long time ago, Bridie. I was a stupid jerk back then. I'm sorry for that, sorrier than you'll ever know, but you never gave me a chance to explain, you just took off and . . . I didn't get another chance to apologise.'

'What was there to explain?' The memory of that horrible night made her stiffen with humiliation.

They'd been laughing at something they'd discovered they had in common; her silly schoolgirl heart had been pounding in her ears as he sat close to her on the uncomfortable old lounge chair on the back verandah. She knew he was about to kiss her, she saw him moving closer, and her mind had gone into a state of euphoric anticipation: Shaun Broderick was actually about to kiss her—*her*, Bridie Farrell!

It was then that the back door had swung open, hitting the wall behind it with a loud bang. The jeers and shouts from the other guys Shaun had been talking to earlier broke the spell, and the bitter truth of who she was—and who she would always be, at least in Tooncanny—hit her squarely in the face.

She'd leapt up from the lounge chair, intending to run away, but Shaun had stood up quickly and blocked her escape. She hadn't allowed him time to speak; she'd swung her fist, catching him off balance and sending him sprawling backwards onto the chair, before running as fast as she could from the laughter that followed her departure.

'Bridie, it started out as a dare, a stupid dare that I wish I had never taken, but you have to believe me, the minute you looked at me and smiled, I was a goner. I wasn't talking to you because of a bloody dare, I was talking to you because I couldn't take my eyes off you.'

'Well, pardon me for remembering it differently.'

'How do you remember it?'

'As you using your Broderick charm to get into my pants.' She shook her head as he opened his mouth to protest, then turned to unlock her car. 'It doesn't matter, you're right; it was a long time ago and it was stupid, so let's just forget it.'

'Wait a minute.' He leaned over and took the keys from her cold fingers. 'It *does* matter. Bridie, I don't want the past to get in the way of the here and now.'

'It already has,' she snapped, turning on him. It hurt. She wasn't sure why she suddenly felt the sting of tears behind her eyes, but it hit her hard and fast. 'I don't have the time or the energy for this, Shaun. If you're after a one-night stand you're wasting your time. You've got the wrong Farrell— go try any one of my cousins, I'm sure they'll gladly help you out.'

'Would you just wait a minute,' he said, raising his voice. 'I've already apologised for being a jerk as a kid—I'm *sorry*,' he emphasised again. 'Believe me, I paid a heavy price for that night in more ways than one.' Bridie could hear the pain in that admission. 'But that was then. We're different people now. I've never got you out of my head, even after all this time. I've been working up the nerve to talk to you ever since I came back to town.'

The sudden uncertainty in his voice seemed out of character for the usually confident Shaun Broderick. Biting her lip, Bridie let out a shaky breath.

'I get that you felt betrayed, but give me a chance to prove I've changed,' he said.

'Why? Are you really willing to feed the gossip mill around here? What about your family? I don't know your parents, but I'm fairly sure they won't be thrilled if you're linked to a Farrell.'

'In case you haven't noticed, I'm an adult. Who I'm linked with is my business.' He must have seen the indecision in her face because he took a step closer. His voice was low and it sent a small shiver along her spine. 'Let me prove it.'

God help her, she wasn't made of stone, even though she wished she were. She didn't fight it when his lips touched hers; she couldn't, her body had overruled her common sense. How was she supposed to resist this man when his very presence sent off fireworks inside her? The explosions were still there when she opened her eyes and it took her a minute to realise they *were* fireworks—real ones!

Shaun slipped his arms around her waist and gently pulled her against him, turning her so she could face the display erupting in the sky above them. She wasn't sure whether it was the deep sonic boom of the fireworks or her own heart beating in her chest, but either way she was grateful for the strong arms holding her close.

As the last of the lights fell from the sky, darkness settled around them once more, and weary show-goers, carrying tired children, began to filter into the car park ready for home and bed.

'I better go or I'll be stuck in the crush to leave,' she said in a voice barely above a whisper.

'Will you think about it, Bridie?'

What could she say when just a simple kiss made her feel light-headed? She managed a nod, and a slow grin spread across his face.

'Can I come by tomorrow? I have to help pack up here in the morning, but I'll be finished by nine.'

'Okay.'

'Goodnight, Bridie—drive safely,' he said and kissed her once more before handing back her keys.

For some reason, not only could she barely form a single word but she was all thumbs too. She fumbled to fit the key into the lock. 'See you tomorrow then,' she said, finally managing to unlock the car and slide inside.

'Count on it,' he grinned.

Bridie forced herself to concentrate on driving. She double-checked her mirrors and carefully reversed out of her parking spot. Risking a quick glance in her rear-view mirror, she saw him silhouetted in the steady stream of lights that bumped their way through the paddock car park.

What have you got yourself into now? she wondered as she dragged her eyes back to the dark stretch of highway before her.

Ten

Sunday mornings were usually sleep-ins and late break-fasts, since it was the only day Bridie didn't work, but after tossing and turning most of the night after the show she decided to get up and clean.

When she was tense, she took it out on the house, changing sheets, reorganising cupboards and moving the furniture around. It gave her a way to work off her nervous energy and be productive at the same time.

By nine o'clock she felt somewhat calmer and was just taking cinnamon swirls out of the oven when she heard a vehicle pull up.

She ran her hands through her hair and took a deep breath before opening the front door. For a minute she stared at him, lost in those dark eyes, and then she regained her composure.

In the kitchen she jumped at the chance to make coffee so she had something to do with her hands.

'I brought you something,' he said with a small smile, handing over a bag. Bridie peeked into the bag and then turned to him with a bright smile. 'We didn't get to dessert last night, so I stopped by to grab you some this morning before they packed up.'

The bag contained three huge serves of fairy floss in sickly-sweet shades of pink, yellow and purple, and half a dozen ruby-red toffee apples. 'Oh my goodness, this will be enough to last until next year's show.'

He gave a small shrug but seemed pleased with her reaction.

'Thank you. This is one of the nicest presents anyone's ever given me,' she said quietly. She selected a bag of pink fairy floss and placed it in the centre of the table between them, then sat down. She tore off a piece, placing it in her mouth; the light fluffy cloud of floss dissolved into grains of sugar, transporting her back to her childhood in an instant.

'You really like fairy floss,' Shaun said, watching her with an amused grin.

Bridie felt a blush creep up her throat. 'It reminds me of when I was a kid. Thank you for bringing it over.'

'No worries. Glad you liked it.' He took one of the cinnamon swirls. 'These look pretty good too. A woman who not only cooks, but also pulls a mean beer—what more could a guy ask for?' he joked.

'There's no end to my talents,' she said sarcastically.

They were on their second cup of coffee and Bridie was laughing at Shaun's account of him and his brother Jared trying to unbog a four-wheel drive before their father found out, when Luke emerged from his room, all sleepy eyes and tousled hair.

'Morning,' Bridie said. 'Luke, this is Shaun—'

'Broderick—yeah, I know who he is.' Luke turned his back and pulled the milk out of the fridge.

'Luke,' Bridie said warningly.

'How you doin'?' Shaun's expression gave nothing away.

'I'm going to Spider's,' Luke said, ignoring Shaun's greeting.

'Luke!' Bridie snapped.

'What?'

Bridie clenched her jaw and kept her voice low and calm. 'Say hello to Shaun.'

'Hello Shaun,' he mimicked. 'Can I go now?'

'As much as I'll miss your cheerful presence . . . Be home by five.' When he pushed open the back screen door without a reply, Bridie called out, 'Luke! Five!'

'Yeah, I heard ya,' he yelled, before vanishing around the corner of the house.

'Well, that was fun,' Bridie said.

'It's a hard age—what is he, fifteen, sixteen?'

'Sixteen. He'll be seventeen at the end of the year. He's already started the application process to join the army after his birthday, if he can stay out of trouble that long.'

'You don't mind him joining the army?' Shaun asked.

'Not really. I think it'll do him some good to have a bit of discipline in his life. Keep him on the straight and narrow.'

'Boys usually manage to get themselves into trouble at some point in their lives—goes with the territory.'

'Not if I can help it,' she said firmly.

'You can't always be there to watch him,' he warned. 'I remember it pretty much sucked to be that age. You're not a kid any more, but you're not quite an adult either.'

'I can't see you running wild with the wrong crowd at sixteen,' she said with a small smile.

'I was away at boarding school most of the time, and when I was back on Jinjulu, Dad kept me too busy working to leave any time to get into mischief. But that doesn't mean I didn't think about it,' he grinned.

'We just have to make it through until the end of the year.' Then she could get her own life back on track . . . or started. Getting it back on track suggested that it had once been *on* track. She hadn't even left town yet.

The phone rang in the next room and Bridie excused herself to go and answer it. Shaun took advantage of her absence to check out his surroundings. Across from him a row of photo frames sat on a waist-high wall divider; he got up to take a better look.

There were school photos of Luke from a range of years, and one of Bridie and Luke together. Bridie was hugging her brother, who held a trophy. Bridie's eyes shone as she stared into the camera, her long hair held back by a pair of sunglasses on her head. At the back were two older photos; one, he assumed, of her parents, and a smaller unframed photo that sat propped up against the other one. It was of a young woman who looked a lot like Bridie, taken in what looked like the late seventies, on some kind of boardwalk by a beach.

He looked around. The house was certainly never going to be featured in *Better Homes and Gardens*, but he could see the effort Bridie had put into her home. The lino had a printed pattern of timber floorboards that at least gave the room a contemporary look, and the kitchen's old chipboard cupboards had been given a coat of white paint that helped to brighten the place up. There was nothing she could do about the Kermit-the-Frog green of the counter tops, but she'd made the most of the room's best feature, a large square window that overlooked the paddocks beyond her minuscule backyard.

He thought of his own house. His father had forked out a fortune for an interior decorator to fly in from the city to revamp the place, simply because his mother had decided that it no longer suited her tastes—even though its last makeover was a mere five years old.

He had stood by and watched the destructive path his parents were on. Part of him felt sad that they both allowed it to continue; part of him was outraged that they weren't trying to change it. Douglas took almost no interest in his wife and yet he handed over fistfuls of cash to pander to her every desire. It was guilt money, pure and simple. He bought peace of mind by keeping his wife happy. It was how Douglas Broderick eased his conscience, how he apologised without having to admit he had been wrong.

Bridie came back into the kitchen. 'Want another refill on the coffee?'

'Sure.' He'd deal with his father and his inevitable wrath at Shaun being late home. Let them manage without him for a bit; he was sick of always being Mr Dependable.

He stole a glance across at Bridie as she made the coffee.

Her long hair was pulled back into a ponytail and it gave her a soft, feminine look, making him itch to kiss her again. The faded jeans she wore hugged her tight in all the right places.

Bugger Dad and the consequences—he'd worry about them later.

~

Bridie was surprised to see it was almost one. 'Do you want to stay for lunch? I have soup.'

'If you're sure you have enough. I can go down the street and grab something from the store if you want.'

'No, I have plenty. I can't seem to make soup in small batches for the life of me.'

They heated up pumpkin soup and she took a loaf of bread out of the freezer. She heated it up in the oven so the crust was crunchy. 'Now all we need is a rainy afternoon and it'll be perfect,' she said.

'Keep wishing, we could use some rain.'

They ate in silence for a few minutes, until Shaun complimented her on the soup. 'Where did you learn to cook like this?'

'My mum. She was a fantastic cook. She always dreamed of opening her own restaurant.'

'It's a shame she never did,' he said, and she caught the honest sympathy in his gaze. 'So you took care of her? When she got sick?'

Bridie nodded.

'How old were you?'

'Seventeen.'

'That's a big responsibility for a seventeen-year-old kid.'

Bridie shrugged. 'There wasn't anyone else to do it.'

'What about family on your mother's side?'

Bridie stirred the soup in her bowl. 'When Mum fell pregnant with me and refused to end her relationship with my father, her parents disowned her. They were quite old when they had her and I guess she'd been a bit of a handful for them.' It still made her blood boil to think about parents refusing to have anything to do with their child. For all their faults, the one thing Farrells did *not* do was turn away family. She guessed that had been, in part, what had kept her mother here when it would have been easier just to leave. The Farrells had taken her in and embraced her as family, while her own flesh and blood had wiped their hands of her.

'How did you manage school and taking care of your mum?'

'I dropped out halfway through my last year.' She didn't look at him as she spoke—she knew that someone who'd been to boarding school and university wouldn't be able to comprehend dropping out of high school.

He was quiet for a long time and Bridie went back to sipping her soup to hide the sudden awkwardness she was feeling.

'I think it's pretty awesome what you did for your mum,' he said at last. 'I can't imagine how difficult it must have been to watch someone you loved get so sick.'

'It wasn't much fun,' she said dismissively. But something in the genuine warmth of his gaze made her go on. 'As bad as that time was, it was also one of the best I had with my mother.' She put her spoon down carefully. 'We talked about so many things—we spent hours lying side by side on her bed while she told me all the things she wanted me to know about life. She had a list.'

Her mother had been trying to cram a lifetime of advice and memories into a few short months. It was both touching and heartbreaking. Bridie knew that Beth was desperately sad at the knowledge that she wouldn't be around to witness her children grow into adults. She didn't wallow in self-pity, though—instead she wrote letters to leave with Bridie for every significant occasion she could think of. Bridie had opened one on her eighteenth birthday, and another on her twenty-first. She treasured those letters and kept them in the carved hope chest at the end of her bed. There were also letters for Luke's birthdays, and she knew there was one for her wedding day and another for the birth of her first child . . . They were kept safely tucked away for a time too distant to seem real to Bridie.

'As painful as it was to watch her fade away before our eyes, at least we had a chance to say goodbye. I can't imagine what it would be like to lose someone unexpectedly with no chance to say everything you wanted to say.' As soon as she said the words her eyes flew to Shaun's face and she caught the flash of pain there. 'Oh my God, Shaun, I'm so sorry, I didn't think before I spoke.'

He brushed away her concern with a sad smile. 'Don't be. It's okay.'

'No, it's not,' she said softly, mentally kicking herself for saying something so insensitive.

'Losing someone you love hurts no matter how it happens. I'm really glad you had the chance to get to know your mum better before she passed away, because regrets suck.'

She gave a nod of agreement. 'Life can be full of them.'

'What about you, do you have any regrets?'

She laughed. 'Only if I never get out of this place. I'd like to think there's still hope for me.'

'You want to leave Tooncanny?' He sounded surprised.

'More than you could possibly know.'

'Where do you want to go?'

'Surfers Paradise,' she answered without hesitation.

'Why?'

'Why? Are you serious? The Gold Coast . . . Queensland?'

'Yeah, but it's like some holiday tourist place—why would you want to go and live there?'

She gave an offhand shrug and stared into her bowl. 'It's just somewhere I've always wanted to go.'

'Then why don't you just go there for a holiday? You don't have to move there, do you?'

'The point is, I want to live just about *anywhere* other than this place. The where isn't important. It's just the *when*.'

'If you hate it so much, how come you've stayed here this long?'

'Because I have a brother to think about, and I can't afford to move anywhere else while I have him to take care of. I've almost finished paying off this place; by the time I have, he'll have finished school and hopefully he'll be in the army. Then I can sell up and move somewhere else.'

'You've got it all worked out.' His reply held a note of reluctant admiration.

'I've been planning my escape for a long, long time.'

'Sounds like it.'

'What about you? Have you always wanted to come back here?'

'Yeah. I've always planned on returning to Jinjulu. Although there are times when I wonder what the hell I'm doing here.'

'What do you mean?'

It was his turn to shrug. 'Dad's got his own way of doing things and he isn't exactly open to anyone else's opinions. We butt heads a fair bit.'

'That must be hard to deal with on a daily basis.'

'I'm working on helping him see the light,' he grinned.

Bridie pushed her bowl aside and smiled back. 'Well, here's to us—may our dreams become a reality,' she said, raising her water glass towards his bottle of beer.

As he reached across to tap his bottle against her glass, his expression seemed slightly guarded. She couldn't be sure, but she had a feeling it had something to do with her plans to leave town some day. She was relieved to have laid her cards on the table; he knew where she stood now. She wasn't planning on offering him anything more than she had to give.

～

Bridie watched Shaun lifting the heavy bags into the work ute and tried to tell herself it wasn't technically considered perving if you had nothing more interesting to look at in the main street on a slow Tuesday afternoon.

The boy could certainly fill out a pair of Wranglers, she thought wistfully. She'd been taking her break at the café when she'd noticed him pull up across the street.

The clatter of her cappuccino being set down roughly on the table startled her from her wayward thoughts, and she looked down to see a fair portion of the contents had sloshed into the saucer.

She quickly steadied the cup. Cheryl took a small step back, her arms folded belligerently across her bare midriff, chewing her gum with an annoying snap of her teeth. 'That's all, thanks Cheryl,' Bridie said pointedly. She had almost turned around and walked out of the café when she realised Cheryl was serving behind the counter, but the aroma of strong coffee overrode her good sense.

Now Cheryl gave a nasty laugh. 'You really think you have a chance with Mr Moneybags over there, don't you?'

Bridie forced herself to be calm. 'Shouldn't you be getting back to work?'

'I saw you at the show—*everyone* saw you with him. You should have heard 'em all talking. "What's he doing with a Farrell?"' She mimicked the old gossips around town a little too perfectly. 'You know he's only sniffing around you because he wants to annoy his olds, don't ya? Everyone knows he and his old man are always at each other's throats. No better way to stick it to Douglas Broderick than to dangle some tramp in his face,' she continued gleefully.

'Then how come he isn't hanging around you?' Bridie asked sweetly.

Cheryl's eyes narrowed dangerously, and her face, which could have been pretty if she'd scraped off the heavy makeup, twisted into a scowl. 'One day you'll get what you deserve, and I can't wait to be there when it happens,' she snarled.

'Did you ever ask Tyler how he got his face rearranged?'

Her question took Cheryl by surprise. 'He was in a fight.'

'Maybe you should ask him what happened that night—and if I were you, I'd give that guy a wide berth from now on.'

'Like I'm going to take advice about men from you, the ice maiden of Tooncanny.'

Bridie shrugged.

The slam of a tailgate drew her attention back across the street. Shaun had finished loading up his ute. He looked up and tilted his hat back on his head. She saw him give his dog's head a rough rub before making his way to the café.

Bridie stifled a groan and again she wished she'd decided against coming here as she caught Cheryl thrusting back her shoulders and presenting Shaun with her cleavage. Shaun barely gave her a second glance; instead, he gave her his order then pulled out the chair opposite Bridie and flashed her that grin she was getting entirely too fond of. She didn't miss Cheryl's huff as she turned away to get the coffee.

'I was hoping I'd get here before you finished,' Shaun said. 'Are you on a break? Or finished for the day?'

She caught the warm fragrance of masculine sweat and felt suddenly warm. 'Just on a break. I was watching you . . . I mean, you know, I saw you there . . .' She blushed as she realised she was babbling.

'Bridie Farrell, were you checking me out?' he teased, his grin broadening.

'As if your ego needs that,' she scoffed.

'Here's your coffee, cowboy,' Cheryl drawled as she leaned across him to put his coffee on the table.

'Er, thanks,' he murmured, this time copping an eyeful of her cleavage whether he wanted to or not.

'Cheryl, get your boobs out of the man's face, he's trying to drink his coffee,' Bridie said quietly.

Cheryl flounced off and Shaun laughed. 'I'm thinking that would have to be an OH&S violation.'

'She'll know it if they fall into someone's hot cup of tea,' Bridie grinned. 'Sorry about that.'

'Why are you sorry?'

'I should have warned you that Cheryl makes it her priority to get her hooks into any man that comes within ten foot of me. She considers it a personal challenge.'

'She was with Tyler the other night, wasn't she?' He frowned, watching Cheryl disappear out the back of the café.

'She's my cousin.'

'Really?' He seemed genuinely surprised by the fact.

'How could you not know that? This is Tooncanny— everyone knows who's related to who around here.'

'I never really spent much time in town when I was back from boarding school or uni . . .' He was quiet for a moment. 'I wanted to ask you to come out for dinner at Jinjulu on Sunday—you don't work on Sundays, right?'

'To Jinjulu? With your family?'

She must have looked horrified because he laughed. 'It's just dinner.'

'No . . . I don't think that's a good idea.'

'Why not?'

'Your parents won't approve . . .' They were going to go freakin' ballistic when they realised their precious son had invited a Farrell to dinner.

'I don't need them to approve. You said the other night you weren't into casual, so I wanted to show you that I'm serious. Besides, it was Mum's suggestion.'

Bridie squirmed in her seat. 'I *really* don't think it's a good idea.'

He leaned back in his chair, watching her. He seemed to be trying to peel away her layers and figure her out. She wasn't entirely sure she liked the feeling.

'I should go, my break's almost over,' she said, getting up and tossing down the last of her coffee, which was now cold and bitter.

'Bridie, hang on,' he said, leaving his coffee untouched and throwing some money on the table. He followed her out of the café and across the road. 'Hey, wait up.' He jogged past her and then turned, blocking her path with his body. 'I'm serious.'

'Knock it off, Shaun. You don't really believe your family is going to welcome someone like me to Jinjulu, do you?'

'Look, showing them I'm not hiding you will shut them up and stop them meddling in my private life, but more importantly it will prove to you that I'm serious about getting to know you.'

'I'm not the kind of girl your mother wants hanging around with her son.' She couldn't state it any more clearly than that.

He clamped his hands on his hips and stared at her angrily. 'Despite what you think, my mother does not choose who I see. I thought you had more guts than this, Bridie.'

'Yeah, well, I'm not into setting myself up for certain humiliation. I don't need to prove anything to anyone, Shaun, your family included.'

'So come out to dinner.'

'No.'

'Chicken,' he taunted softly, then leaned close and kissed her, coaxing her into submission with his clever lips. 'Say yes,' he whispered against her mouth.

'No,' she murmured, but she didn't know what the hell she was fighting against any more.

'Say yes, Bridie,' he persisted, slipping his hands around her waist and pulling her to him.

Sweet Lord, she thought, desperately trying to keep her head; what hope did she have when she felt like this about him?

'Fine,' she groaned, pulling away slightly to send him a stern glare, 'but only to prove a point.'

'What point is that?' His gravelly voice sent a shiver of desire through her.

Good question . . . She fought to recall her train of thought. 'That you've got your head buried way too deep in the sand about us, and that this will finally prove it,' she said, finding the strength to pull out of his arms and take a step away from him. The man was temptation on legs— the things her vivid imagination were conjuring up were nothing short of scandalous.

'It's a busy time of the year, so I'll be working all day, but I'll pick you up at four,' he said as she turned to walk away from him.

'Fine.' She didn't turn around; she wasn't sure she was strong enough not to run back into those all-too-persuasive arms.

She heard his soft chuckle behind her and shook her head at her pathetic lack of willpower where this man was concerned. She didn't want to think about Cheryl's state-ment that people were talking about them. They certainly hadn't helped matters with that kiss. What on earth did he think was going to come of this?

Trouble. That's what he was, and she didn't need any more in her life right now. But she was damned if she could make herself listen to her own advice.

Eleven

They turned in to an elaborate bricked entrance with *Jinjulu* sculpted in fancy ironwork across the front. A neat hedge grew at the base of the brick wall, adding a splash of colour and breaking the plains of crops growing all around them. The driveway was a good three kilometres long; looking out the window, Bridie saw that any paddocks which weren't planted with crops had sheep contentedly grazing in them.

She was no farmer, but she could tell this place was run by someone who took a great deal of pride in it. There were no sagging fence posts here; the driveway was in better condition than the main road out the front of the gate!

Up ahead was a grove of trees, and behind that a sprawling homestead. Made from sandstone and timber, the house seemed steeped in history. Wide timber verandahs ran around the bottom storey, while the second floor looked out over the surrounding countryside. The gardens were gorgeous, while rows of roses of every imaginable colour and size adorned the houseyard, which was lush and green.

Shaun had already described the house to her, but nothing had prepared her for seeing it for herself. She didn't belong here. She'd never before set foot in a place remotely like this.

Bridie forced her fingers to uncurl from the edge of the passenger seat as they pulled up in front of the grand homestead.

'It won't be so bad.' Shaun sent a lopsided grin her way and leaned across to place a gentle kiss on her lips. 'They're probably sweating bullets about meeting *you*.'

Bridie gave a very unladylike snort at the thought of his mother sweating at all. Even in the heat of summer, the woman wouldn't be so uncouth as to perspire. 'I'm sure they're quaking in their boots. Come on, let's get this over with.'

She pushed open the door and climbed out. She smoothed her hands down over her top that fell just below the waist of her black jeans and took a deep breath, straightening her shoulders. The top was her favourite, a blouse in pretty shades of purple and green; she'd grabbed it in a rare moment of shopping madness last time she was in Dubbo. She wasn't used to getting dressed up. It'd been quite a while since she'd had to impress anyone.

The loud echo of Shaun's boots on the verandah pounded in time to her heart. What was she doing? Why had she agreed to this? It was crazy. She didn't belong here *socialising* with the Brodericks over dinner.

Shaun stopped in front of a large door and reached across to open it for her. She caught the scent of his after-shave and a surge of longing raced through her. No man had a right to smell that good.

Shaun had told her that the original homestead dated back to the late 1860s and the rest of the house had been built around it. Looking around now she could see that over the years each generation had added more rooms and luxuries as the property had prospered; rather than creating an architectural monstrosity, the result was in fact harmonious and attractive. The foyer had pale green walls and black and white tiles, while tasteful shades of turquoise and cream dominated the lounge-room furnishings. It was hard to believe the place housed men who worked with smelly sheep and came home with muddy boots.

Discreet and expensive down-lighting gave the place a soft dreamlike glow, and Bridie felt as though she'd walked into the pages of a fancy lifestyle magazine.

She glanced over at Shaun, and noticed that he wasn't as calm as he'd seemed a few minutes ago. *He's nervous too*, she thought anxiously. *That can't be a good sign.*

Bridie hardly had time to register any more details before Shaun's mother walked in. She was immaculately dressed, as always, and elegantly beautiful. She had wavy silver-blonde hair that fell to her shoulders in a thick, shiny mass. Her dark eyes were a perfect match to Shaun's but her face was sharper and thinner, making her seem rather cool and aloof.

'Mum, this is Bridie Farrell,' Shaun introduced them. 'Bridie, my mother, Constance.'

117

'Hello, Bridie. We've heard so much about you. It's nice to meet you at long last.'

Although Constance seemed relaxed, Bridie couldn't shake the feeling that she was eyeing her a little too intensely, as though searching for something . . . a weakness maybe? Telling herself not to be so paranoid, she smiled and said, 'It's nice to meet you as well.'

'My son tends to pretend we don't exist, so it's always a treat when he brings someone home,' a deep voice boomed. Mr Broderick was a big man, almost as tall as his son and solidly built. There was a presence about him—something powerful and more than a little intimidating. He was older than she'd expected, but he carried his age well and she could tell that time would be just as kind to Shaun. Father and son shared the same dark hair and handsome facial features, but that's where the similarities ended. There was a coldness about Douglas, a certain arrogance in the set of his jaw that Shaun didn't have.

'My father, Douglas,' Shaun said.

'Thank you for the invitation to dinner.' Bridie smiled, politely she hoped. The man had a very intense gaze and she found it difficult to hold. He gave a gracious bow of his head.

'So, Bridie, how did you and my son meet?' Constance asked, settling into the corner of the lounge and leaning forward slightly to give Bridie her full attention.

For a moment Bridie felt like a deer trapped in the headlights. What was she supposed to say here: 'Your son was dared to see how long it took to get into my pants'? Somehow she didn't see that going down well. Thank goodness, Shaun stepped in smoothly, saving her from having to answer.

'We've known each other for a while. We met a few times at parties when I was home from school.'

'Oh? Old friends then?' His mother smiled a little hesitantly.

'You have a lovely home,' Bridie volunteered to fill the silence.

'Thank you, dear. I'm very fortunate to have an excellent interior decorator. He's worth every penny.'

'I wish it only cost me pennies,' Douglas said sarcastically as he moved towards the sideboard, which held an impressive collection of expensive bottles of scotch, port and wine. 'Can I offer you a drink?'

God yes, Bridie thought desperately, *and don't bother putting the bottle away*—the way this was heading, she was going to need all the help she could get. She thanked him as he handed over a crystal glass that probably cost more than she made in a year.

'Drink, son?' he asked, raising an eyebrow as his hand hovered over a second glass.

'No, thanks. I'm driving Bridie home later.'

'I thought you had a big day tomorrow, dear,' his mother said.

Shaun gave his mother a small smile. 'It's okay. I'll make sure I'm back in time for work.'

This apparently didn't reassure his mother any if the slight frown on her face was any indication. Surely a fully grown man didn't have a curfew?

The sound of footsteps on the polished floors announced Shaun's sister's arrival. She flounced into the room and flopped onto the sofa.

'Have you met our daughter, Phoebe?' Constance asked. Phoebe smirked as she waited for Bridie to answer.

'Yes, we've met,' Bridie murmured and hoped she'd managed to sound civil.

'So, what did my big brother have to promise you in exchange for going through with this?'

'Phoebe,' Shaun frowned.

'I hope it was something worthwhile. Dinner in this place is not for the faint of heart,' she added dryly, then noticed the beginnings of a frown across Shaun's brow. 'What?' she asked, looking up at him innocently.

Shaun didn't get a chance to respond, as a little round woman now bustled into the room with a platter of hors d'oeuvres. She gave Bridie a welcoming smile.

'Bridie, this is Daisy.' There was genuine warmth in Shaun's tone, and Bridie could see that these two shared a strong bond.

'Nice to meet you, love,' said Daisy. 'Get some of these horse-doovers into ya.'

Bridie grinned and took a small puff-pastry case with creamy tuna and cheese spooned carefully into its centre. 'Oh, these are lovely, Daisy.' She almost moaned in delight as the pastry melted in her mouth. Shaun hadn't been kidding about the woman being a great cook.

'Just a little somethin' I threw together.' The older woman shrugged, although she seemed pleased by the compliment.

'You should start your own catering business,' Bridie said, reaching for another tiny pastry case.

'Too old to start that rot now, darlin'. I'll see out my last few years servin' her ladyship 'ere, I reckon.'

'Last few years, my foot—you'll outlast the lot of us, Daisy,' Shaun said, scooping up two of the pastry cases as the platter passed him.

'Oh, for goodness sake,' Constance muttered as she gave Daisy a disapproving glare. Presumably she didn't much like the 'her ladyship' remark. It seemed strange that she would feel the need to make sure everyone was on their best behaviour for Bridie's sake. Clearly it didn't matter who the guest was, appearances were appearances—although someone had obviously forgotten to send Daisy the memo!

The silence that followed Daisy's withdrawal to check on dinner bordered on uncomfortable until Constance dragged up her how-to-be-a-gracious-hostess manners and politely asked Bridie about her job.

'I work at the Drovers Hotel.'

'Oh. And how long have you worked there?'

'Ever since I was eighteen.' Bridie took a sip of her wine and resisted the urge to toss it all down in one large gulp.

'And do you enjoy the work?'

Bridie tried to ignore the slightly incredulous tone of the question. 'In Tooncanny, you're grateful just to *have* a job. There isn't a great deal of choice.'

'Have you thought about leaving the area? Surely you could find better opportunities in other places?'

'Mum,' Shaun cut in smoothly enough, although Bridie detected a slight edge to his voice.

'It's a legitimate question. I don't understand why people continue to loiter around a town where there's no work. Why not move?'

'I guess without a proper education, they aren't guaranteed better options anywhere else. Most prefer the safety of a familiar place. It's a scary world out there without money.' Bridie held the older woman's gaze steadily.

'It's a free country—there's money out there to be made if you're willing to work for it,' Douglas Broderick piped up.

'For some. Others get stuck working hard all their lives and never get anywhere.'

'Then they simply aren't trying hard enough,' he dismissed arrogantly.

Bridie fought to keep a rein on her temper. Douglas Broderick might know all about hard work, having been a farmer all his life, but he had no idea what it was like to be broke and trapped in a low-paying job with no hope of ever getting ahead. He had grown up with wealth and privilege; he assumed that everyone had the same advantages.

It went against the grain to hear him dismissing everyone who was in a minimum-wage job as simply not working hard enough. Did he have any idea how hard most people worked just to keep a roof over their heads? Not everyone in Tooncanny was lining up for a dole payment each fortnight.

'Dinner's served, come and get it.' Daisy's cheerful call from the doorway saved further comment, and Bridie was glad—she wasn't altogether sure she could have remained civil for much longer. She hoped this would end soon; she could feel a headache coming on and it wasn't from the wine.

❧

Shaun gave his parents an angry scowl as Bridie walked out of the room ahead of him, but it bounced off them without registering. They seemed not to know how naive and superior they sounded. He guessed he'd been like that himself before he'd gone away to uni. It was university that had stripped away the sheltered cocoon he'd been living in all his life. He'd discovered that some of his fellow students had to work two jobs while studying just to be able to survive. He met single parents scrimping and scraping to put themselves through university so they could better their lives and provide a future for their children. Not everyone had it as good as the Brodericks, and he'd felt guilty for not realising this sooner.

'More wine?' he asked Bridie as they sat down at the large table in the formal dining room.

'Please.' She smiled at him, but he noted the small lines of tension around her full, kissable mouth. Pushing aside all thoughts of her mouth and all the things he wanted to do with it, he concentrated on pouring her wine without spilling it.

He sent her what he hoped was a 'hang in there' look. If he had anything to do with it, this would be the quickest dinner party Jinjulu ever had. He was doing what he felt he had to in order to prove his point to his parents and Bridie, but it would be a relief when it was over.

He caught Bridie eyeing the extra place setting across the table and hoped he wouldn't have to explain. His family had hardly endeared themselves to her already—a discussion about *this* would probably send her running.

'So Jinjulu runs sheep?' Bridie ventured.

'Among other things, yes,' his father acknowledged with an amused expression. 'Do you have an interest in sheep?' he enquired with exaggerated politeness.

Bridie looked over at Shaun. 'Only if they're in the same sentence as "baked dinner".'

'Lucky for you, Shaun, another meat eater,' Phoebe said sarcastically as she accepted a big plate of salad from

Daisy. 'I'm a vegetarian. Personally, I deplore the slaughter of animals, especially animals as gentle and adorable as sheep.'

'I don't know,' Bridie said doubtfully. 'Their bulging eyes kinda freak me out.'

Shaun coughed, then took a sip of his wine and caught his mother's disapproving glare; no doubt she was thinking, *Choke quietly, dear.*

'Thankfully not everyone is as neurotic as my daughter. Good news for sheep graziers,' Douglas said. 'I suppose my son's told you all about his grand plans for Jinjulu?'

'Not now, Dad,' Shaun said wearily, feeling the tension in the room amplify.

'Here's your chance to preach to the uninitiated,' Douglas said, waving a fork towards Bridie. 'My son here thinks he knows everything about farming. He's had a few years at university so he now knows everything about the land. What would I know, I've only been farming for what, the last fifty years?'

Shaun sensed Bridie shifting uncomfortably in her chair at his father's bitter tone. He tried not to rise to the bait. 'All I've said is that there are more cost-effective ways of farming.'

'Sent my boy away a farmer and he comes back a bloody greenie.'

'Just because you want to save the environment doesn't mean you're a greenie, Dad. I would have thought that you'd want to make Jinjulu a more sustainable property.'

Douglas's eyes narrowed as he leaned across the table and glared at his son. 'Now, you listen here, boy! There isn't a single thing in this world I value more than this place. It's been in this family six generations. Don't you go telling me about what's best for Jinjulu.'

'You heard him, Shaun—there isn't anything more important to Dad than Jinjulu,' Phoebe put in, slicing up her salad carefully.

Fantastic. Welcome to the family, Bridie. Nothing quite like an initiation by fire. From the corner of his eye, Shaun saw Bridie look down at the plate placed in front of her. She thanked Daisy quietly.

'Can we all please just eat in peace?' Constance's voice cut through the growing tension around the table and a grudging silence followed. The meal went from bad to downright uncomfortable after that, the silence only broken by the occasional clink of silver cutlery against bone china. Shaun forced himself not to shovel down his food just to reach the end of the meal faster and get the hell out of there.

࿐

'Well, I think you got your proof. Your family hates me,' she said with quiet acceptance as they drove home.

'No they don't, that's just the way they are. Give it time. They're an acquired taste.'

Outside her house he turned off the ignition and they sat in silence, listening to the tick of the engine as it cooled.

'I don't think you should read too much into us,' Bridie said slowly.

He went still, hardly daring to breathe. 'Well, how do you see it?'

'As something that shouldn't get too serious.'

'I thought you were the one who didn't want a fling?' He tried to swallow but his mouth was dry.

'I didn't want to be used as a one-night stand,' she corrected him. 'But I think we'd just be setting ourselves up for heartache if we thought this was ever going to be long term. Once Luke finishes school, I'm leaving. It's something I've had planned for years. But even if I stayed, your parents would never make life easy for us.' He was silent. 'I admit there's an attraction between us, but I can't afford a serious relationship right now, and it wouldn't be fair to you if I didn't tell you that upfront.'

'You can't plan your life on a "maybe". You might *not* leave and then where would you be? Anything could happen between now and the end of the year. Why do you keep throwing up roadblocks every time I try to get close to you?'

'You're not listening to me,' she huffed.

'I am.'

'You're not! I'm telling you that I'm leaving town at the end of the year and you're shrugging it off like it's no big deal.'

'So, what, we're supposed to ignore this thing between us for the rest of the year? Even though it could be the best thing that ever happened to either of us?'

'I don't know!' Bridie threw up her hands in frustration and looked out the front windscreen. 'It's just that every time I think I'm about to get out of this bloody town, something always happens to stop me leaving.'

'Maybe something's trying to tell you that leaving isn't what you really want to do?'

'I'm leaving at the end of the year, Shaun.'

'Then I guess that's it,' he sighed.

'I guess so,' she said.

They sat for a while in silence, the gentle moonlight casting a subtle glow inside the cabin of the ute. Shaun tried to imagine how it would feel to see Bridie around town for the rest of the year and have to ignore the feelings he had for her. It would be impossible.

'I suppose I'd better let you get home. You sound like you have a busy day tomorrow,' Bridie said, cutting into his thoughts.

'Yeah.'

Neither of them moved and Shaun glanced over at Bridie. He thought that maybe she wasn't exactly thrilled about her decision to stop this thing between them in its tracks either. He watched quietly as she tentatively lifted her gaze to meet his, and relief washed over him as he saw the same sadness reflected in her eyes.

Her conflicted look dragged a small moan from his chest and he bent his head to touch her lips in a kiss that was intended to comfort, but one taste and all his good intentions flew out the window.

Beneath his mouth, he felt her respond and he moved her back against the door, framing her face with his hands as he savoured the fresh lime scent of her hair. Pulling away, he looked down at her and felt something kick low in his gut. Christ, she was beautiful.

'I'd like to have it noted for the record that I think your idea to end this sucks.'

Bridie bit her lip, her breathing unsteady. 'What else can we do? If this gets serious, how are we going to walk away at the end of the year?'

'Why don't we just see where this thing goes and forget about the future for a while?'

'I don't know if it's a good idea, Shaun . . . I feel like I'm out of control when I'm around you,' she admitted softly.

'And being in control is important to you—yeah, I get that. But why not, just this once, stop trying to dictate everything and see what happens?'

He could see that giving up the tight grip on her control wasn't easy for her. She liked to think she was in charge of her destiny, and he understood why, but he also knew life had a way of letting you believe you were in control just before it blew all your beliefs out of the water.

'How about I come over tomorrow and cook dinner to say sorry for tonight?' he suggested.

'You don't have to apologise. You didn't do anything wrong.'

'I'd still like to make you dinner.'

He stared at the tip of her tongue as she lightly ran it across her lips. 'I'd like that,' she said finally.

It took all the willpower he could summon to let his hands slip away from her body. What he really wanted to do was pick her up and take her to the nearest bed, ripping her clothes off as he went.

'Shaun?'

He snapped out of his fantasy to realise she'd asked him something that he'd completely missed.

A sly smile crossed her lips; she must have known *exactly* where his thoughts had been. 'I said, do you want me to bring anything home from work?'

'No, I'm cooking. Just bring yourself home,' he said, his heart rate picking up even more at the thought of spending the evening alone with her.

'Are you coming inside?' she asked hesitantly.

'I'd really like to,' he said, thinking: *Like you wouldn't believe*, 'but I have to get up early tomorrow to make a start on the drenching.'

He saw the flicker of emotion in her eyes and wasn't sure if it was disappointment or relief. *Idiot! What kind of dumb-arse turns down a beautiful woman for sheep drenching?* But hell, he didn't want to sleep with her and then get up and leave her as though she was some sort of easy conquest. He wanted to be able to wake up with her the next morning . . . and start all over again. His thoughts were heading back to the bedroom; he had to get control of himself.

'I better get inside too, it's late,' she said. 'I'll leave the key under the pot plant on the top step so you can get in.'

He leaned forward and kissed her goodbye, this time reining in his desire. 'See you tomorrow.'

He waited until he saw her close the door before he reversed down the driveway, then turned Cold Chisel up really loud to distract himself from what he was leaving behind.

Twelve

Arriving home from work the next evening, Bridie saw lights blazing inside and a Jinjulu farm vehicle parked out on the street.

Inside there was a wonderful aroma of garlic and spices. 'Something smells great.' She sniffed at the oven appreciatively and received a swat on the fingers with the tea towel when she tried to open the door for a peek inside.

'You have to kiss the cook before you get to do that.'

'You want me to go all the way down to Marilyn's café to kiss her?'

He winced. 'How did you know I bought it from Marilyn's?'

She nodded over at the bin near the counter. 'I saw the empty cartons as I walked past,' she chuckled.

'Damn it, I thought I'd covered everything,' he muttered,

then grinned with pleasure as Bridie went up on tiptoes to kiss him anyway.

'You still deserve a kiss. I don't care who cooks dinner, as long as it isn't me,' she smiled sweetly.

A growl of disgust intruded on their moment and Bridie stepped back, feeling guilty, as Luke stalked into the kitchen and opened the fridge door.

'Dinner will only be a few minutes, mate,' Shaun said from behind her.

'I'll get my own.'

'Luke,' Bridie warned. 'Shaun's come over to cook dinner. The least you can do is eat with us.'

'No thanks,' he said, just about slamming the fridge door shut.

Bridie moved to follow him out of the room, but Shaun slipped an arm around her waist and pulled her back against him. 'Leave it. He's just sniffing about because there's a new dog in his territory. He'll come around.'

'Do you realise you always explain things in animal or farming terms?'

'That's because humans aren't that much different from animals.'

Bridie let out a contented sigh as his lips nuzzled her throat; she could almost feel herself relax, but then heavy footsteps coming back down the hallway put a stop to that.

'Get a room,' Luke snarled as he stalked past to the cupboard to grab a glass.

'Don't speak to your sister that way. She deserves more respect than that, mate.'

'Firstly, I'm not ya mate. Second, you're the one groping

her, so maybe *you* should be respectful and stop trying to get in her pants.'

Bridie felt Shaun try to step around her, but she pushed a hand against his chest in warning. 'Luke, just stay in your room if you're going to be like that.'

'Why do you think he's hanging around so much? You think he's not like everyone else around this place? Everyone knows the Farrell women put out, isn't that right, Broderick?' he snarled.

'Luke!' Bridie gasped, shocked and hurt by her brother's cruel remark.

Shaun quickly reached around her and grabbed a fistful of Luke's T-shirt. 'Apologise to your sister,' he growled.

'Make me.'

'Stop it, both of you!' Bridie yelled, pushing them apart and turning her angry glare upon her brother. 'What the hell has got into you lately? You were never this rude before you started hanging around that bloody Spider Jennings!'

'At least they don't treat me like some little kid!'

'No, obviously not—it shows how much they care when they ply you with alcohol and let you find your own way home.'

'I'm not a baby any more!' he shouted.

'You're not an adult yet either, Luke. You're a kid. And you're my responsibility until you're old enough to take care of yourself.'

'Well, I'm sick of being your responsibility!'

'Tough! You are. So get over it.'

Luke made to turn and walk out of the kitchen, and Shaun stepped in front of him. 'There's no excuse for speaking to your sister like that, so apologise.'

'Go get fu—'

'Luke!' Bridie cried in horror. She couldn't believe how rapidly the situation was getting out of hand.

'He thinks he's so damn high and mighty just because his family has money. How's your ute going, mate? Got it fixed yet?' Luke's face twisted into something cruel and nasty and Bridie felt her heart tear a little. This was not her baby brother.

'What do you know about it?' Shaun asked quietly.

Bridie saw Luke's expression slip slightly and watched as he shifted his weight onto the balls of his feet as though in preparation to flee. 'I don't know nothing,' he answered sullenly.

'I think you do. Was your big-mouth mate, Spider, boasting about that dropkick, Tyler Jennings?'

'Spider wasn't boasting about it, *I* was, so shove that up ya arse, *mate*,' Luke shouted.

Bridie gaped at her brother. 'Luke—just shut up. Shut up now!' She turned to face Shaun. 'He's not serious. He wouldn't have done that. He's just angry and lashing out.'

'Bullcrap,' said Luke. 'I'm not scared of him. I was there that night and I helped smash the shit out of ya ute. And you know what? I don't even feel bad about it.'

Shaun's outraged growl barely registered as Bridie stared at the stranger who seemed to be inhabiting her brother's body. How could the little boy she'd loved as though he were her own child be capable of such a thing? 'Why would you do that?' she asked, feeling numb.

'Because he struts around the place as if he owns it, thinking he's so great—well, you're not! You don't belong here, so piss off, and leave my sister alone.'

'You don't have any idea why they went back to the pub that night, do you?' Shaun said.

'I just told you why,' Luke snarled.

'They told you it was because I deserved it, but they didn't tell you what I *did* to deserve it, did they?'

'You beat the livin' shit out of Tyler.'

'And *why* did I beat the livin' shit out of Tyler?'

Bridie turned towards him and shook her head. 'No, Shaun, don't.'

Shaun ignored her. 'Well? Did they tell you why?'

'I don't care why,' Luke said, but his eyes darted to his sister's uncertainly.

'You know, I can almost understand how you'd think hanging out with Jennings and his mates would be cool. But I can't figure out why you'd go along and smash up the car of the guy who came out and stopped Tyler Jennings from raping your sister.'

'Shaun, that's enough!'

'You're a liar!' Luke yelled, his disbelieving gaze wavering back and forth between Shaun and Bridie. 'You're a goddamn liar.'

Bridie shook her head and sank down onto one of the chairs at the kitchen table, too weary to fight any more.

Luke was watching her and when she looked up she saw in his eyes that he was almost begging her to tell him it wasn't true. She wanted to summon up the strength to deny it but she was so damn tired. 'It doesn't matter. Shaun stopped him in time,' she said quietly.

'Why the hell didn't you tell me?' Luke demanded, his face taut and almost as pale as her own.

'Because it's none of anyone else's business!' she said,

casting a dangerous glare at Shaun. 'Now you know why I don't want you hanging around with them.'

'You should have told me!'

'When was the last time you bothered to listen to me?'

The shrill ring of the oven bell cut through the air and Luke ran from the room. A few seconds later, they heard the slam of the front door. Instantly Bridie stood to follow him.

'Leave him,' said Shaun. 'He'll be all right.'

'Why did you do that?' Bridie demanded, turning around to face Shaun.

'He smashed up my bloody ute! He needed to hear the truth, Bridie,' he said, and the creases in his forehead were deep gullies of disapproval. 'He's idolising thugs who tried to rape you—have you forgotten that part?'

'He didn't need to hear it like that,' she snapped. She felt betrayed and sick. The absolute last thing she wanted was for her little brother to know about what had happened to her.

'Well, at least he won't be hanging around them any more, so that solves one of your problems.'

'It wasn't your place to tell him.'

'Dinner's ready,' Shaun said with an air of exasperation.

'I'm not hungry.'

'You know, he's right on one score—he isn't a little kid any more. If you keep running after him, he'll never grow up. Look, I might have lost my temper there for a minute, and maybe I should have kept my mouth shut, but he just admitted to smashing my ute.'

His quiet intensity brought her back to reality. This man had the power to ruin her brother's life. 'What are you going to do?'

Shaun shook his head. 'I don't know.'

He didn't know? Bridie held her breath as a wave of terror washed through her. Everything Luke had been working towards was about to amount to nothing. She'd failed. She was supposed to be keeping her little brother out of jail, helping him make something of himself, and look at what had happened.

'Bridie, if I could only get the others charged, I would, but once I give Tim their names, he'll need Luke's testimony. He won't be able to stay out of it.'

She nodded slowly. 'Do what you think is best. I can't ask you to stay quiet about this.' She wouldn't do that. Shaun was the victim here, and even though she wanted to protect her brother, she knew he had to face the consequences of his actions. It was going to kill her to see him in trouble with the law, but there was no excuse—he'd been raised to know right from wrong and he'd made his choice. 'I'm sorry you went to all of this trouble with dinner, but I can't do this tonight, not right now.'

Shaun rubbed the back of his neck in frustration. 'I'm sorry, okay?'

Bridie clenched her teeth; she could understand him being angry with Luke, but he had no right to betray her confidence. Refusing to meet his eyes, she nodded.

'Bridie,' he moved across the room and stopped in front of her, 'let's just eat and wait until he gets home, then I can apologise to him and work out what to do about the cops.'

'It wasn't your place to tell *anyone* what happened that night. It was *my* business, not yours.'

'Would you have made it your business to go to the police if they'd finished what they started?' he demanded.

'It didn't happen.'

'The point is, Bridie, it *could* have bloody happened if I hadn't come downstairs when I did!'

'I don't want to talk about it any more,' she said, pushing away from the edge of the kitchen bench and stepping around him.

He moved sideways and blocked her escape, tilting her chin to make her look at him. 'Would you have gone to the police, Bridie?'

'No! All right? No, I wouldn't have gone to the bloody police. Happy?'

'Why the hell not?'

'Because they would have said I deserved it. Christ, Shaun, open your eyes! Look at my family's track record. I have cousins like Cheryl . . . Everyone in Tooncanny knows a Farrell is an easy lay. Do you honestly think the police would listen to my side of the story?'

'Of course they would. People aren't blind.'

She jerked her face out of his grip and he stepped back, raising his hands in a gesture of surrender. 'You know what your problem is? You've been conditioned to believe that everyone thinks you're worthless. Look at your life, Bridie—you work your guts out to make a home for you and your brother. You think people around here don't see that you're different from the rest of your family?'

'I don't want to talk about this any more, please just go.'

'If you had half as much faith in yourself as you do in this warped view of your own reputation, there wouldn't be a problem,' he said, walking away. 'Give yourself a break, Bridie—who knows, you might actually see what anyone with half a brain sees.'

A moment later she heard the decisive thud of the front door and something inside her chest constricted.

Bridie turned off the stove and removed the baking tray with the chicken kiev, golden and crispy, surrounded by baked potatoes and pumpkin. A tug of regret pulled at her heart; she so wished tonight had gone to plan instead of turning into a nightmare.

Taking a seat back at the table she rested her head on top of her folded arms and closed her eyes. She just needed a minute to get her head around it all . . .

Thirteen

The ringing in her ears intensified and for a moment Bridie wasn't sure where she was. Then she was instantly awake and scrambling for the phone. Her groggy 'Hello' was interrupted by a firm, no-nonsense explanation and within moments she'd hung up and was running down the hall and out the front door, the keys to her ute clenched in her fist.

The hospital seemed such a daunting place at midnight. The bleach and antiseptic smells reminded her of visiting her mother before Beth had begged to be allowed to go home to die. Hospitals held nothing but painful memories for her.

The last time she'd been to the emergency room was when Luke had fallen off his skateboard and broken his wrist. Here she was again, running through the halls, battling a clawing panic, but this time Luke wasn't in her arms and he wasn't ten years old, he was in the emergency room and she had no idea what state he was in.

She'd been told to take a seat until someone was free to speak with her. Perched on the edge of the hard plastic seats in the small waiting room, she felt as though each minute lasted an hour. After what seemed a lifetime of listening to a baby cry somewhere down the hall and the old man across from her with his smoker's cough, she was finally called up by a nurse.

'Is he all right?' Bridie asked anxiously.

'He'll be fine. He's a lucky boy. He's got some nasty bruising and a few fractured ribs, as well as a fractured hand and slight concussion. Just don't be alarmed by the bruising and swelling—it looks a lot worse than it actually is.'

She hardly had time to digest that little piece of information before the nurse pulled open the blue curtain to reveal her brother, his eyes all but swollen shut and a bandage around his head.

'Luke! What happened?'

'I'm all right,' he said quietly, barely moving his lips, which were split and bloodied.

'All right? Are you crazy? Did Tyler do this to you? Tell me you didn't go over there, Luke!'

'I wanted to hear him admit it.'

Bridie felt sick that Tyler had caused this much damage to a kid of sixteen. What about his mates? Had they just stood by and watched? What were they—animals? She slumped into the chair by the bed and fought back angry tears. 'What on earth were you thinking? They could have killed you, Luke!'

'Well, they didn't. Would you just stop talking for a minute and let me speak?'

Bridie took a deep breath, letting it out slowly.

'I've asked the doctor to call Tim Stanley. I'm going to make a statement about the night at the pub.'

'Luke—'

'No. You can't talk me out of it.'

Bridie stared at her brother's battered and bruised face and fought back tears. 'I just don't get why you did it in the first place—it's so unlike you.'

'*Unlike* me?' Luke winced and Bridie was shocked to see tears running from the puffed-up slits of his eyes. 'I don't even know who I am most of the time. I tried to be who you wanted me to be and I just ended up alone when Daniel left town . . . I tried to spend time with my family and all that did was cause trouble between you and them . . . Spider and Tyler treated me like I was someone. They didn't baby me. I wasn't a *responsibility*.'

'I . . .' Bridie wasn't sure what to say. 'Why didn't you talk to me about it?'

'Because you shouldn't have to be always worrying about me, Bridie. You're my sister, not my mother! Don't you get it? I don't want to be the reason you're putting off living your life. I'm sick of hearing how you're waiting for me to leave school, or you're waiting for me to join the army. You're always waiting, Bridie . . .'

'You've already missed out on so much. You lost both your parents pretty much at the same time. I promised Mum I'd take care of you.'

'We didn't lose Dad—he just isn't here right now—and *you* lost your parents too, Bridie . . . It's like you've forgotten that.'

'Of course I haven't forgotten.'

'You've spent so long being angry at Dad that you've convinced yourself we're all alone.'

'We *are* all alone, Luke!'

'No we're *not*. Uncle Tom might be a bit rough, and yeah, Cheryl and the others aren't anything to write home about, but they're family . . . *our* family, and they aren't as bad as you think they are . . . If you'd just give them a chance you'd see.'

It would take a lot to convince her of that, but she wished she'd realised earlier how hard the situation had been on him. She'd never considered how torn he must have felt. She'd been too busy trying to do the right thing.

'I'm sorry,' Luke said. 'I know I haven't made things easy over the last few months but I'm gonna put things right. Starting with telling Tim about Broderick's ute.'

What could she say? Her little brother wasn't so little any more.

The sound of someone clearing their throat drew their attention and Bridie's heart sank as she saw Tim Stanley.

'Bridie. Luke,' he said with a nod of his head. He took in Luke's swollen face as he moved towards the bed. 'What's the other guy look like?' he asked with his usual dry humour.

'Hey, Tim.' Luke attempted to wave, wincing at the movement, and Bridie let out an unsteady breath as she saw the bandaged hand. It had been splinted in order to immobilise his fracture.

'So what happened?' Tim got straight to the point.

'I didn't call you here because of this,' Luke told him quietly. 'It's about Broderick's ute being smashed up at the back of the pub. I was there.'

Tim frowned. 'Hang on a sec.' He switched his glance to Bridie. 'Before he implicates himself in anything, I'm going to have to make him aware of his rights. Okay?'

Bridie felt sick. 'Okay.'

'Luke, I have to tell you that I'm going to ask you some questions about the incident that took place in the car park of the Drovers Hotel, do you understand that?'

'Yeah.'

'You do not have to say or do anything if you don't want to, do you understand that?'

'Yeah.'

'Anything you say or do may be recorded and used in evidence at court. Do you understand that?'

'Yep.'

'Okay, just start at the beginning and tell me what happened.'

Luke began to talk, starting by explaining how Tyler had come back from the car park after taking a beating from Shaun and recruited his younger cousin, Spider, as well as Luke and one of the other boys to go back and trash Shaun's ute as payback. Bridie listened silently, proud of her little brother for speaking up even if it meant he was now facing the very thing she'd fought so hard to keep him away from—a run-in with the police.

Tim listened carefully, too. When Luke had finished he said, 'Look, you've made admissions to vandalising a vehicle and that's an offence. At this stage you will be charged with destroying or damaging property. You'll have to go to court.'

Bridie closed her eyes and concentrated on taking a deep breath to stay calm.

'I'll bring out the paperwork once I've got it,' Tim said, closing his notebook quietly.

Luke nodded briefly and dropped his gaze to the bed-spread beneath his hands.

'Now. How about we have a chat about how you got to look like you got run over by a bus?'

'Not important.'

'Luke,' Bridie warned, 'Tyler and his mates can't get away with this.'

'So it's okay for you to let them get away with something but not me?' he threw back angrily.

That was different, she thought indignantly. But if she thought about it, she knew it was shame that had prevented her from reporting the attack, as well as fear that she wasn't worthy of justice.

'I'll report mine if you report yours,' Luke said quietly. 'It'll be all right, sis. You can trust Tim.'

Bridie felt her lip tremble and the sting of tears behind her eyes. He was right; even Shaun had seen through her. She needed to stop hiding behind old family hurts. She couldn't very well preach to Luke about standing up to Jennings when she was too chicken to do the same.

Bridie looked up. 'Tim, I need to report an assault,' she said in a voice that was not quite steady, but the small smile on her brother's face gave her courage. Maybe tonight was the first step towards healing a lot of old wounds.

৵

Shaun took off his hat and wiped his brow with the sleeve of his shirt. A white four-wheel drive was coming up the driveway, a plume of dust in its wake. As it drew closer, he saw the police markings on the side.

It had been two days since the dinner date from hell at Bridie's and he hadn't spoken to her yet. He'd needed time to think about what he wanted to do about Luke. He kept seeing the pain in Bridie's eyes as she'd realised Luke had been involved. It had hit him hard to see her so distraught. As badly as he'd like to nail Jennings, he wasn't going to put Bridie through that kind of pain again. He had insurance, the ute would eventually be replaced, but he couldn't put a price on Bridie's wellbeing.

With a hollow feeling inside, he walked across to meet Tim Stanley as he stepped from his vehicle. He hoped she hadn't taken Luke to the cop station; he hated to think of her going through that alone.

'Shaun.'

'Tim. What brings you out here?'

'I've got some good news for you about the vandalism of your ute,' Tim said, and Shaun steeled himself. 'We've charged Spider Jennings and one other kid, as well as Luke Farrell, who've all admitted to being there that night.'

Shaun rubbed a hand around the back of his sweaty neck and let out a long breath. 'How'd you get them to admit it?'

'I was called up to the hospital to see Luke Farrell. He wanted to come clean about it.'

'What the hell was he doing in hospital?'

'Seems he took it upon himself to confront the Jennings boys about it and got badly beaten for his trouble. Not the smartest plan in history, but the kid's got guts.'

'Is he all right?' Shaun felt as if someone had punched him in the solar plexus.

'Could have been a lot worse. He's got a few broken ribs and a broken hand, but he was sent home today, so he's on the mend.'

'What's going to happen to him?'

'I'm willing to bet the prosecutor will go easy on him. It's a first offence and he confessed. The beating he took will be taken into account, too. Tyler will undoubtedly do time for that. He was already walking a very fine line.' Tim paused. 'I'd have liked to add a charge of assault occasioning actual bodily harm, for what he did to Bridie Farrell, but unfortunately, although she reported the assault, she declined to make a formal statement, so I can't take it any further.'

Shaun stared at the cop blankly for a moment. 'She reported it?'

'For all the good it did.' Tim shrugged. 'Not much I can do about it unless she gives a statement to back it up, though.' Shaun stared at the policeman, stunned by the news. 'Maybe someone will be able to talk her into it. Well, I better get going.'

'Thanks for coming out to let me know, Tim. I appreciate it.' Shaun shook the policeman's hand, then turned back to the post he was straightening. He pushed his shoulder against it, the physical strain feeling good, easing the knot of anxiety that had formed in his stomach on hearing Luke had been in hospital.

With the last post in, he packed all his gear into the ute, slammed the tray shut with a bang and climbed into the cabin. He'd been fixing fences all day, but it was time to go and mend some other fences in town. He had some grovelling to do—he just hoped it wasn't too late.

⤳

The knock on the front door caught Bridie on her way out to the kitchen to refill Luke's water glass. She opened the door and a flood of relief washed over her at the sight of Shaun standing there.

He looked so clean and wholesome that she wanted to throw herself into his arms and let him hold her, let him sweep away all the worry of the last forty-eight hours. Instead, she managed a shaky nod and bit the inside of her lip to keep from bursting into pathetic tears.

'I'm sorry, Bridie, I would have been here before this if I'd known . . .' He let the sentence drift off.

'He only just got home this morning—they kept him in a bit longer because of his concussion.'

'Tim dropped by today to tell me. He seems to think Luke won't be getting in too much trouble. I wasn't going to press charges, Bridie. I didn't want to see him ruin his life over one stupid mistake,' Shaun said, stepping through the doorway.

'It doesn't matter now. Apparently he'd been listening a little too closely to my *taking responsibility* lectures.'

'He had a good role model in his big sister. I'm sorry, Bridie—for everything. I had no right to open my mouth like that. I should have gone after him when he left the house. I should have realised he might confront them after what I told him. I blame myself for all this mess.'

Bridie reached out and placed her fingertips against his mouth. 'It's not your fault. This was all simmering beneath the surface waiting to explode.'

Shaun took her fingers in his hand, kissing them gently before he tugged her closer and wrapped her in his arms. 'What can I do to help? From now on I'm here . . . to stay.'

With her face against his chest, hearing the reassuring beat beneath her ear, she knew she should protest, should remind him that this was not long term, but his arms felt so damn good. It was like a weight being lifted from her shoulders and she just wanted a moment to savour it. It couldn't hurt for just a little bit, surely?

She'd set him straight tomorrow.

꒰

The male companionship and the balancing influence Shaun brought to the household was a huge help over the next few weeks. Luke's attitude and his whole outlook seemed to finally be back on track and Bridie could hardly believe the difference in him.

Early on in his recuperation he'd surprised her by saying he was still going to join the army. She was worried that his injuries might not be healed in time for him to pass the fitness and medical exams, but his ribs and hand were healing nicely and the doctor seemed to think that by the end of the year he would be fine to undergo the recruitment tests.

Folding clothes, she smiled at the Xbox battle going on in front of the television. Shaun had come over for lunch and afterwards he and Luke had settled in to play. To hear Luke laugh—actually *laugh*, for the first time in she didn't know how long—was so amazing that she had to blink away happy tears at the sound. With the game destined to continue long after her folding had finished, she picked up the basket and headed off to the kitchen.

'Hey, where are you going?' Shaun called after her.

'There's way too much testosterone in here for me. I'm going outside for some girly time with a good book and a cuppa,' she said over her shoulder.

Shaun paused the game and crossed the room to open the hallway door. 'Don't hurry, we're fine out here,' he said softly. 'You go and take some time out for yourself.'

A lump lodged in her throat. Reaching up on her toes she placed a gentle kiss on his lips. 'You're a good man, Shaun Broderick.'

He flashed his killer smile and moved close for a longer kiss, pulling away only when Luke made a gagging sound from in front of the TV. 'Come on!' he called. 'I'm just about to kick your butt—hurry up and take this thing off pause, will ya!'

With a cheeky wink, Shaun turned and went back to restart the Xbox. Bridie let out a sigh. It was getting harder each day to remember that invisible line she'd drawn for herself, the one that was supposed to keep her from falling for Shaun Broderick. Scarier still was how close she was to actually crossing it.

༄

The morning of Luke's court appearance arrived and Bridie tried to keep her nerves in check. Tim had told them how it would all work, and although he'd been quietly confident that Luke's coming forward meant the judge would cut him some slack, until she heard the verdict herself, Bridie couldn't help worrying about the outcome.

'Relax, sis. It'll be okay,' Luke said, squeezing her hand as he walked past her into the courthouse.

Bridie forced a smile to her face. *Pull it together, girl—you're supposed to be the strong one here, reassuring him!* Shaun put his arm around her waist and gave her a gentle squeeze of comfort, then took her hand to follow Luke.

The courtroom had been cleared for Luke's case, it being a children's criminal matter and therefore not open to the public, and Bridie was relieved. She hated the thought of strangers coming along to gawk at them. The magistrate, seated at the bench, wore a no-nonsense expression, his glasses perched low on his nose as he watched Luke take a seat beside his legal aid lawyer at the end of the bar table. Alan Baker didn't have much of a personality, but he seemed a capable lawyer, and as long as he did his job, Bridie could overlook the fact that she'd never seen the man smile.

Bridie and Shaun gave Tim Stanley a quiet hello as they sat down beside him. 'Thanks for coming, Tim,' Bridie smiled, grateful for the policeman's support. He'd written a personal reference since Luke had started going to the gym again.

The prosecutor walked in and took a seat at the opposite end of the table, taking out his files and shuffling his papers. 'The prosecutor is one of the best. But he's got a reputation for being pretty fair,' Tim said, leaning closer to Bridie, and she managed a nervous smile.

The magistrate gave a nod. 'Yes, Mr Baker?'

Alan cleared his throat and began proceedings. 'Young person before the court, Your Honour, supported by his sister. I have a number of references to hand up.'

The prosecutor made no objection and the court officer handed up the personal references to the magistrate, who then called the prosecutor to address the court.

'Your Honour,' he began, 'the offence for which the young person has been convicted is a serious crime and one that is prevalent in the community. It is a crime in which the victims must endure some hardship at the loss of the property and one in which insurance companies are forced to wear the cost of the offending on behalf of the community, such that the cost of insurance to the general community is affected. It is the view of the prosecution that the young person should face some period of supervision in relation to a bond.' He sat down.

'Mr Baker?' the magistrate said.

Alan stood up again. 'Your Honour, the young person before the court has no prior history, and he has shown contrition for his actions, as can be seen both in his admission to the police and his plea of guilty at the earliest opportunity. Your Honour, I note for the record that he fell in with a bad crowd and was not strong enough, in his own words, to resist what his friends at the time were doing. However, when he went to his friends, wanting them to confess to the offence, he was then attacked by them and the matter was ultimately brought to the police. His sister is in support of him today.'

'What does his sister have to say?'

Bridie frowned. She'd been trying to follow the legal jargon and was surprised when the magistrate peered over the top of his glasses at her.

'Stand up, Ms—' he glanced down at the paperwork before him—'Farrell. What's your brother's behaviour been like since this incident?'

'He's made a big effort to get back into his schoolwork and he's trying really hard, Your Honour,' she said quietly but smiled at her brother, so proud of him for stepping up like this.

'Thank you, you can take your seat again.'

Alan Baker spoke up quickly. 'Your Honour, I'd like to mention that he's made an application to join the army, and his prospects for rehabilitation are very good.'

'All right,' said the magistrate. 'Well, noting what's been submitted to me, the early guilty plea and the contrition shown by the young person, I'm of the view that the matter can be dealt with by way of a caution under thirty-three-one-A.'

Bridie glanced over at Tim anxiously. 'What the hell's a thirty-three-one-A?' she asked, her nerves jangling.

Tim gave her a comforting smile. 'It's okay—it's a good thing.'

'Very well. Mr Farrell, stand up. I am dismissing these charges under section thirty-three-one-A with a caution. I wish you every success in the future and hope that your application to join the military is successful. I hope never to see you again.'

Bridie shut her eyes in relief, whispering a silent thank-you to the universe, before making her way towards Alan and Luke, a huge smile on her face.

Fourteen

Luke usually scoffed his breakfast as fast as he could, barely even sitting down to eat, but this morning he was toying with his spoon in an empty bowl. Bridie looked at him curiously. 'Everything okay?'

'I've been working really hard lately,' he said without looking up.

'Yes, you have.' Bridie kept her voice neutral, even though her mind was already ticking over furiously as she tried to guess where this was heading. It had been weeks since the court hearing and things had been going so well.

'I want you to let me go and visit Dad.'

Bridie went to open her mouth but closed it again as Luke said, 'Before you say no, just listen to me for a minute. I wanted to be upfront with you this time. You said you wanted me to talk to you about things—well, I'm talking to you about it. I want to go and see Dad as my reward for working hard. It's important to me, Bridie.'

After he'd stated his point so calmly and with a maturity that belied his years, Bridie didn't have the heart to object. 'Okay. I'll call and see if I can get your name on the visitor list. I'll take you over there.'

'I don't want you to freak out, but Uncle Tom asked if I'd like to go over with him. Would that be okay?'

The old instinct to immediately veto the idea was still there, but she managed to bite the words back before they escaped. The hopeful look on his face was so much harder to resist than the surly one she'd been dealing with before. 'I guess so.' She couldn't hide her reluctance, but Luke had been working hard and she knew it meant a lot to him to go and see their father. 'Just . . . be careful,' Bridie said lamely. It was going to take a while to get used to not babying her baby brother.

৵

Bright and early on Sunday morning she drove out to Jinjulu. Shaun had invited her out. It would be the first time she'd set foot there since the uncomfortable meet-and-greet with the Brodericks a few weeks before.

For weeks now she and Shaun had seen each other regularly, but rarely alone. Now that Luke wasn't hanging out with the Jennings crew, he seemed always to be around. Not that she was complaining, but having a teenager nearby wasn't exactly conducive to romance. Shaun had never once complained; in fact he'd gone above and beyond what anyone would have been expected to do considering her brother had ruined his car. True to his word, he'd made sure he was there for her as much as possible. But today it was just the two of them.

He was waiting for her out the front when she pulled up. His brown stockman's hat was tugged low, hiding his eyes from her, but she didn't need to see them—she felt them on her.

He wore old jeans that hugged his strong thighs, and his sleeves were rolled up. He was dressed the same as a hundred other men in the district, and yet on him it was inexplicably sexy.

'Okay, so you're going to put me to work?' she asked once she'd happily accepted his welcome kiss.

'Sure am, city girl.'

'Oh yeah—I've driven all the way from the big smoke of Tooncanny,' she scoffed. 'So what delights have you got in store for me today? Shearing? Crutching?'

'Ah, no. Not time for shearing yet. Have you ever done shearing or crutching?' he asked doubtfully, and grinned at the dry glance she sent him. 'Just as I suspected—city girl. No, I thought you might like to come and take a look at my big business venture.'

'Oh.' She was a little disappointed. 'I've always wanted to see shearing up close and personal.'

'You can come back at shearing time. You'll probably be over sheep by then. The novelty wears off after the first few hundred.' He whistled for Mick to jump into the back of the ute and the dog leapt up, looking at Shaun with big brown eyes and a doggy grin.

They drove down to the paddocks where the first of his new crops were growing and she listened to the excitement in his voice as he explained his vision and the reasons behind this new direction of conservation farming. Even with her limited knowledge of farming techniques, Bridie could see the logic in his arguments. His passion for the land was unmistakable. Clearly, farming was his life. She felt a burst of pride in his confident nod of approval as they walked through the paddocks. The large yards set up to hold a herd of sheep were the other side of his venture.

'So what's this all about?' Try as she might, she couldn't figure out what was so special about the massive yards holding so many smelly, noisy sheep.

'This is what I want to show Dad. I'm leasing this land to prove to him that veering away from traditional grazing and adopting sheep lots will help protect paddocks from soil erosion. There's an increasing market for meat that's been fattened and finished in a feedlot. This lot are almost due to go to sale and I'm confident they'll bring me a higher price than Dad's. These are a new Damara/Wiltshire cross. I'm hoping they'll be able to handle drought better. They'll be able to produce more often and they're a sought-after breed for their meat, weighing in at a bigger size at a younger age.'

'I don't get it—how is this more environmentally sustainable?' Bridie asked.

'Sheep cause a lot of erosion as they graze, which makes things worse during drought. Keeping them contained limits the amount of damage they do to the soil, plus it frees up valuable land that could be used for crops,' he explained patiently. 'See, Jinjulu has always split grazing with crops, but the sheep do so much damage to the land that we're limited in how much of it we can use for crops. I want to prove to Dad that my way can free up the land for crops and still make a bigger return on the sheep.'

'Wow. You really know your stuff,' Bridie smiled.

'I should do, I've been researching this for a long time, trying to sway Dad to my way of thinking.'

'You think this will work?'

Shaun sighed, turning his attention back to his sheep. 'He won't be able to deny the figures once he sees them for himself—but then again, he's a stubborn old bastard, so who knows?'

Bridie had thought *her* family dynamics were all screwed up. Shaun seemed to be going to a lot of trouble to get his father to show him a little respect . . . She wasn't sure she would have persisted this long.

༂

As they drew closer, the line of trees gave away the river's location and Bridie was struck by the beauty of the scene before her.

'You like it?' Shaun asked, the quiet pride evident in his shining eyes.

'It's gorgeous. What a great spot.'

'This section widens out here into a deep pool that's great for swimming.'

'It looks well used,' she said, spying the rope and tyre hanging off a big sprawling willow that drooped over the water, and the small clearing with a brick barbecue and timber table and bench seat.

'We practically lived down here as kids. It's a great place to camp.'

They climbed out of the ute. Bridie helped unload the esky with their food and drinks and placed the goodies out on the table.

'Let's go for a swim. Come on, last one in is a rotten egg,' he said as he backed away from her, pulling off his shirt and changing into board shorts.

'Oh, for goodness sake, how old are you?' Bridie grumbled, quickly slipping off her sandals and waiting until he turned around on the bank before she stripped off her own shirt and shimmied out of her cut-off jeans to reveal her swimsuit beneath.

'Old enough— Hey!' he called as she streaked past him and ran into the water, taking him by surprise. Her chuckle of delight at catching him off guard turned into a strangled shriek as the icy water took her breath away.

'Oh my God, that's cold,' she gasped. Shaun dove from the bank to emerge in the centre of the pool, shaking the water from his hair.

Goosebumps covered her body as she stood thigh deep in the cold water, but she barely noticed as her gaze wandered over Shaun's bare chest.

'Just dive under. It's only cold for a second,' he promised.

Transfixed by the tanned muscles of his torso and the beads of water that clung to his chest, she found it hard to move.

Their eyes met, and she saw that his had darkened as he caught the heat in her gaze. Wordlessly he moved closer, coming to a halt a mere breath away from her. All around them she could hear insects droning and birds singing, and in the distance the sheep were bleating. But beneath it all, she heard the rush of blood through her veins.

The first touch of his warm lips sent a hot pulse of desire through her and she raised her arms and slid them around his neck. They kissed feverishly, with a kind of desperation brought on by weeks of reining in their desire. The heat from his skin ignited her own, and the extreme cold water against her overheated, overstimulated body made her arch against him in response.

Shaun didn't give her a chance to react to the sensation; instead he gathered her close and swam them across to the opposite side of the waterhole to a bank of soft long grass.

She felt the warmth of the sun-kissed ground against her back as Shaun laid her down, covering her body with his own. He stared down into her eyes and Bridie felt a jolt of electricity pass between them. Reaching up, she pulled his head towards hers, searching out the warmth of his mouth and showing him that she was just as much a part of this decision as he was.

'I was hoping our first time would at least be in a bed,' Shaun said, breaking their heated kiss.

'If you suggest we stop right now, I think I'll scream. Do you have any idea how badly I've wanted you?'

'Well, I did kind of get the idea—it's not like we've kept our hands off each other the last couple of weeks.'

'Not that you'd know it! You've had more than one chance to stay over, you know.'

'Yeah, but your place is so small, and I feel weird having your kid brother in the room right next door. Not to mention I don't think I could make myself leave the next morning, and I can just imagine how much my father would love me calling in sick.'

'Well, Broderick, are we going to lie here and continue to debate this problem, or are we going to do something about it?' She gave him an arch look.

'I'm a hands-on kinda guy when it comes to problem-solving,' he said, and lowered his lips to hers.

∽

If she was honest, Bridie had known she was in trouble the first time the man had kissed her. Lying here now, feeling his need, she was well and truly a goner. For weeks now she'd fought her frustration when every night he kissed her senseless, then said goodnight. Part of her was grateful Shaun had shown so much restraint—she knew that he was trying to take it slowly for her sake, to prove he was serious. But she was beginning to feel things for Shaun that she couldn't afford to feel. She was leaving town—she wasn't supposed to be falling in love.

As Shaun's clever hands moved over her body, Bridie forced away her lingering doubts. She was tired of fighting herself. They were two consenting adults, for goodness sake! Shaun knew what her plans were, and when the time came they'd deal with it.

Shaun slipped the straps of her swimmers from her shoulders and slowly traced their path with his lips, sending a shiver down her spine. Interlocking his hands with hers, he raised her arms above her head, and held them there, effectively pinning her to the ground beneath him. She should have felt exposed and vulnerable, but seeing the blaze of desire in Shaun's eyes as he took his time surveying her body, she suddenly felt powerful . . . and beautiful.

Untangling her hands, she lightly trailed her fingers across his chest, smiling as she felt him shudder.

Bridie pushed against him, and he moved so that she could sit up and face him. 'You're wearing far too much clothing,' she said, her hands moving to the top of his board shorts. She watched with a stir of excitement as he covered her hands with his own, stilling her movements as he slowly got to his feet before her and took over, easing the shorts lower. He seemed to enjoy the anticipation in her eyes as he revealed his lean body inch by agonising inch, until finally he stepped out of the shorts and stood before her in all his male glory.

Bridie couldn't help but think she'd been robbed all these weeks when he'd kept himself hidden beneath his clothing. He dropped down to his knees before her and Bridie traced the thick column of his neck with her tongue, tasting the salty tang of his sweat.

She heard him groan softly next to her ear, and she urged him onto his back, following him down until she straddled him. His surprised chuckle soon faded and was replaced with an intense look as he cupped her face in his hands, holding her gaze silently for a long moment. The depth of feeling in that one shared look made Bridie quiver with a mixture of emotion and lust. Leaning forward, she kissed him, pouring into the kiss the feelings she knew she couldn't voice.

His hands slipped to her waist, holding her firmly as she began to move slowly against him. The gentle moans of their mutual need drifted away on the breeze above them.

�

Everything about the day was perfect. The hum of busy insects all around them and the warm sun, gentle at this time of year, made for a peaceful backdrop. Once summer hit it would be unbearable to sit out in the sun and bask as they were today.

Bridie stretched out, her head resting in Shaun's lap as he sat with his back against a big gum tree. Out here it was easy to believe they were the only two people in the whole world. She let out a long sigh of contentment as he ran his fingers through her hair.

'Can I ask you something?' Bridie asked quietly.

'Sure,' Shaun said easily.

Bridie paused a moment. 'What did you mean when you said you'd paid a heavy price for that night of the bet?'

She felt his hand go still in her hair and turned so that she was in a better position to see his face. It surprised her to see he was struggling to find the words to answer her.

'I should never have gone to that party. I wasn't supposed to, but I was pissed off at Dad and too wrapped up in my own problems to think about anyone else.' Shaun gave a sad shake of his head and went back to playing with her hair. 'I should have been at Jinjulu helping Jared, but I went to the party instead.' At her frown of confusion, he dropped his eyes to hers. 'The night of the party was the night he died.'

Bridie felt her breath catch at the look of despair in Shaun's eyes.

'He was always the responsible one. He was supposed to inherit Jinjulu—that's how it's always been, from eldest son to eldest son. We all knew that, but even so I guess I always hoped Dad'd change his mind and let both of us run the place.'

'But he didn't,' Bridie guessed.

Shaun gave a snort of disgust. 'He made it clear a few days before the party that I wasn't responsible enough to run Jinjulu.' He stopped abruptly, his gaze lifting to take in the land around him. 'It just about gutted me. I couldn't imagine myself anywhere else, doing anything else. The thing is, he was right to a certain extent. I *did* like to party. I got in a bit of trouble at school—nothing too bad, but I was a little wild for a time and Jared was the complete opposite. In Dad's eyes Jared was the right son for the job. I could stay on at Jinjulu but only as a glorified labourer. It shattered me. I guess pride got in the way because I decided that if I wasn't good enough to help run Jinjulu then I wasn't sticking around to get walked on.'

'What did your brother think about all of this?'

'He was stuck in the middle. He loved Jinjulu as much as I did and he worked hard. He didn't get in trouble at school, he didn't argue with the old man, he was good at following orders and keeping the peace, but he didn't agree with Dad about this. He hadn't gone to uni—he'd just wanted to be out working on Jinjulu. The first time I ever heard them fight was a few nights before he . . .' Shaun let the words trail off. 'He tried to tell Dad that we'd be able to run the place together but Dad wouldn't have a bar of it. That night I talked Jared into coming into town with me. We went to the pub and drowned our sorrows—stayed out all night and turned up the next morning hungover and sick as a pair of dogs.' Shaun smiled a little at the memory. 'Dad was fuming. He let Jared have it big time, said he expected nothing less of me but that he thought Jared was smarter than that.'

Bridie frowned. What kind of parent put down one of their kids in front of the other?

'Anyway, for the next few days Dad hounded Jared,

and of course Jared felt bad for letting Dad down. When I got word that party was on, I was supposed to be helping him finish up a job, but I was still pissed off at Dad and, I guess, hurting about never being considered good enough. I wanted Jared to come with me but he wasn't going to risk getting grilled by Dad again, so he stayed back and I went into town.'

'So what happened?'

Shaun looked down, but he didn't meet her eyes. He really didn't feel like reliving all this now. Today had been so unbelievably good; finally being able to do what he'd been dreaming of doing to Bridie for years had made him happier than he had been in a very long time. It was understandable that she'd want to know about Jared—obviously she'd heard about the accident—but he'd never talked about it to anyone before.

'I wasn't in the mood to hang around the party after you left,' he said quietly. 'There was a storm. It was still raining heavily out at Jinjulu, and when I got home everyone was still up.'

Shaun had parked the farm ute and was walking towards the house when his mother hurried across the front yard towards him.

'Jared's not back yet.'

Shaun was momentarily confused, thinking Jared must have changed his mind about going into town and he'd somehow missed him at the party.

'From the back paddock. He hasn't come back yet,' she clarified. 'He's not answering his phone. Shaun, I'm worried.'

Shaun squinted at his watch and swore. It was ten-thirty. 'Why the hell hasn't anyone gone out to look for him before now? Where's Dad?'

His mother's face hardened. 'He says he's teaching him a lesson.'

Shaun brushed past his mother and headed inside. He found his father seated at his desk and immediately demanded, 'Why isn't anyone out looking for Jared? It's pouring out there.'

Douglas looked up from the papers on his desk and glared at him. 'He's a big boy—a bit of rain won't hurt him. In fact, a long walk back in the wet might help him remember he needs to be responsible if he wants to run Jinjulu.'

'Anything could have happened to him out there.'

'Then you should go out and bring him back. Bit of time out in the rain won't hurt you either.'

Shaun turned away in disgust. The weather outside was not improving; in fact, the lightning was getting a little too close for comfort. He left the office, grabbed a long water-proof coat from the rack by the back door and headed out to the ute.

The rain was coming down so hard that it was diffi-cult to see through the windscreen. The dirt track he was following was slippery and it took all his concentration not to end up in an irrigation ditch. When he'd finally reached the paddock where he and Jared had last been working, Shaun got out of the ute and searched up and down the fence line. There was no sign of Jared.

He drove to every place he thought Jared might have holed up in, waiting for the rain stop, but there was no sign of him. Then, as he began very slowly to retrace his route back towards the homestead, he noticed some freshly churned-up dirt and his headlights caught the glimmer of something metallic.

He phoned the house to get his mother to call in the neighbours. He needed more lights. Something was very wrong.

Within an hour, Shaun had seen the trail of lights as a group of vehicles headed towards him, but they had barely registered . . . They had all been too late . . . *He* had been too late.

Shaun couldn't look into Bridie's eyes. He knew he'd find compassion and sadness there, and he couldn't deal with that if he wanted to get to the end of his story.

'He'd lost control of the bike and hit a tree. By the time I found him he was already dead.'

Bridie sat up, dismayed. 'Finding him like that must have been terrible.'

'I should have been there, Bridie. I should never have left him to finish up alone.'

'You were a kid—' she started before he cut her off roughly.

'I was nineteen, Bridie. Old enough to know better. It was my fault he was out there.'

Most of the rest of that night had been a blur. The ambulance had been called, but it was clear to the others, just as it had been to Shaun when he'd found him, that Jared was gone and there was nothing anyone could do for him. But one thing he remembered clearly was the arrival of his parents. His mother had been hysterical, but it was his father's reaction that was branded onto his mind forever.

'You left him out here, you bastard!' Shaun had yelled at Douglas as he'd stood staring down at the twisted metal of the bike wrapped around the tree.

'Don't put any of the blame on me, boy,' Douglas had said, his voice booming in the rain and gloom of the night.

'He was out here on a bike, for Christ's sake! Why didn't you come out and look for him?'

'And why was he on a bike in the first place? Because *you* took the work ute into town to go out and party. I hope it was worth it,' Douglas had growled, before turning away and trudging back to his four-wheel drive.

'It wasn't your fault. It was an accident,' Bridie said gently.

Shaun shook his head. 'He stayed behind to finish a job I was supposed to help him with. I took the work ute. Nothing can change that.'

After the funeral he'd made a decision: he owed it to Jared to change. He'd needed some time away to deal with his grief, and he hadn't been able to face going back to uni straight away, but he'd vowed to use everything he learned to make sure Jinjulu thrived. It had been Jared who'd been ahead of his time with environmental sustainability. It had been Jared's idea to implement some of the new ways of thinking, Jared who had inspired Shaun with the possibilities of what they could do with Jinjulu once they were given the run of the place.

'Everything pretty much changed that night. Don't get me wrong,' Shaun said, 'my family has never been your typical happy family. My father has always been difficult, and my parents have never been openly affectionate to each other, or to us kids really, but when Jared died it was like part of this place died too, part of all of us.'

⟋

Bridie felt a heavy weight on her heart at the sadness and guilt she heard in Shaun's voice.

She didn't remember hearing much about Jared's death at the time. It had coincided with her father's arrest and her mother's deterioration and she'd had enough to cope with without another tale of family tragedy.

Shaun went on, 'There was quite a lot of condemnation of the way Dad handled the whole thing—leaving it so late before anyone went out to look for Jared. He took it pretty hard—he'll never admit it bothered him, but it did. His reputation around the district had always meant a lot to him, and having people judge him so openly knocked him back a bit. I don't think Mum has ever forgiven him for not going out when she began to get worried.

'This place was never the same after that night. It was still home to me but I couldn't be here for a long time afterwards. Dad made it clear he didn't think I was up to the job—too young and full of too many weird ideas to be let loose—so I went out and started working in the mines. I did the rest of my degree online, then worked on different properties to learn more.' He fell silent.

'Then you came back,' she prompted.

Shaun didn't answer for a while. 'I guess it was time to face things. I missed Jinjulu.' She watched him twirl a small stick between his fingers. 'I still half-expect to see Jared walk through the door at any moment.'

Bridie knew what that was like. Before she'd moved into her own place, everywhere she looked in their small family home had reminded her of her mother.

'Things don't seem to be improving with your parents though?'

'They haven't let go of the past. It's like they're holding what happened over each other's heads or something.'

'That can't be healthy.'

Shaun gave a hollow chuckle. 'Mum still insists on setting Jared's place at the table.'

So that was why there had been an extra place setting at dinner that day. 'Why does she do that?'

Bridie saw a flicker of something like anger cross his face. 'To remind my father what he did.'

'Seriously?'

'Yeah . . . well, that's my theory. There should be a photo of my parents in the dictionary under "dysfunctional".' He grimaced wryly, but she could tell it bothered him a great deal. 'So you see, your family's looking pretty good in comparison, isn't it.'

'I don't get why you stay if your father won't listen to what you want to do.'

'It's my heritage.'

'Not until he decides to hand it over,' she pointed out. 'You could buy your own place, run things the way you want. I just don't get why you're prepared to stay this frustrated.'

'Before I left that afternoon . . . I said some things to Jared that I shouldn't have.'

Bridie watched as a parade of emotions crossed his face.

'I was so angry at the old man, and angry at Jared—but it wasn't his fault, he was just stuck in the middle trying to please everyone . . . When he started lecturing me about pissing off Dad and proving that I was reliable, I told him he could keep Jinjulu, that I was leaving and I didn't want a bar of it . . . Now I owe it to him to stay here and run Jinjulu. Putting up with Dad goes hand in hand with it.'

It seemed obvious to her that this whole family was trapped by their guilt. 'You're putting up with your father because you feel guilty about leaving Jared that night? Shaun, you can't let him walk all over you because of something you think you owe your brother.'

'You don't get it.' He stood up and pushed away from the tree. She saw the stiff set of his shoulders and knew she'd touched on a taboo subject. *You don't stick your nose into Broderick family business.* He pulled his hat off and ran a hand through his hair, then turned to face her.

'You know, you're the last one who should be pointing out where I'm going wrong with my father. What about you? At least I've spoken to mine in the last decade. You haven't even gone to see yours.'

'That's because he's in *prison*.'

'Last I heard, you were allowed to visit.'

Bending down to throw together the picnic things, Bridie gathered the basket and the blanket and stormed over to the ute. 'Now look who doesn't get it,' she snapped as she slammed the tailgate shut.

'Family dynamics are hard to explain to someone else, aren't they?' he said quietly. Bridie clenched her jaw but didn't comment.

With the carefree mood of earlier gone, it seemed to take forever to get back to the homestead. She was angry that they'd let a conversation about their fathers, of all things, spoil what had been a fantastic day, but worse than that, she felt as though she'd been chastised like a child.

It irked her that he had a point, though. What was she doing commenting on anyone else's family problems? She had enough of her own to deal with.

When they pulled up at the homestead Shaun turned off the ignition and they sat in silence for a few minutes. Through the open windows came the sound of the work dogs barking somewhere off in the distance. He turned his big frame to face her, no easy feat in the confines of the work ute, and slid one arm behind her.

'Bridie, I'm sorry if I bit your head off back there. I didn't mean to lash out at you like that.'

A sigh escaped as she shook her head. 'No, you were right. I was preaching and I had no business doing that. I'm sorry too.'

'Stay for dinner? Daisy always makes enough food to feed a small army.'

As tempting as the offer of Daisy's cooking was, she wasn't sure she was up to a repeat performance of dinner with the Brodericks.

'Come on, just a drink then. Luke won't be back for hours yet.'

She didn't want to leave him just yet, not after what they'd shared down by the creek. She'd thought she'd be strong enough to keep things low-key after sex, but she was forced to concede now that she'd been having herself on. It wasn't just great sex with Shaun—she had feelings for him.

A little voice warned her that she should get out while she still could, but she didn't want to hear that now. Today had been as near to perfect as she could have imagined, and she didn't want it to end just yet.

The house seemed empty as they made their way inside. Shaun led her out to the kitchen to find Daisy and rustle up something to eat.

'I see my picnic lunch did the trick then,' she chortled, her laughter gaining strength when she saw Bridie's cheeks redden. 'Ah, to be young and in love again,' she sighed, moving around the huge kitchen like a mini tornado.

Bridie refused to meet the glance Shaun shot her; she wasn't ready to talk about it yet, and especially in front of Daisy.

'Where is everyone?'

'Drinkies by the pool.' Daisy tossed her head in the general direction of the entertainment area out the back of the house. 'If you're going out there, take this out and save me old legs a trip,' she said, thrusting a tray of dips and biscuits into Shaun's hands.

'Come on, Bridie, let's go feed the starving hordes.'

'Starving? Not bloody likely in this place,' Daisy called after him. 'All I do is cook!'

'How long has Daisy been with your family?' Bridie asked as they headed outside.

'She started working for my grandparents.'

'Wow, that's a long time to work in one place—and for one family.' *For this family, and not go insane*, she added silently.

'She was engaged to my granddad's older brother, before he went off to New Guinea in the war. He was killed in action.'

'Poor Daisy.' Bridie's heart went out to the woman. She couldn't imagine how painful those war years must have been for the girlfriends and wives of soldiers who went off to fight, never to return. You only had to read the list of names on the war memorial in the centre of town to see the devastating effect the two wars had had on little

towns like Tooncanny. In its prime, Tooncanny had been a
thriving town on the way to rivalling Dubbo. Then, when
so many young men died in World War I, topped by further
catastrophic losses in World War II, the town all but died.
Farming families with no sons to take over the properties sold up and left town. Women with no prospects of
marriage due to a shortage of eligible men left in droves
as soon as they were old enough to go in search of work.
Tooncanny's dreams of a grand future crumbled in the dust
along with the bodies of the fallen soldiers overseas.

'My grandparents kept her on here because she didn't
have any other family nearby. She ended up marrying a
stockman who worked for my granddad. He died a few
years later. I guess old Granddad kept her on to make sure
she was taken care of.'

Bridie's eyebrows lifted in surprise. She wondered how
the woman could handle being treated as an employee
when, had the brother she was engaged to survived, she
might have been running Jinjulu. Douglas and Constance
wouldn't be residing in the main house, it would have
been Daisy's.

The thought unsettled her. The grandfather had kept
Daisy on as his employee out of the goodness of his heart?
Gee, what an offer. *You're no longer going to be a member
of this family, but you can cook and clean for us, how's that?*

As Bridie and Shaun emerged through the French doors
that opened up onto the verandah, angry voices greeted
them. Bridie hesitated behind Shaun as she registered the
tension between his parents.

'Decided to come home, I see,' his father drawled sarcastically.

'Hello, Mr and Mrs Broderick,' Bridie cut in to announce her presence.

'Oh. Hello.' Constance's surprised expression was quickly transformed into a polite mask of welcome as Shaun pulled out a patio chair for Bridie.

Phoebe sat on a lounge beside the pool, busily sketching on a large artist's pad, her earphones fixed firmly in her ears. She looked up as Shaun and Bridie approached, but instantly dismissed them without a greeting, returning to her drawing.

'It's nice to see you've been making good use of my son lately,' Douglas said to Bridie as he reached across to take a biscuit from the tray.

'I'm not sure what I would have done without him the last few weeks,' she said carefully, certain his comment had been meant to sting, even though he smiled easily across at her.

'So I take it I can actually get him to do some work now?'

'I'm sorry if I took him away from anything important.' Bridie sent an alarmed glance towards Shaun and saw that he was frowning. She stifled a groan. God, this family was exhausting to be around—how did Shaun handle it?

'I have to go and book that conference,' Douglas said to Shaun. 'You just make sure you get things organised with your little experimental plot. I don't want you lumping Pete with it while we're away—he's got his own work to do.' He got up and stalked away down the long verandah.

'Conference?' Bridie asked Shaun after his mother had excused herself as well and headed in the opposite direction.

'Yeah, I forgot all about it. Dad and I are going to a conference down in Sydney.' His dark expression indicated he wasn't exactly looking forward to the event.

'That's a good sign, isn't it? I mean, if he's going to a conference with you, doesn't that mean he's warming to the concept of new ideas?'

Shaun gave an irritated sigh. 'Not really. He's dragging me along to listen to arguments against the push for what I'm trying to do. I thought if I was willing to go and listen to his side of the argument, he might come and listen to mine as soon as I find a speaker hosting an information seminar.'

'That's a good plan. Very mature of you,' she congratulated him.

'What do you think the chances are that he'll repay the favour? Still, it seemed a good idea at the time. We've had this planned for months, but I'd almost forgotten about it. I don't want to go now.'

'It won't be so bad—I think it's a positive move on your part.'

'No, not that. I don't want to go now because it means I'll be away from you.'

Bridie felt a shy grin spread across her face. 'I'll miss you too.'

'Let's go to your place.' He smiled back. 'Luke won't be home till dark.'

She couldn't ignore the excitement that rose in her as she met his eyes. He was like a drug; she couldn't get enough of him.

They were up out of their seats in a heartbeat, heading towards the car. She kept glancing up to catch him in her rear-view mirror all the way back into town. She didn't want to leave her ute out at Jinjulu, so they were taking two vehicles into town.

They spent the rest of the evening in bed, scrambling out guiltily when they heard a car pull up outside later that night. By the time Luke came inside they were seated at the kitchen table, dressed—barely—and trying to look as though they hadn't almost been sprung. They might have got away with it too, if it hadn't been for one thing . . .

Bridie smothered a giggle as Shaun got up from the table to grab a beer from the fridge and she saw he'd pulled his T-shirt on inside out in his rush.

Early the next morning, Bridie took her cup of coffee out and sat on the back step, watching the cows pulling at the lush grass that grew by the back fence. Right now she envied them. How nice would it be to have nothing more to think about than where your next mouthful of grass was going to come from?

Bridie had a feeling that, after yesterday, her life was about to get a hell of a lot more complicated than she'd counted on. She was happy—deliriously so if she was going to be entirely honest with herself—but last night she'd had a dream. She'd been standing in the middle of the road while a truck barrelled towards her. Everything had happened in slow motion. She knew she had to run but for some reason found herself frozen, unable to move out of the way. Was it an omen? She wasn't sure. All she knew was that the truck was getting closer and that very soon she'd have to make the decision to jump out of the way if she didn't want to be run over.

Fifteen

It was still dark and the morning air was chilly as they stood on the platform of the Dubbo train station.

Bridie had to count the lines on the paving to keep her mind from the fact that her baby brother was about to leave home. Luke had made a complete recovery, passed all his medicals and had been accepted into basic training.

For the last couple of weeks things with Shaun couldn't have been better. They didn't speak about his family and she refused to dwell on Luke's upcoming departure. If she thought about that too much, she'd have to consider the fact that she no longer had an excuse to stay in Tooncanny—and that was just too confusing to think about at the moment.

Shaun had insisted on coming along for the drive, and secretly Bridie was relieved. She wasn't sure she could have held herself together if she were alone. At least having him here would ensure she did her best to stay composed.

'Make sure you call me when you get there,' she reminded Luke for the third time since they'd left the house.

'I said I would,' he told her without trying to hide his exasperation. He, at least, couldn't wait to start his big adventure. She, on the other hand, was wondering why she'd been pushing him towards this moment for so long. Now that it was here, she was suddenly overwhelmed by a suffocating helplessness. For the first time in her life she would be completely alone.

The sound of the approaching train made her heart sink. Swallowing past the tightness in her throat she turned to Luke and clung to him tightly. 'Just make sure you keep your mouth shut and do what you're told, okay?'

'Bridie, you gotta let me go now,' Luke whispered, and his arms tightened around her briefly in comfort.

She tried to blink away the tears and quickly wiped at her face as she took a step away from him. 'Call me,' she croaked.

'When I get there—yeah, I know,' he grinned and she rolled her eyes.

Shaun leaned across her and shook Luke's hand, and a fresh wave of tears threatened. It was as though her kid brother had matured into a young man overnight.

With one last look at his sister, Luke turned and walked down the platform to climb into his carriage.

She watched as he took a step into the train. An overwhelming rush of pride and love clenched her throat, making it ache with the pressure of holding it inside. She had to tell him before it was too late. 'Luke!' Bridie called, and he paused as she hurried to the door of the carriage. 'I'm proud of you, mate.'

She saw him swallow and give her an awkward nod. 'You too, sis. Love you,' he said, before turning and making his way to his seat.

With her arms wrapped around her middle, Bridie watched as the train disappeared down the track. Just like that, he was gone.

She was grateful that Shaun had left her alone for the last few moments. She'd needed time to say goodbye to a part of her life that was over now.

Silently she walked back to where he stood, leaning against the station wall, waiting patiently. This was what she liked about him. He knew how to be patient, to wait and watch and just . . . be.

He searched her tear-filled eyes and sent her a crooked smile that managed to be both tender and downright sexy at the same time. 'Come on, I'll buy you breakfast before we head back.'

Earlier she'd been too unsettled to even think of eating, and now daylight was only just beginning to stretch its arms out wide and yawn. Shaun found a nearby café and ordered breakfast.

'He'll be fine,' he said as he spooned sugar into his coffee.

'Yeah, I know. I think it's me who won't cope so well.'

'You'll be fine too. I'll be around to keep an eye on you,' he grinned.

She watched his big hand as he stirred the coffee. In all her planning and dreaming, at this point she just packed up and drove away. There was no one 'keeping an eye on her' to leave behind.

This was supposed to be *her* time—at long last.

The thought unsettled her more than she cared to admit. Could she afford to put her plans on hold, yet again, for a relationship? Or, more to the point, could she afford *not* to?

⁓

Bridie was in an irritable mood as she drove home after a busy shift at work. She hadn't slept well the previous night. Shaun had been away for three days, in Sydney with his father at the farming conference. Three. Long. Days.

In the lead-up to Shaun going away, Bridie had been looking forward to inserting some independence back into her life, but right now she was failing miserably. Instead of basking in all the free time she had without Shaun to distract her, she was fretting. Her. Fretting!

It shouldn't be like this. She hadn't realised just how much time they'd been spending together until he wasn't there and she was left with a gaping hole.

She smiled as she thought back to Shaun's phone call last night, and the memory momentarily erased her sadness.

'I wish I was there with you right now,' he'd said.

'I wish you were too,' Bridie had replied, fighting a wave of loneliness. The house was just too quiet nowadays with Luke gone and no Shaun to distract her long into the night.

'What are you wearing?'

His question sparked surprised laughter from her. 'You sound like some internet sleaze.'

'Come on, Bridie, I'm dyin' here. Just hearing your voice makes me miss you like you wouldn't believe.'

'Shaun Broderick! Are you asking me to have phone sex with you?' she asked, feigning shock. 'What would your mother say if she knew that was the kind of kinky stuff her son was into?'

'I'm telling you, Bridie, you should see the size of—'

'I get the picture!' she cut him off quickly. Oh boy, did she get the picture! 'I'm not really into the whole phone-sex thing, you know.'

'Can't say I've ever done it either—but come on, think of it as an adventure.'

'Oh, for goodness sake.'

'Thatta girl—come on, talk dirty to me.' She heard the grin in his voice and knew he thought she wouldn't go through with it. *Okay, Mr Smarty Pants*, she thought with a smug smile, *let's see about that.*

'Well, I've just got out of the shower and all I'm wearing is this very . . . small . . . towel,' she said, lowering her voice.

'Really?'

'Yes, really . . . Oops, well, I *was* wearing a towel . . . now I'm standing here . . . naked. Oh, and I'm still all wet from the shower. Are you still there?' she asked when he didn't say anything.

'Yeah—I'm here. Ah, so what are you doing now?' he asked, clearing his throat.

'I'm lying down on my bed . . . thinking of you,' she said in what she hoped was a seductive purr.

'Tell me what you're thinking about.' His voice had lowered and for a minute Bridie lost her smirk as a shiver raced through her, even though she wore a very unseductive pair of blue and white striped flannelette pyjamas.

'I'm thinking about the way you kiss me. About the way you can melt me with just one glance. I'm thinking how good it feels when you touch me and how badly I want to touch you right now. I want to run my mouth all the way down your—'

A loud thump on the other end of the phone jolted her out of her lustful thoughts. 'What was that?' She could hear a long string of profanities down the phone. 'Shaun? Are you okay?'

'No, I'm not bloody okay.'

'What happened?'

'I fell off the bed and hit my goddamn head on the bedside table, and it's bleeding all over the damn place, that's what happened.'

'Is it okay? Do you need stitches?'

She heard him moving around the room—presumably into the bathroom to check it out. 'Nah, it's not a big cut—just bleeding a lot.'

Bridie bit back a laugh. It wasn't funny—he could have really hurt himself, and how would he explain *that* to the casualty department?

'Jesus, Bridie!'

'What?'

'I thought you said you'd never done this before.'

'I haven't.'

'Could've fooled me,' he grumbled.

'Dare I ask how you managed to fall off the bed?'

'It's not as easy as you'd think to do things one-handed,' he said dryly.

'Well, that's it. No more phone sex for you, mister—clearly it's not something amateurs should partake in.'

But Shaun had had the last laugh. He might have nursed a bit of a headache, but it had been a long night of tossing and turning for Bridie, feeling frustrated and irritable thanks to her skyrocketing libido.

Now she parked in her driveway and gathered up the bags of groceries. As she put her key in the lock she heard the phone start to ring inside. Normally she wouldn't risk breaking her neck over a phone call, but the thought that it might be Shaun made her scramble to open the front door.

She made a dive for the handset as she launched through the door. 'Hello?'

There was silence on the other end and for a moment she thought that whoever had been calling must have hung up. Then: 'This is Constance Broderick. How are you, dear?'

Bridie couldn't have been more surprised if a snake had stuck its head out of the mouthpiece and hissed at her. 'Ah, hello, Mrs Broderick . . . I'm fine, thanks.'

'I was wondering if you'd be able to come out tomorrow for morning tea.'

'Ah . . .' Bridie's mind went blank. Morning tea? *Seriously?* Bridie wasn't under any illusions that the Brodericks had changed their minds about her and suddenly welcomed her presence in their son's life. They barely tolerated the fact that he spent every moment he wasn't working with her. Why would the woman invite her out for morning tea as if they were old friends?

'I have something very important to discuss with you,' Constance said smoothly. 'I'll be expecting you at ten tomorrow.'

She hung up and Bridie was left blinking uncertainly at the abrupt summons.

∽

As she drove out to Jinjulu, Bridie almost turned around several times, but suddenly the impressive gates were before her and it was too late. She had a horrible feeling she was being dragged towards something unpleasant, but she seemed incapable of stopping it.

Daisy answered the door and one glance at her tight-mouthed expression made Bridie's heart sink to her boots. Before Daisy had a chance to greet her, Constance was bustling towards them.

She swept Bridie into the hall and out through the tall French doors onto the patio overlooking a beautiful manicured garden. 'Thank you for coming out at such short notice. I just thought we should take the opportunity to get to know each other a little better while the boys are away. Shaun's always hovering whenever you come out and we don't get a chance to chat, girl to girl,' she smiled.

'Sure, no problem.' *Now if only I could get rid of this feeling of impending doom hanging over my head,* she thought wryly.

Daisy deposited the tray of tea and coffee onto the patio table and Bridie wondered why she looked so cross.

'Thank you, Daisy, that will be all now,' Constance dismissed the woman with a tight smile.

As Constance poured the coffee, Bridie was distracted by a movement in the pool. She stared as a graceful water nymph of a woman emerged from the water and bent to retrieve a towel, dabbing at the droplets that ran down her body. The woman was too tall and willowy to be Phoebe. Bridie glanced at Constance but she seemed oblivious to the stranger's presence. Bridie watched the woman make her way across the lawn and disappear inside open doors further down the verandah.

Bridie sat nervously on the edge of the lounge chair, feeling Constance's gaze upon her.

'I asked you out here because I wanted to talk to you alone about something,' Constance said.

Bridie braced herself.

'I'm worried about Shaun's intentions.'

For a moment Bridie wasn't certain she'd heard right. 'Excuse me?'

'Please don't get upset, dear—I know it isn't my place to butt in, but I really don't want to see you get hurt. I'm just not sure you're aware of Shaun's bigger plans.'

'Mrs Broderick, I don't think this is any of your business.'

'Darling, everything about this family is *business*, haven't you figured that out yet? Nothing happens here unless it will somehow benefit Jinjulu and, unfortunately,' she paused, then softened her tone slightly, 'you're not considered of any benefit.'

Bridie blinked, stunned into silence.

'I'm afraid that he's using you to make some kind of point to his father and me. I just felt you deserved to know the truth before you got too involved and risked being hurt.' She reached over and patted Bridie's hand. 'Jinjulu means everything to him, and he knows that unless he keeps his father onside, his dream of running this place will never eventuate. If it comes to choosing, he'll pick Jinjulu over . . . anything.'

Constance was only saying out loud all the things Bridie had already thought herself, but hearing it from someone else stung as painfully as a slap.

'Just don't get your hopes up that you have any kind of future with Shaun. I really would hate to see you hurt.'

Bridie was saved from having to respond when the woman she'd seen earlier wandered down the verandah and took a seat opposite Bridie, smiling over at Constance with a comfortable familiarity.

'Bridie, I don't think you've met Alisha, have you?'

'Umm, no, I haven't.' *Alisha? Who the bloody hell is Alisha?*

'Bridie, Alisha is a very dear friend of the family. Her mother and I went to school together, and she and Shaun are very close friends. She's come to visit for a few days.'

'How nice.' *Close friends?*

'Pleased to meet you.' Alisha's voice was as smooth as her appearance.

'Shaun and Alisha were inseparable as youngsters,' Constance said with an indulgent smile. 'So, anyway, Bridie, Alisha and I were just discussing Shaun's birthday party.'

'His birthday?' Bridie repeated blankly.

Alisha gave a tinkerbell laugh that reminded Bridie of one of those annoying wind chimes. 'We thought it would be fun to throw a party. Of course, you're most welcome to come along. You *did* know it was his birthday soon?'

Bridie placed her cup back down on its saucer, rubbing her lips together for a moment as she took a calming breath. She didn't know Alisha but she hated her already. Maybe she was being irrational, but after Constance's little warning a few minutes earlier, Bridie wasn't entirely sure that the woman's sudden visit was completely innocent. 'No, I can't say we've got around to talking about birthdays yet.'

'Oh,' Alisha said, putting a wealth of emphasis on that one little word.

A spark of pride straightened Bridie's spine and she forced a carefree smile. 'Well, you know how it is, all that hot sweaty sex we have, we don't actually get time to talk about little things like birthdays.'

It gave Bridie a small moment of satisfaction to see Shaun's mother, with her impeccable manners, splutter her mouthful of tea across the table.

'Sorry,' Bridie said, shrugging. 'I sometimes forget that mothers don't want to know everything their sons get up to.'

Constance looked flustered as she dabbed at the corner of her mouth and blotted the tea stains that dotted the front of her blouse.

Bridie stood up. 'I should get a move on. I have to get ready for work soon. Thanks so much for inviting me out, Constance. It was a lovely idea, and it was very nice to meet you too, Alisha.'

She fumed as she stalked out the front door. She felt ready to inflict grievous bodily harm on anyone who was silly enough to get in her way. Luckily, nobody crossed her path and she made it to her car without incident.

꒰

For the third time in the last hour, Shaun tried to phone Bridie's mobile. He listened to the number ring out again and muttered a curse as it switched to message bank.

He saw his father poke his head out of the large conference room doors searching for him. Damn it. He couldn't even get five bloody minutes alone without the old man keeping tabs on him.

He stayed behind the man-sized potted plant and waited until Douglas turned and went inside. Then he sent a text to Bridie, hoping he'd be able to get hold of her later.

It wasn't like her not to at least text him back. Something was wrong, he knew it—he could feel it. He had no idea what had happened; he'd been racking his brain to come up with an explanation for why she might ignore him like this, but for the life of him he couldn't think of a single reason. When he'd left, he could have sworn she'd been eager for him to get back.

The day by the creek had been so much better than he could ever have imagined, and since then they'd had trouble keeping their hands off each other. It was more than the sex, which was awesome; he felt closer to her than he'd felt to anyone before. They hadn't talked about what it all meant, though. He'd tried to bring it up a few times but Bridie had brushed it off, and the truth was he was too cowardly to force the issue. He wasn't entirely sure Bridie was as certain of their relationship as he was and that scared the hell out of him.

The only upside was that he'd spied one of his uni lecturers at the conference and introduced him to his father, leaving them to discuss some of the new crop-rotation techniques. Douglas wouldn't listen to Shaun but he might listen to a university professor. It was worth a try, anyway.

With a frustrated sigh, Shaun shoved his phone into his pocket, steeling himself to head back into the conference room once more. The sooner this was over, the sooner he could return to Tooncanny and find out what the hell was going on with Bridie.

೨

Bridie moved along the bar to her next customer, her smile faltering as a kaleidoscope of emotions whirled inside her. Relief, *desire*, anger . . . *desire* . . . 'You're home,' she pointed out needlessly.

'I am. Now, what did I do?' At her raised eyebrow, he said, 'You haven't returned my calls. I get the feeling you're ticked off about something and I have no idea what it is.'

'I'm at work, Shaun. Can we talk about this later?'

Shaun did a slow sweep of the room. There were three people in the entire pub, counting the two of them. 'Yeah, I can see you're rushed off your feet at the moment.'

'I wasn't ignoring you,' she lowered her voice. 'I was just too angry to talk to you.'

He shook his head in bewilderment. 'About what? I haven't even been here to do anything to piss you off.'

'It wasn't you. It was your *mother*.'

'What's she done now?'

'She invited me to morning tea,' she bit the words off with surgical precision.

'That doesn't sound too bad,' he answered cautiously.

'Have you been home yet?' she challenged, throwing him for a minute.

'No. Pete picked us up at the airport and I got him to drop me off here first. I wanted to see you.'

'Well, let's just say there's a really big surprise waiting for you when you get there,' she snapped.

'Bridie!' he growled.

'I don't want to talk about it, Shaun. I'm over all the drama that goes along with your family.'

'What happened?'

Whatever game his mother and Alisha were playing she wanted nothing to do with it. No doubt they expected she'd have reported their little tea party to Shaun by now. Her jaw clenched angrily at the memory. Well, they were going to be sorely disappointed, she thought. She had no intention of playing a part in their little soap opera. In fact, she could imagine Constance feeling rather deflated that Bridie hadn't thrown a tantrum and called Shaun as soon as she'd left Jinjulu. Well, tough.

'Look, while you were away I just realised a few things.' She braced her hands against the side of the bar and looked up to meet his frustrated expression.

'Like what?'

'Like your parents are never going to accept me and nothing I do is going to change that.'

'They don't have any say in my life, Bridie. For God's sake, I'm a grown man, give me a little credit.'

'I don't need all this crap right now, Shaun. I've had more than my limit the last few years with a teenager at home!'

He looked at her helplessly. 'What do you want me to do? Tell me, Bridie, so I can fix it.'

She shook her head slowly. 'I don't know.'

'When do you finish here?'

'In about half an hour.'

He gave a brisk nod, and ordered a beer. She wanted to tell him to go home and leave her alone, but the truth was she missed him like crazy and all she could think about was getting him alone and ripping that shirt from his shoulders so she could—

'Bridie!'

190

She dragged her gaze from Shaun's chest and stared at the customer at the end of the bar. 'Sorry, Jack. What can I get you?'

'Whatever you were thinking about giving him would be just fine, love,' he said, chuckling.

She sent Shaun a dark glare as he laughed at the blush creeping up her throat. 'At this very moment that would be a good clip around the ear,' she snapped, taking the used glass and replacing it with a fresh beer.

⌇

As soon as she unlocked the front door, Shaun backed her against the wall. 'God, Bridie. I missed you so much,' he whispered roughly against her mouth as she pulled at his shirt.

'Bedroom—now,' she managed to gasp between kisses.

'I love the way you think, woman.' He dipped his face to bury it in the sensitive hollow of her neck as he bent to sweep her into his arms.

Clothes were strewn across the bedroom floor, and Bridie sighed as she felt his warm skin against hers, his big body covering hers. God, she'd missed him. She pushed away all the doubts and good sense she'd been talking herself into while he was gone. Reality would be waiting for her as always, but for just a few minutes she could pretend it wasn't.

'You had me worried for a minute this afternoon,' Shaun said later as they lay in the dark room, their breathing not quite back to normal and their bodies still sleek with sweat. 'I thought you were trying to give me the shove-off.'

When she didn't reply, he raised up onto one shoulder and looked down into her face. 'Bridie,' he commanded, and she gave a weary sigh.

'It crossed my mind,' she admitted. 'It made sense when you weren't here to distract me.' He ran his fingers lightly down her arm and she pushed his hand away. She couldn't concentrate when he touched her. 'I'm just not comfortable around your parents, not when they make it more than obvious they don't approve of me.'

'I'll talk to Mum when I get home, but if it's any comfort, she and Dad are like that with everyone.'

'No, actually, Shaun, it's not much comfort. Who the hell do they think they are?'

'I don't want to argue, Bridie—not now. I don't want to talk about my family, I just want to catch up on lost time away from you.' He leaned over and captured her lips in a long kiss that wiped out any further conversation for the rest of the night and well into the early hours.

༈

The screen door banged shut behind him as he walked into Jinjulu homestead the next morning.

'Surprise, darling,' his mother crooned from the kitchen. 'Look who came for a visit.'

Shaun stared at the woman sitting at the table. This wasn't happening. 'Alisha?'

Just about the last thing he'd been expecting to find when he came home this morning was the woman he'd been engaged to barely a few months earlier. After last night, he thought he might be hallucinating from too much sex and not enough sleep.

'What are you doing here?'

'I invited Alisha to help celebrate your birthday,' Constance put in.

'My birthday?'

'We thought it'd be nice to have a big party. It's been so long since Jinjulu had a social event, so we've been busy planning it while you were away.'

'Did you know about this?' Shaun demanded, swinging his outraged glare to his father at the opposite end of the table.

'What gives you the idea that anything your mother does gets run past me first, son?' Douglas asked in a bored tone.

Shaun stared at his mother and shook his head. No wonder Bridie had been upset ... Oh Christ, had she already met Alisha? The thought made him panic for a moment. He'd never quite got around to bringing up Alisha and the fact that not so long ago he'd been engaged to be married.

'I don't have time for a party,' he pointed out, weakly. Shearing was due to start next week—they were going to be flat out.

'Of course you have time for a party,' said Constance. 'We've already started on the arrangements.'

Shaun shook his head again. 'I can't deal with it now—I've got too much to do. We'll talk about it later, Mum.'

He headed towards his ute and tried to ring Bridie, but her phone went straight to voicemail. He left a message telling her he'd call back later tonight so they could talk, then disconnected and tossed the phone onto the seat beside him.

He should have told her about Alisha before this, but Bridie was skittish enough about a relationship without him bringing up the fact that he'd been engaged not so long ago. He thought if he told her it would give her an excuse to use against him. He knew she'd think she was some kind of rebound fling or something.

He knew he'd been a coward not bringing up Alisha before now, but he also knew deep down that Bridie would have slipped out of his life again if he had, and that was something he *wasn't* willing to risk. Indeed, after returning to town and seeing her again, he'd realised that he'd never felt around Alisha the way he felt just looking at Bridie.

Sixteen

Shaun had plenty to work on in the shed and he was determined to avoid the main house for the rest of the day, but just after lunchtime he glanced up to see Alisha picking her way towards him. She was dressed in white linen trousers and a blue silk top, and was wearing high heels, of all things. She looked great—but totally out of place.

'You missed lunch. I didn't want you to go hungry on account of avoiding me, so I brought you something to eat.' She set the basket she was carrying down on the ground by his feet.

Shaun ignored the food, even though his stomach growled in protest—he'd been planning on having breakfast when he arrived home this morning but had lost his appetite as soon as he'd seen his mother's 'surprise'. 'What are you really doing out here?' he asked.

'Your mother sounded worried about you last time I spoke to her. You don't just stop loving someone overnight, you know. I thought I'd come out to see if you were okay.'

'Alisha, you know as well as I do that our parents wanted that marriage more than either of us did.'

'What we had was good.'

Shaun looked at the woman he had come very close to marrying for all the wrong reasons. Alisha was the daughter of another well-off farming family who now lived and worked in Sydney. They'd been friends as teenagers, both going to nearby boarding schools. A year before he'd decided to move back to Jinjulu they'd got together at a function in the city, and afterwards it had just seemed easier to go with the flow when both sets of parents had begun hinting at wedding bells. To tell the truth, most of the fight had gone out of him. Back then all he had really been interested in was coming back here to prove to his father that he had skills to make an important contribution to Jinjulu.

His moving out here hadn't gone down too well with Alisha, however. She'd made it clear she had no intention of living full-time on Jinjulu, and he'd told her that his desire to live on Jinjulu was non-negotiable. She hadn't pushed the issue again but he hadn't been convinced she was prepared to compromise. When he'd come back to Tooncanny and spotted Bridie again, he'd been shocked by just how powerful his attraction to her was—even after all that time. He hadn't felt the same gut-tightening, sweaty-palmed reaction when he'd been with Alisha, and he'd known in his heart that marriage to Alisha would be second rate in comparison. Even before he'd spoken more than two words to Bridie, he'd gone back to Sydney and ended it with Alisha. He'd spent a few weeks under his parents' roof and seen what their marriage had deteriorated into, and there was no way he was going to follow in their footsteps.

'Why did you really come out here, Leesh?' he asked again.

'I guess I hoped you might have changed your mind after a bit of a break.'

He caught a flash of vulnerability behind her smile and his annoyance dissipated a little. 'It wouldn't have worked between us—you know that. You don't want to live out here and I'm not interested in a socialite wife who's never home. We'd make each other miserable.'

'And you think it's going to be smooth sailing with this Bridie woman? You know your parents are never going to accept her, Shaun, and you're deluding yourself if you think that won't make you both miserable.'

Shaun's jaw clenched at her words. What was it with everyone around here? Did they honestly think he was about to let his parents dictate who he was or wasn't going to marry? He ignored the small voice that pointed out, *Why not? You know you cave in to most other things just to keep them happy*, and the darker voice that reminded him that he was obliged to make up for leaving his brother to die alone in a storm.

'Bridie makes me happy . . . She's not something I'm willing to give up to keep my parents satisfied.'

'I hope you know what you're doing,' Alisha said, turning away. 'Just so you know, I'll be waiting to pick up the pieces.'

She walked out of the shed before he could reply, leaving

him irritated and with the disquieting feeling that something was about to go very wrong.

~

'Hey, sis.' The voice on the end of the line sounded so close she felt as though she could reach out and touch him.

'Luke! How are you?'

'Yeah, good. I got a few minutes to call home, so I thought I'd ring and say hi.'

Bridie heard the fatigue in his voice and was alarmed. 'Are you all right? You sound tired.'

His weary chuckle pulled at her heartstrings. 'You could say that. We've been working pretty hard. We go out bush for three days next week. Boot camp is harder than I thought it was going to be.'

'Hang in there, mate. You're just tired and it's probably all catching up with you.'

'Yeah, I know,' he sighed. 'Hey, on the upside, I'm learning a whole new set of swear words. You should hear the corporals go off when they get really wound up—man, it's so hard not to laugh sometimes.'

He went on to horrify and amuse her in equal measure with tales of all the extra drill they received as punishment for the silliest of things.

She hated hearing about it. She had to stop herself from taking down names and calling these barbarians for putting her baby brother through all this. Thankfully, though, common sense told her to keep her mouth shut and let him handle it.

She understood why the army did it. It was designed to strip the new recruits down and recondition them from scratch. Discipline and teamwork were what made soldiers function under extreme pressure. That was cold comfort, however, to the instinct in her that only wanted to protect her brother.

She loved getting his letters; they came in weekly intervals and she spent hours reading and rereading them, laughing almost hysterically over certain parts and then feeling indignant and angry over others. Phone calls were a bit of a luxury; there was usually a long line for the weekly call they were allowed, as the thirty-odd recruits apparently had to go everywhere together.

She was looking forward to watching him march out, although it seemed such a long way away still. For his sake she hoped the next few weeks went by fast, the poor little bugger. He was certainly tougher than she was. Just the thought of someone screaming in her face was enough to make her hyperventilate.

After a few more minutes of conversation he had to go, and Bridie stared at the phone in her hand, feeling melancholy after hearing his voice. He sounded so grown up.

She missed him more than she had ever dreamed she would. Was it possible to be suffering empty nest syndrome at only twenty-four? Sometimes she forgot how old she was; she didn't feel like anyone her own age around here. They all seemed so immature and self-centred when they came into the pub.

⌇

When Bridie looked up to serve a customer at lunchtime the next day, the last person she expected to see was Phoebe Broderick.

'What can I get you?' Bridie asked cautiously. She wasn't sure what it was about this young woman that put her on edge. The sombre clothing gave her pale skin an almost sickly look, but the heavy dark eyeliner and mascara emphasised her large emerald-green eyes.

'I'll take a bourbon and Coke. A double.'

Bridie was an expert at hiding her opinion—it wasn't her job to question what a person drank—but it had barely gone noon and for such a small-framed individual it really did seem like an unwise order. However, she made the drink and gave it to Phoebe without comment.

Handing over the change, Bridie was about to turn away when Phoebe called her back. 'So are you coming to the big birthday bash?'

'I wasn't planning on it,' she said politely. She had about as much intention of attending the party as running down Main Street in the nude.

'I think you should come.'

'Why? Did the entertainment cancel?'

Phoebe cocked her head slightly. 'I'll be honest—I'd like to see Mum and Dad's feathers ruffled a bit, but I actually think that if you don't show up you'll be leaving my brother alone in a snake pit . . . Alisha's just looking for an opportunity to win him back, and if you don't show up you'll give it to her.'

Bridie paused. 'Win Shaun back?'

'They were engaged up until a few months ago,' Phoebe said, eyeing her strangely. 'He didn't *tell* you about her?'

Bridie straightened her shoulders and took a calming breath. There was no way she was going to allow Phoebe to see just how much that news had shocked her. She turned away and moved up to the other end of the bar to continue serving. *Engaged?* No wonder Alisha and Constance had looked so comfortable together . . . *Old friend, my arse!*

Arriving home that evening, she checked the letterbox on her way up the front path. She flicked through the three envelopes listlessly; two had little cellophane windows, which automatically had her shuffling them to the rear— she was not ready to face any bills before she'd even had a chance to kick off her shoes! But the third had a handwritten address; she flipped it over and froze. The sender's name was Brian Farrell.

Slowly she put the mail into her handbag so she could insert her key into the front door. As she put the kettle on, she eyed her handbag as though it contained something dangerous—which, depending on what was in that letter, could very well be the case.

This wasn't the first time her father had written to her; in fact, for a while he'd written to her once a week, but she had never replied and eventually his letters had stopped. Nowadays he only sent them at Christmas and on her birthday.

At first it had upset her to read them, but then she'd begun to resent them. What was the point of reading about how sorry he was and how he wished things had been different? It didn't help her and Luke in any way, didn't pay their bills or help her take care of her brother. She'd stopped reading them and simply put them into the bottom drawer of her dressing table unopened. Receiving a letter now, so unexpectedly, threw her off balance.

Making herself a cup of tea, she turned her back on the bag and headed instead for a long hot bath. She wasn't ready to read the letter yet.

Bridie ignored her ringing phone and Shaun's voicemail request to call him when she got in. She ran the bath and even took time to cleanse her face—something she usually forgot to do—before picking up the phone as it rang again.

'Hey, you're home late. Everything okay?'

'Everything's fine,' she said, keeping her tone cool. 'So when exactly were you going to tell me that you and Alisha were engaged?'

There was a guilty silence on the end of the phone, and then he gave a long sigh. 'Yeah, I know I should have said something—'

'You think? The fact that you'd been engaged up until recently was not something I enjoyed finding out from your sister!'

'It was months ago—and Phoebe should have kept her mouth shut,' Shaun growled.

'Oh, *months*. That's much better. And at least she told me—which is more than you did!'

'Bridie, it wasn't like it was some big secret . . . I didn't know she was going to turn up unannounced like that. I would have got around to telling you eventually. It's really not that big a deal.'

'Well, no . . . except that your ex-fiancée and your mother are planning your birthday party, and Alisha *obviously* still has feelings for you,' Bridie said, more than a little exasperated.

'I had no idea she was coming out here. Besides, Alisha and I have talked and she knows I don't have any feelings for *her*.'

Bridie sighed quietly. She could imagine Shaun running a hand through his hair in frustration as he waited for her to speak. 'Why are you the only one who can't see that this is not going to work out?' she asked softly.

'Must be that annoying desire to bash my head against a brick wall.'

'I'm serious, Shaun!'

'What do you want me to say, Bridie? I didn't invite Alisha out here. I told her I was in a relationship with you. There's not a whole lot about this situation I'm actually responsible for, and yet I'm copping all the flak over it.'

He was right, and she did believe he'd had nothing to do with Alisha turning up unannounced, but she really didn't like the fact that his mother had invited her out to morning tea to show her *exactly* the kind of woman she had in mind for her son.

He tried again. 'Look, let's just get through the damn party. Having you there with me will put an end to Mum's schemes. Everyone will know that you're my girl, not Alisha.'

'I'm not going to the party, Shaun.'

'Okay. I'll come over Friday night and stay the weekend,' he said easily.

'*This* weekend?'

'Yeah, this weekend.'

'Aren't you forgetting something? Like, maybe, *your birthday party*?'

'If you're not going, I'm not going.'

'You can't not go to your own birthday, Shaun!'

'Sure I can. I never agreed to it in the first place. I'm not going somewhere you don't feel comfortable.'

Oh, for goodness sake! Bridie shut her eyes. 'If you don't go, then they'll just blame me for that as well, and it'll make things even worse.'

'I'm not going without you,' he said, and she could picture him shrugging one big shoulder in that annoyingly offhand way he did sometimes.

'Damn it, Shaun! Fine. We'll go to the stupid party!' she snapped.

'I'll pick you up.'

'No, I'll drive myself out there . . . thanks.' She might be going to the party—under duress—but she wouldn't be staying long, and taking her own car ensured she could leave whenever she liked without dragging Shaun away.

'It'll be okay,' he said. 'I'll be right there beside you.'

She wasn't sure that was going to make any difference this time.

꒰

Jinjulu was in all its glory. The gardens were decorated with fairy lights; floating candles and flowers were scattered across the surface of the pool, and Chinese lanterns had been strung between trees. A live band was setting up on the lawn and a long table seemed ready to collapse under the weight of the huge buffet.

Bridie gave a low whistle and searched the milling crowd for the birthday boy. She hoped she looked okay. She hadn't been too sure of the dress in the fitting room, but the bossy assistant had clapped her hands and done a little happy dance, assuring her it was a knockout. It clung *everywhere* and had a plunging back, which meant she had to buy special jelly-like cups to hold her breasts in place. She'd questioned the wisdom of her choice and bundled up the garment several times to return it to the shop. But each time she did, something held her back. Maybe it was sheer martyrdom— the need to punish herself a little more for even thinking she had a future with Shaun Broderick. Whatever it had been, though, it had messed with her good intentions long enough to prevent her finding anything else in time, and here she was, dressed to kill and feeling like a complete idiot.

She smiled as Pete came up to say hello. 'Wow, Bridie, you scrub up well.'

She blushed. 'Hi, Pete. Have you seen Shaun? I haven't been able to spot him so far.'

'He and his old man went to have a heart to heart in the study. Poor bugger'll need a stiff drink when he finally gets away, I reckon,' he grinned, then someone he knew caught his eye and he left her with a jaunty wave.

'Suck it up, Bridie, my girl,' she muttered. 'Just get in there and mingle—they aren't any better than you.' She placed one foot in front of the other until she was in the middle of the growing crowd and no longer lurking on the fringes.

She spotted some familiar faces, mostly neighbours of the Brodericks'. There were quite a few pub patrons, though, and she nodded politely as she passed them. She noticed some surprised glances between the guests. They'd be wondering why the Farrell girl from the pub would be at a Broderick party. But she ignored them and straightened her shoulders. She'd endure this for Shaun's sake, stay a while and then get the hell outta here.

At the bar, Bridie helped herself to one of the glasses of wine that had been poured and left on the silver tray for guests to help themselves. Wandering over to the buffet table she picked up a napkin and speared a tiny meatball. At least eating would give her something to do other than stand around looking lost.

A movement near the house caught her eye and she smiled as she saw Shaun jog down the few steps to join the party. He looked good enough to eat, in his black suit, red shirt and boots. He'd made the effort to shave for the big event, but it didn't make him look any less dangerous. He was still way too sexy for her peace of mind.

She saw him scan the crowd and could almost feel the physical touch of his gaze as it landed on her. He smiled and waved as he made his way over to her, accepting birthday wishes and handshakes along the way, but not stopping to talk. Bridie watched his progress with growing excitement, holding her breath in anticipation as he came to a stop in front of her.

'You look amazing, Bridie,' he murmured, his eyes taking her in hungrily before he leaned in and grazed her cheek with his lips. 'Later, I intend to show you just how amazing,' he whispered before drawing back.

'Happy birthday,' she said. Her breathing had shortened as she felt the warmth of his breath against her neck. The scent of his cologne triggered erotic images of that hard body beneath his suit, memories that made her knees go weak.

'I've missed you,' he said, and the simple truth of the statement momentarily rushed her senses. God help her, she'd missed him too.

Just then Constance rushed towards them. 'Shaun, darling, there you are. Come along, you're the guest of honour. There's people to mingle with, and I think your father has someone he wants you to have a chat with about the conference.' She smiled at Bridie. 'You don't mind if I steal my son away for a while, do you, dear? Can't hog him all to yourself on his birthday!'

Bridie saw Shaun's brow crease and jumped in to forestall an argument. 'Your mother's right, you have guests. I'll be okay,' she assured him, holding up her glass of wine. *That's right: me and Mr Riccadonna here will be just fine.* She smiled through gritted teeth. 'Go mingle.'

He sent her a doubtful glance, but his mother had latched onto his arm and began to drag him away. Bridie turned her back on them and reached for a refill. This was going to be one hell of a long night.

꙳

Shaun was a man on the edge.

He'd been feeling like a caged tiger the last few days, but with just one glimpse of Bridie he'd felt his mood shift, his world fall back into alignment once more. Then she'd turned around and he'd caught sight of her smooth, naked skin and something *other* than his mood shifted.

He performed his duties as guest of honour faultlessly, but at all times he kept Bridie in his line of sight, waiting for the moment when he could finally get her alone and run his hands over that soft smooth skin . . .

'Shaun!'

He let his gaze slide from Bridie, who was chatting to the middle-aged couple who ran the neighbouring property, and turned his attention back to Alisha.

'You weren't even listening,' she pouted.

'Yes, I was,' he lied. The truth was he'd stopped listening to his mother reminiscing about his and Alisha's childhood about twenty minutes ago. All night his mother had been introducing Alisha as a very dear, *close* friend, and it was beginning to wear thin.

'Shaun, why don't you and Alisha go and stand by the cake and we'll get ready to cut it?'

'It's not a bloody wedding. I can cut my own damn cake,' he snapped. *And once it's done, so am I*, he thought.

'Shaun, for goodness sake, it's *your* birthday, you're expected to talk to all your guests.' His mother's waspish tone did nothing to improve his mood.

'My birthday party, that *you* organised. I don't even know why we're having one.' However, it would be coming to a screaming halt very soon. He wanted to spend time with Bridie and he wasn't going to let anything—not even his meddling mother—come between them.

※

Bridie turned to find Douglas beside her, sweeping a stray crumb from the tablecloth. There was no hint of a smile on his face.

'You can see why everyone thought they made such a wonderful couple,' he said, watching Shaun and Alisha across the lawn.

Bridie took a sip of her wine. They did make an attractive couple, Alisha with her willowy grace and Shaun broad-shouldered and handsome beside her.

'Why don't you like me?' Bridie asked, tired of being polite. 'What have I done to make you so hostile towards me?'

For a moment she thought he wasn't going to answer, but then he turned his shrewd glance upon her. 'There is no way I will ever allow my boy to bring someone of your background into the family.'

'You talk as though your kids are sheep. You can't pick and choose a blood line for your children—it's ridiculous!'

'What's ridiculous is any hope you continue to hold of getting your hooks into my son. How much will it take?'

'I beg your pardon?' Bridie gaped at the man.

'How much will it take to get you to leave my son alone?'

Tempted to throw the remainder of her drink in the man's face, Bridie had to force herself to replace the glass on the table and take a step away. 'Even *you* don't have enough to pay me off, you arrogant bastard. How dare you treat me like some second-class citizen.'

He gave a chuckle, but his eyes were hard as granite. 'Everyone has their price, girl—you just remember that. Even Shaun. Don't say I didn't give you a fair chance.'

'You don't give your son anywhere near enough credit.'

'Make no mistake, my son has his price, and if it comes to choosing between you and Jinjulu, you won't stand a hope in hell.'

She was shaking as she watched him walk away. She'd had just about all she could handle of the Brodericks for one night. Looking around she couldn't see Shaun anywhere. Somehow she felt dirty after Douglas's proposition—so she went in search of Shaun to tell him she was leaving.

Inside, the house was as impeccable as usual, but Bridie didn't waste time admiring it. She heard noise coming from the kitchen and walked through the door to find Daisy bustling about preparing desserts.

'Hello, what are you doing back here? Do you need something, love?' she asked, pausing to give Bridie a quick once-over. 'Don't you look swish. Bet you've caused a stir out there tonight, me girl.'

'You could say that, although not in a good way,' Bridie said dryly as she automatically gathered a stack of dirty glasses and began to pack them into the empty dishwasher.

'What happened?'

'If I had any doubts that I wasn't welcome out here, I had them well and truly confirmed tonight. Why do they hate me so much?'

The housekeeper paused in her scraping of plates for a minute and regarded Bridie's gloomy face. 'It's not you personally, love.' Bridie reached for the dishes Daisy had just scraped. 'It's not you, it's . . .' She trailed off.

Bridie looked at the kindly old woman. 'My family's reputation,' she finished, sounding hollow and defeated. 'It doesn't matter what I do, or how hard I try to separate myself, they continue to drag me down with them.'

'Well now, we can't pick our relatives—we just got to make the best of what we're given.'

'Why do you stay, Daisy?' Bridie asked curiously.

The old woman's face hardened slightly. 'Unlike you, I don't have any relatives left—good or bad. I've been here so long I'm used to their ways, and I guess I've always stayed because of the kiddies.'

Bridie bit back a smile at hearing Shaun referred to as a kiddie, but she saw the genuine warmth in Daisy's eyes and understood that, to her, Shaun and Phoebe were like grandchildren and she loved them dearly.

Daisy went on, 'They may be wealthy and think they're better than the rest of us, but I can tell you one thing, they've suffered terrible grief and they have to live with the consequences of the choices they've made. Believe me, for all their airs and graces, they're still just people and they've had their share of heartache just like the rest of us. You count yourself lucky for the family you've got, my girl, 'cause I can tell you now—there are some out there a whole lot worse off than you.'

Bridie stared at the housekeeper, waiting for her to elaborate, but she didn't; instead she gave Bridie's arm a pat. 'Go and have some fun, eat their food, drink their wine and keep making that boy of mine happy. Despite what they think, you've been a breath of fresh air around here, and I've never seen Shaun so content.'

'I can't compete with Alisha, though,' Bridie said sadly.

Daisy squeezed her hand gently. 'More like *she* can't compete with *you*.' She smiled kindly before bustling off to put the finishing touches on the last of the desserts.

Bridie made her way back through the house, but she paused when she heard raised voices coming from behind a half-shut door. She backed away, intending to find an alternative route outside, but stopped as she recognised the male voice as belonging to Douglas Broderick. There was something about the menacing tone he used that made her linger outside the doorway to listen. The young woman he was talking to was easily identified as Phoebe.

'Art is my life! Why can't you just support me in this *one* thing?'

Bridie bit her lip as she heard the vulnerability in Phoebe's voice.

'Support you? All I've ever done is support you, and look what happened. I ended up *supporting* your drug habit and paying a fortune for that fancy counsellor. Don't talk to me about support! It's time you started pulling your weight around here, girl.'

'Oh please! As if I could ever do anything right around here. You don't give a damn about anyone or anything except this bloody farm!'

'It's the only thing that doesn't continue to disappoint me.'

'I pity you, Dad, I really do,' Phoebe spat. 'You're going to die a lonely, miserable old bastard.'

'How dare you speak to me in that tone! Who do you think you are?' Douglas roared.

'I'll tell you who I am, Dad ... I'm the person who knows *exactly* what happened that night between you and Jared,' she said in a soft, dangerous voice.

Bridie held her breath.

'I want you off Jinjulu. Do you understand? I'm no longer responsible for you. I've had enough of your dramatics.'

'Worried, Dad? You never told anyone about the fight you and Jared had just before he died, did you? I didn't think so,' Phoebe said. 'You have every right to be worried.'

A slap sounded loudly and Bridie gasped. She heard Phoebe's strangled cry, followed by the sound of heavy footsteps on the other side of the room, which snapped Bridie into action. Spinning around, she raced for the first door she came to and scrambled inside. It appeared to be a spare bedroom and she figured if she were discovered in here she could just say she was looking for a bathroom.

Bridie waited until the sound of Douglas Broderick's boots faded into the distance, then released the shaky breath she'd been holding. She wasn't sure what to think. Phoebe obviously knew something about her brother's death that Douglas didn't want anyone else to know about. She debated whether checking on the girl might do more harm than good, seeing as Bridie would be the last person Phoebe would probably want to see right now, but then again maybe she was hurt.

She cautiously edged her way out into the hall, and took a tentative step towards the doorway she'd been outside only a few moments earlier. The door was now wide open and Bridie could see the room was empty. She hurried outside and did a quick scan of the crowd, but she couldn't see Phoebe anywhere, or Douglas for that matter.

'There you are. I've been looking for you everywhere.' Bridie jumped guiltily, and relaxed only slightly when she realised it was Shaun. 'Come with me,' he whispered into her ear, before leading her around the back of the house to a secluded corner of the garden.

They stopped in the shadow of a large archway of roses and Shaun pulled her against him, covering her mouth with his own in a deep, desperate kiss. It seemed to go on forever, and she became so caught up in the electrifying sensation that Phoebe and Douglas faded from her mind.

Shaun slowly lifted his head and she searched his hungry gaze. The solid strength of his body against her own felt so safe and familiar. She slid her arms around his waist and hugged him to her tightly. 'I missed you,' she said quietly.

'Listen, after tonight, Alisha will be on her way home. I've already spoken to Mum and it ends now. I don't want to embarrass her in front of all her friends—although she deserves it—but I promise, this is over.'

'I don't think it's going to make any difference. If it's not Alisha, then they'll find someone else they consider better suited to you. It's never going to be me.'

'Bridie, they can't choose the woman I'm going to marry,' he told her gently.

'It seems no one's told them that,' she sighed miserably.

'Well, I have a solution.'

She pulled away so she could see his face, and all of a sudden she had a premonition of what was about to come and her heart raced in blind panic.

'Marry me, Bridie. I know I want to grow old with you, and once we're married they'll give up this stupidity.'

'Marry you?' she whispered, her head suddenly feeling light.

'I love you, Bridie. I think I always have, even way back on that very first night when you knocked me on my arse for taking that bet.'

Bridie shook her head. 'I can't marry you, Shaun, they'd disown you, or . . . or something worse—it wouldn't work,' she stammered.

'They won't disown me,' he scoffed.

'You didn't hear—' She stopped quickly. There was no point repeating his father's warning—the last thing she wanted tonight was to cause some kind of spectacle.

'Didn't hear what?'

Bridie shook her head and backed out of his embrace. 'You know what your dad is going to say. He's going to hit the roof.'

'It won't matter. Once we're married, they can't do a damn thing about it. We'll go overseas. You can get married in Hawaii with just a day or so's notice. We can get married on the beach, have a honeymoon and be back before they even realise we're gone.'

'Shaun, would you just think about this for a minute. What if we did that and he kicked you out of home? What if you ended up losing Jinjulu because of me? I won't be responsible for that. I *won't* be the reason you lose the chance to run this place.'

'Don't decide now then, think about it for a few days,' he said, his jaw clenched tightly.

'Shaun.' She heard his mother calling out for him somewhere nearby.

'Oh, for God's sake,' he muttered under his breath. Then he spoke urgently. 'You have a week to think about it, and then I'm coming back for your answer.' He kissed her, a long, slow, spine-tingling kiss that almost made her swoon. He rested his forehead against hers for a moment, then stepped away to put an end to his mother's search.

Bridie was happy to remain hidden in the shadows, away from the judgemental eyes and snide whispers.

Then she remembered Phoebe and wondered whether she should tell Shaun what she'd overheard. He had a right to know if it had some bearing on Jared's death, but then again, it might just add to his grief. She needed to stay out of his family's dramas—they were none of her business. She wished she'd never overheard the horrible argument in the first place.

By now guests were starting to make their farewells and Bridie decided she would too. As much as she wanted to stay and spend time with Shaun, she was shaken by his proposal. She needed time away from him to think—his presence always seemed to rob her of her common sense. Slipping out the back way, she almost ran to the ute, certain that Shaun would try to stop her. *He'd proposed to her!* She didn't know what to think. All she knew was that she couldn't deal with any more tonight. It had all been too much.

She was halfway back to town when her mobile sprang to life inside her handbag. She didn't look at the screen. She knew who it'd be. Yes, she should have waited to say goodbye to him, but he'd have insisted on coming home with her and she needed time alone.

Maybe he'd regret his rash proposal once he had time to think it over. If she gave him enough space, surely he'd come to his senses . . . But what if he did mean it? What about her plans? It was ludicrous, she couldn't marry the man, she was planning to leave town by the end of the year, early next year at the latest. This was her time. *Her* chance to do something just for herself—finally.

Why, then, had she not immediately disregarded the idea? Deep down inside, she wasn't horrified by the proposal—surprised, yes, but not horrified. Actually, the idea made her feel warm inside, and glad—excited too—but she didn't want to acknowledge that, because how would she ever leave then?

Giving herself a determined glare in the rear-view mirror, she pushed down a little heavier on the accelerator. Right now she needed to put as much distance between herself and Shaun Broderick as she could. She couldn't think straight when he was close.

She should have stayed away from him.

He was trouble.

He was dangerous.

He was already under her skin.

Seventeen

Two days.

Forty-eight hours.

That was how long it took to work up the courage to drive to her house and confront her. It felt like a week.

He'd understood that his proposal would have sent Bridie running as far away from him as she could get in order to think things through, but in all honesty his proposal had shocked the hell out of him as well. Once it was out, though, he hadn't regretted it. It felt . . . right.

But if he'd had the chance to do it all over again, he would have maybe gone slower and taken into account Bridie's aversion to surprises, given her a little warning.

After the first night when she hadn't returned any of his messages he'd stopped calling; he'd been panicked at the thought of her taking off without a goodbye. She just needed some time alone—he got that. He was patient, he was a farmer after all; nature took its own time. He'd had plenty of practice waiting, so he forced himself to take a deep breath and sweat it out in silence. It wasn't like he had nothing to do—the shearing had started and Jinjulu was a hive of activity. But he hadn't been able to stop thinking about it and he knew she must be feeling just as anxious as he was, so he'd decided to end the torment and go see her.

His heart beat erratically when she answered the door. She offered him a half-smile, not exactly encouraging but it was better than slamming the door in his face.

He spoke quickly. 'I know I said I'd be back for an answer in a week—I'm not here to pressure you, but I couldn't stay away.'

She let out a long sigh, and when she lifted her eyes to meet his, he saw the uncertainty in their depths.

He pulled her close and held her. She felt small and soft in his arms, and so damn good that it hurt. *Please don't have let me stuff this up*, he pleaded silently.

After a few minutes, she pulled away and led him into the house. 'Do you want coffee?' she asked as they walked into her small kitchen.

'No. I want you,' he told her bluntly.

'Shaun—'

'I'm sorry I sprang it on you the way I did, but it feels like the right thing to do.'

'You're just angry at your parents and reacting to their interfering. You weren't planning on asking me to marry you before you lost your temper with your mother and Alisha that night, were you?'

'That's not—'

'Were you?' she said, cutting off his protest.

He gave a short frustrated sigh. 'No, but once I did, it made perfect sense.'

'It was a reaction, that's all.'

'No it wasn't. I meant it. I want to marry you, Bridie.'

Bridie turned away from him to fill up the jug. 'We hardly know each other, Shaun.'

'We know each other better than you think. I know *you*, Bridie.'

'You *think* you know me.'

'After you got home from the party you went straight outside to sit on your back step,' he said, leaning against the kitchen bench with his arms folded across his chest, watching her calmly. 'You know how I know that?' he prodded when she refused to comment.

'You have my house under surveillance?' she muttered mockingly.

'I know that's what you would have done because being out there makes you feel calm. I also know that you probably took that photo of your mum out there with you and thought about her, and I know that because you always look at that picture when you feel unsure,' he finished softly.

She took her time before turning to face him. 'So you're observant, but it doesn't mean you really know me.'

'We'll learn all about each other as we go,' he shrugged.

'I think you need to sort things out with your family before you think about making any major life changes.'

'Like how?'

'Like, you have no say in how you live your life now—what do you think your father will do when you come home and announce that we're married? Not only will you still be at his mercy without any say in how Jinjulu is run, but we'll all be living together under his roof—can you imagine how awful that would be?'

'We wouldn't have to live at the homestead. There's an empty workmen's cottage we can live in.' His heart sank. He had a feeling he knew where this conversation was headed. 'I can handle working with my father—it's nothing you need to worry about.'

'What would you do if he made you choose?'

'Choose?'

'Between me and Jinjulu.'

'He wouldn't do that.'

'I wouldn't be so sure. What would you do if he gave you an ultimatum, Shaun? If it was me or Jinjulu?'

'I'd pick you, of course,' he growled.

'Which would leave us where? Here? You'd be happy to work in the pub? Or go back to work out at the mines? Work on someone else's property again?'

What she was saying was ridiculous. There was no way his father would make him choose. And yet a tiny niggle of doubt began to plague him. He wished he could hit rewind and start this conversation all over again. 'So what would you suggest I do to improve the situation?'

'You could buy your own place and tell your father to go jump if he isn't going to at least listen to your ideas for Jinjulu.'

'Because it's that easy,' he said sarcastically.

'I didn't say it was easy, but it could be done. If you took a proposal to the bank, surely they would consider you a viable proposition?'

'Jinjulu is my home.'

For a long moment she held his gaze without speaking. 'I think to a certain extent that's true, but I also think you believe you owe it to Jared to stay and be treated like crap. It's not right, Shaun—would your brother really want you to be living like this?'

'Look, I don't want to talk about Jared right now.' He stalked to the window and looked out over the paddock down the back.

'I know you loved your brother, and I know you feel guilty about not being there that night, but you weren't to blame. You can't spend your whole life trying to make up for something that wasn't your fault.'

He couldn't speak; her words had knocked the wind out of him. No one spoke about Jared—not him, not the family, no one—and yet here she was, throwing around his name as though she knew what the hell she was talking about. Well, she didn't.

'It drives me crazy to see you so miserable and your father pulling all the strings. You're not happy, and Phoebe sure as hell isn't happy.'

He swung around and met her gaze angrily. 'And your family is so much more functional,' he said, then regretted it as he saw her face fall.

'Shaun, it wouldn't work. Not the way things are at the moment.'

'I'll give you until the weekend to think it over,' he said, heading back to the front door. He had to get out of here now, before she told him something he didn't want to hear.

'I don't need to think it over, it won't change anything,' she called after him.

He didn't want to think she was right. Not about this.

Because if she was right, then that would mean he'd have to sit down and make some pretty big decisions—decisions that all came with a hefty emotional debt.

～

The sun felt good on his back. It was another long hard day in the sheep yards, vaccinating them and treating them for lice. Every sheep had to be treated once they came out of the shearing shed, and there didn't seem to be an end to them in sight. It was a tiresome procedure.

'Bloody sheep.' Shaun wrestled another one when it tried to turn around in the race.

Pete flashed him a grin across the yard. 'Almost done.'

'I reckon after this it's gotta be your shout down at the Drovers,' Shaun called.

'You just want to go and ogle your woman while she's at work.'

'You think of something better to ogle?'

'I might just take you up on that offer,' Pete laughed.

'You just get to buy the drinks, mate,' Shaun grunted as the sheep jerked its head and hit him a little too close to the groin for comfort. 'No way I'm letting you ogle my future wife,' he tossed back with a growl.

After a few minutes Shaun realised Pete hadn't responded, and he glanced over. Pete was smiling at him thoughtfully.

'You serious? You're thinking about asking her to marry you?'

Bending to lift another sheep upright, Shaun shook his head. 'Already did,' he grimaced. Nope, he wasn't going to admit defeat yet—he knew Bridie would need some time to get used to the idea. He was patient; he'd just wait her out.

She hadn't technically said no . . . *She just said it wouldn't work*, a small voice reminded him sarcastically.

'So when's the big day?'

'She hasn't said yes yet.'

Silence followed and this time Shaun refused to acknowledge it.

'You know she will. She's just playing hard to get. Women like to do that. You'll be right,' Pete offered, but Shaun didn't miss the hint of uncertainty in his friend's tone.

They finished up the last of the sheep and loaded the equipment into the ute, then drove back towards the sheds.

'You smell something?' Shaun asked as he put the ute into low and eased to a stop.

Pete stuck his head out the window and sniffed the air, then swore as he threw open his door and sprinted towards the shed where Douglas's prize rams were penned. 'The shed's on fire!' he yelled.

Shaun grabbed the fire extinguisher from the ute and followed Pete across the yard, yelling for him to wait. Shouldering his way through the tin door, he saw Pete trying to reach the distressed animals at the far end. Flames formed a barrier between the men and the rams still shut in their pens, bleating loudly over the roar and crackle of fire.

Shaun emptied the contents of the extinguisher at the flames but it made little difference. The fire had already taken hold of the shed.

'Shaun, we have to get out of here,' Pete called, coughing.

Through the smoke his father approached then barrelled past, catching Shaun by surprise. 'Dad!' he called. His lungs were burning with the thick acrid smoke. 'Dad! We have to go—come on,' he yelled.

'Shaun, the roof's gonna come down on us. We have to get out,' Pete shouted.

'I can't find Dad.'

Shaun dropped down and moved across the floor on his hands and knees, searching blindly for his father, groping about until he found him slumped on the ground. He grabbed hold of Douglas's shirt and heaved him back towards the doorway. His eyes stung and his throat burned. It was slow going, dragging his father's not inconsiderable bulk, barely able to see where he was going, using Pete's voice to guide him. Making it to the doorway, he fell out onto the dirt, gulping huge lungfuls of fresh air. Quickly he rolled his father over onto his side and was relieved when he began to cough and gasp.

Shaun heard Pete on the radio calling the house to get an ambulance. He began coughing himself, trying not to panic at the feeling of suffocation in his lungs.

The noise from the sheep had ceased, but the groan of timber and tin still came from the depths of the fire. Struggling to his feet, Shaun unrolled the hose across the yards and began to water down the outside of the shed. There was no hope of putting out the fire, but he wanted to make sure it didn't spread to the other sheds.

Behind him he heard his father murmuring incoherently; he was obviously still dazed and confused, unaware that the sheep were long past saving and he had only narrowly escaped the same fate himself.

Pete's shout made him turn sharply; his father was struggling to sit up.

Bridie's Choice

'Dad!' He threw down the hose. 'It's too late, they're gone.'

Douglas pushed him weakly, his red, smoke-blurred eyes full of rage and pain. 'Why didn't you try to get them out?'

'I couldn't reach them.'

'You didn't even try.'

'Dad, for God's sake, there was no way we could reach them. We were bloody lucky to get you out in time,' Shaun said, furious that his father wouldn't listen to reason.

'Bullshit! You just didn't try. None of you bloody try. Useless, the lot of you,' Douglas snarled, before staggering to his feet, pushing his son away when he tried to stop him.

Shaun picked up the hose once more and kept directing the water at the blaze. It took a further forty-five minutes to burn itself out.

☙

'Come on, mate, I'll drop you home,' Shaun said wearily, waving Pete over to the ute. The short distance to the small cottage Pete lived in was made in silence, both men drained from breathing in smoke and still in shock at what had happened.

'Will you be right? Sure you don't need me to take you to hospital to have them check you over?' Shaun asked as Pete climbed out of the vehicle.

'Nah, mate, I'm good. Just a bit of smoke. She'll be right once I have a coldie or two.'

Shaun waved, then put the ute in gear and headed back to the homestead. When he walked into the house, he could hear his mother's alarmed voice.

Daisy came down the hall and caught sight of his blackened face and singed clothing. 'Get into the kitchen and let me take a look at you,' she demanded, her no-nonsense voice cutting through his shock and exhaustion. Shaun followed her without argument, sitting patiently as she administered cream to superficial burns. They stung like blazes but wouldn't need any further treatment. 'We've called the ambulance, but your father's being his usual stubborn self and probably won't let them see to him.'

At the sound of raised voices Daisy and Shaun exchanged a brief glance. A few minutes later heavy footsteps pounded down the tiled hallway and into the kitchen.

'I want answers,' Douglas shouted, slapping his palms down on the table.

'You need to get to the emergency room—you're in no condition to be demanding anything at the moment,' Daisy snapped at him.

'You need to remember your place, woman, and stay out of this,' he snarled, then turned back to his son.

Shaun moved to stand, enraged by his father's rudeness to Daisy, but she put a hand on his shoulder and gave him a quick reassuring pat.

'What the bloody hell happened out there?'

'Pete and I came back from the yards to find the shed on fire,' Shaun said. His voice was husky and raw from the smoke he'd breathed in.

'Where the hell were the shearers?'

'Already knocked off for the day.'

'Well, I want to know what the hell happened! Christ! We lost six top bloody rams. Did you clear away that bin of offcuts I told you to get rid of?'

Shaun paused; it had been on his list of jobs to do, just not one of the more pressing jobs. His father jumped on his hesitation immediately. 'You see! This is what happens when you don't bloody do as you're told! The dags and offcuts are flammable—don't you know that?'

'Christ, Dad, the rams are your bloody pets. I'm already working my guts out doing the rest of the goddamn jobs you hand out every day. I'm only one man. I can't do it all,' Shaun yelled.

'Pets? They're the lifeblood of this property, you damn fool. We've just lost six good breeding rams—can you get your thick head around that? Where the hell are we going to replace them from, do you think?'

'It wasn't the offcuts that started that fire. There was nothing there that could have spontaneously combusted like that.'

'So you bloody say!'

Daisy spoke up. 'He saved your life—can't you for once just give him a little bit of credit?'

'It was his fault the fire started in the first place!'

'Bullshit, Dad!' Shaun yelled.

'Don't you raise your voice at me, boy,' Douglas warned.

'You're never going to bloody change, are you? I've tried to keep my mouth shut and do what I had to do, hoping one day you'd come around, but nothing I do is ever going to be enough for you, is it?' Shaun snarled, shoving his chair away from the table and getting to his feet.

'Sit back down,' Douglas's voice boomed.

'Go to hell! I'm not going to be your bloody whipping boy any more.'

'You leave and you'll get nothing, boy! You hear me? Not a brass razoo from Jinjulu. You're out of the will and you're dead to this family!'

Shaun watched the veins in his father's neck stand out and a dangerous shade of purple-red creep up his face. 'Shove your fuckin' will, you old bastard. I don't want anything from you,' he shouted.

'What have you done, Douglas?' Constance's shocked gasp drew his father's attention.

'I hope you're happy—you've managed to ruin *all* your children,' he hissed.

'Me? I'm not the one driving them away from here— that's always been you.'

'And then there was one,' Phoebe drawled from the doorway.

'Shut your mouth, girl,' Douglas roared.

Shaun looked from his sister to his father in confusion.

'Oh, you've missed the latest scandal in the Broderick household, have you, big brother? I think we should let him in on it, don't you, Dad?' She was slurring her words and Shaun thought she must have been drinking most of the afternoon.

'You are as dead to me as your brother—do you understand? Get out of my house!' Douglas lunged across the room at Phoebe, but stumbled and crashed to the floor.

'Douglas!' Constance screamed, running to his side and rolling him over.

'Where's that ambulance?' Shaun said, kneeling beside his father on the floor.

'Silly old coot—I knew he wasn't well,' Daisy piped up from across the room.

'Phoebe, call and find out how far away the ambulance is. Tell them Dad's collapsed,' Shaun said, leaning over to check his father's breathing. He glanced up to see Phoebe staring at Douglas with a look of shock and horror. 'Phoebe!' he snapped, and she blinked rapidly then scampered across the room to the phone.

Shaun loosened his father's clothing. To his relief he saw that Douglas was still breathing, although his breath seemed laboured and raspy.

Within minutes the ambulance arrived, its siren loud in the quiet of the bush.

What a lousy shit of a day, Shaun thought to himself as he stood on the verandah and watched the ambulance take his father away.

꒰

The shed was still smouldering, its tin walls leaning precariously.

Shaun picked his way through the blackened rubble, his eyes falling on the charcoal remains of his dad's prize rams. It didn't make sense. He supposed the generator could have caught fire, but it was only new. He was circling back to take a look at the generator when something caught his eye. The drum of wool containing the offcuts was where the worst of the damage seemed to be. It was too much of a coincidence. Drums of wool didn't just explode on their own, no matter what his father might say. But the lanolin in the wool was highly flammable if it caught on fire—or was *set* on fire.

He was no fire investigator, but if he had to he'd bet his money the fire had been deliberately lit.

Shaun headed for the machinery shed and started up the bulldozer. He had an idea who had started the fire, and he wasn't about to let his father make an example of her. Without a doubt Douglas would order an investigation into the fire. His rams, which had been his pride and joy, had been killed. He'd make sure he got to the bottom of it and then he'd press charges against the guilty party, daughter or not.

Well, not this time. Shaun wouldn't stand by and let his father take out his rage and vindictiveness on another of his children. They'd all put up with it for too long. Douglas would be furious that they wouldn't be able to claim insurance on his bloody rams—that wouldn't be possible without a report to the fire chief and a burnt-out shed as evidence—but he could yell all he liked. There was no way in hell Shaun was going to sacrifice his sister for the sake of insurance money to replace his father's damn sheep.

By the time Shaun was finished it was dark. All that remained of the burnt shed was a charred area on the ground. He parked the bulldozer back in the machinery shed and went back to the homestead to wash away the disappointment and fatigue that went along with peace-keeping in his war-torn family.

Eighteen

The morning air was fresh and clean, the horizon an explosion of pink, blue and orange. Shaun sucked in a huge breath, contentment settling on his shoulders. Today was going to be a good day.

Christ, it couldn't be any worse than yesterday. What a mess. He still hadn't got the whole story out of anyone about Phoebe's cryptic announcement. She'd disappeared at some stage. Shaun hoped she was just licking her wounds somewhere nearby—if she didn't show up by this afternoon he'd go out and look for her.

His father was in hospital; his collapse yesterday had been put down to the after effects of smoke inhalation and shock. The doctor had kept him in overnight, but Shaun had no doubt he'd sign himself out at the first opportunity. He could just imagine Douglas fretting in his hospital bed, fearing Jinjulu would be falling down without him there to bark out his orders.

The truck was coming to get *Shaun's* sheep today, and if things went the way he'd planned, he'd finally be able to show his father that he'd made a smart investment. The canola crop would be ready for harvest soon and then he could plant wheat into the canola residue to provide mulch and help retain the moisture in the soil. Next year he planned on putting in barley. The stubble remaining once it was harvested would provide an ideal light mulch for the next crop of canola. Once he was able to adapt this to the rest of Jinjulu, the profits would multiply, but more importantly, the land would be rejuvenated and protected. No longer would valuable topsoil be blown away by wind or washed away by rain.

As he drove the ute down the track, his thoughts drifted to Bridie. He hadn't had time to fill her in on the details last night—he'd been too worn out to try to explain how atrocious the day had been. He wished he could just hold her and pretend everything was all right, but he wasn't entirely sure it was. He couldn't bring himself to accept she wasn't going to say yes. Bridie was unlike any woman he'd ever known. He'd realised that even back when he was a kid, but he'd been too stupid and inexperienced to do anything about it. She was independent, opinionated and a survivor. She wasn't the kind of woman who needed a man to feel complete or safe. She'd learned to depend on herself from a young age and she thought she didn't need anyone. He'd change her mind—he had to. He wasn't sure he could bear thinking about a life without her right now.

He glanced out through the windscreen, then looked again, disbelieving. It took a few minutes to register what he was seeing . . . or, more to the point, what he *wasn't* seeing—his sheep.

The gates, all of them, were wide open. The mobile stockyards he'd built were empty!

Shaun sped down the track, reaching for his mobile. He jabbed the number for Pete's phone and swore violently while he listened to the phone ringing.

'I need you down here,' he barked when Pete answered. 'Someone's let the bloody sheep out. I've got a truck coming any minute and no bloody sheep to load! Bring as many of the boys from the shearing shed as you can find.' He listened briefly to Pete's voice on the other end then cut in loudly, 'I don't give a shit what Dad will say—get the men here and I'll deal with Dad later!'

He tossed the phone onto the seat beside him and slammed his hand against the steering wheel. What the hell was going on? There was no way the gates had come open by accident . . . not *all* of them!

Right now, he had to find the sheep and hope Pete could bring enough men down to help get them all back into the yards by the time the semi got here. What more could possibly go wrong?

༄

Three hours later Shaun sat on the open tray of his ute, head braced in his hands, completely exhausted. They'd found the sheep all right. The good news was that they hadn't strayed too far from the yards; the bad news was that the reason they hadn't strayed too far was because they'd found the canola he was supposed to be harvesting in a few months.

God knows how long they'd been out for, but the little bastards had been making good use of their new-found freedom—they'd eaten their way through a good twenty percent of the crop.

'It's not too bad. We got 'em on the truck, so they'll get to the sale on time, and you'll still have most of the crop,' Pete pointed out calmly, having sent the rest of the men back to the shearing.

Shaun nodded silently, too drained to reply.

'Any word on Phoebe?' Pete asked.

Shaun looked up suspiciously at that. 'Why?'

'Just worried about her, that's all.'

Shaun eyed his friend closely. He'd had his head crowded with Bridie and their problems for so long that he'd completely missed the signals he should have seen. 'You got something you want to say?' he asked.

Pete glanced away from Shaun's hard look, then seemed to reach some kind of conclusion and straightened his shoulders. 'Yeah, actually, I do. I like your sister—a lot.'

'How long has this been going on for?'

'Well, it's not exactly going on . . . we're just mates,' Pete admitted, cracking his knuckles. 'I've been hoping one day she'll finally realise she likes me too.'

'You and Phoebe?' Shaun said, still staring at his friend.

'Yeah, I know I'm not good enough for her as far as you Brodericks are concerned . . . but I get her,' Pete shrugged.

'I didn't even know you guys . . . What exactly do you two do?' Shaun's eyes narrowed slightly.

'We talk. That's all we do—we talk. Look, I know you all think she's some screw-up, but she's not. She's smart, real smart, and she's got talent—you should see some of the stuff she draws . . . We're friends, that's all.' Pete kicked a clump of dirt with his boot but Shaun saw the hurt in his friend's eyes.

Shaun wasn't sure what to say. Who was he to give out any advice? He couldn't even handle his own love life at the moment. But thinking about his sister suddenly reminded him of something he'd been tossing around in his head all morning. 'You didn't happen to be with her last night, did you?'

'No. I figured with all the excitement she'd be busy up at the main house. That's why I was worried about her this morning. Why?'

'It's just a bit of a coincidence that she goes missing at the same time someone lets out the sheep.'

'Now hang on, you don't really think she did this?'

Shaun picked up his hat and ran his fingers along its brim. 'They didn't let themselves out of that yard, and they didn't set fire to that drum in the ram shed either.'

Pete paused before answering, and Shaun knew it must have also crossed his mind. 'She's been under a lot of pressure lately, but I don't know,' he said with a nod in the direction of the sheep yards, 'that's kinda extreme.'

They were both quiet for a moment before Pete raised another possibility. 'You know, it might not have been her that released the sheep. There's someone else who had more to gain by seeing you fail than Phoebe.'

Shaun looked across at his friend in surprise. 'You mean Dad?'

Pete shrugged then gave a grunt as he slid off the tailgate

of the ute. 'Well, your day is about to get considerably worse,' he said, slapping Shaun's shoulder in commiseration. 'Maybe this is your chance to find out.'

Shaun lifted his head and stifled an irritated groan. 'Great.' The dust billowed out behind his father's four-wheel drive as it roared across the paddock towards them.

'You get going, I'll handle Dad,' Shaun said, easing his weight onto his tired legs. He felt as though he'd aged ten years in the last few hours.

'He's not going to be happy,' Pete warned.

'That's my problem. And mate, thanks for getting here so fast. Couldn't have done it without you. Tell the boys I'll shout them a beer or two down at the pub this afternoon.'

'If you're still around when your old man gets through with you,' Pete joked, but Shaun detected a somewhat nervous edge to his voice.

'If I'm not, throw a round on me as a parting gift,' he muttered as he watched the vehicle come to a halt, the dust barely settling before the door was open. He saw his father climb out awkwardly, a wince of pain on his face proving he hadn't completely recovered from yesterday's excitement. 'Make yourself scarce, mate,' he said to Pete, walking across the rough ground to meet his father halfway.

'What the bloody hell do you think you're doing?' Douglas demanded, a menacing look on his face. 'I've just come from the ram shed—what the hell were you thinking? This is why you'll never run this place! What kind of moron cleans up before the insurance assessor gets a chance to look at the claim? Stupidity! Then you have the bloody hide to take my shearers off the job to come out here and stuff around.'

'Shouldn't you still be in hospital?' Shaun pointed out, trying to keep his cool. He'd known all hell was going to break loose after he'd used the shearers on his job—he just had to suck it up and deal with it.

'I asked you something, boy! What the hell were you thinking?'

'Someone opened the yards last night. I didn't have time to ask your permission—I had a semi on the way and sheep loose in my canola . . . I figured you'd understand it was an emergency.'

'Well, you figured wrong. You were covering up for someone or something in that shed—that's why you cleared it, isn't it? You tell me right now what you know or I'll be calling the police in to interview you.'

'You're unbelievable.' Shaun shook his head and turned away, too angry to speak.

'Don't you turn your back on me, boy!' Douglas roared, grabbing Shaun's forearm and spinning him back around.

Instinct brought Shaun's fist up, but sheer will stopped it connecting with his father's jaw. He might hate his father, but he was not going to sink to his level by hitting him. A flash of surprise flickered in Douglas's eyes as Shaun lowered his fist and shook his arm free of his father's grasp.

'I gave you and your brother everything and I still don't get the respect I deserve,' Douglas spat.

'Gave us everything? Don't kid yourself, Dad—you've never given anyone anything.'

'No one gets a free ride in this world. Better you learn it here than out there. Even so, this family has never gone without anything—ever.'

'Except the things we most want.'

'What the hell's that supposed to mean?' Douglas demanded.

'Open your eyes, Dad! You've been so busy telling everyone what to do that you can't even see how miserable everyone is.' Shaun shook his head.

'What do any of you have to be miserable about?'

'You refuse to listen to my ideas to help run the place . . . All these years you've treated Phoebe as though she's some second-class citizen. You made Jared feel like a piece of crap whenever you had the chance. I don't remember one thing you ever congratulated him on, it was always criticism, even when he was doing everything he could to please you . . . It's no wonder things are so messed up.'

'Bloody crybabies. It's your mother's fault, she let you kids get away with everything.'

'Yeah, blame everyone but yourself,' Shaun said with a humourless chuckle. 'At least you're consistent.'

'We'll see how high and mighty you are soon, boy—the deal's off. I'm not leasing the bottom paddock to you any more. Once this is harvested, that's it. No more. I've had enough of this greenie crap. We go back to my way and that's the end of it.'

'You can't renege on a deal. We agreed. I have the lease for five years.'

'I don't believe I signed anything saying that, did I?'

'You can't do that, Dad!'

'I can and I just have, and if you ever use my men again without asking me first, I'll hit you up for a day's wages for all of them.'

Rooted to the spot, Shaun stared at his father's back as he stormed to his vehicle. He watched him drive away. This was the way it was always going to be. Why was he trying to fight it?

Shaun reefed open the door of the ute and swore loudly. Throwing the gearstick into first, he took off with a spin of tyres. He needed to go somewhere to think—somewhere he wouldn't risk running into his old man again.

৵

The tree still stood in the centre of the field. It was old; no one knew exactly how old, but it had been there for generations—Shaun had seen it in black and white photos in the family album. It was just a tree, there was nothing remotely sinister about it, and yet it had killed his brother—his best friend—on that miserable rainy night seven years ago.

Nowadays no one else came out here unless they had to, but he came. For some reason, he felt close to Jared here. Resting his back against the tree, he shut his eyes and let the anger and frustration he'd been carrying around all day leave his body.

'Jesus, Jared, I miss you,' he said quietly.

As always his mind went back to that night, asking how such a stupid accident had happened. Yes, he could concede it was an accident, but that didn't mean he was any less responsible for it. He should have been here . . . He could have stopped it happening.

Shaun swallowed past a tight lump in his throat, swearing softly as the sharp burn of tears stung behind his eyes. What a shit of a day, he thought again.

Nineteen

As had been Bulldog's habit since the night Bridie had been attacked by Tyler Jennings, he waited by the back door until she was inside the ute, then he waved a big paw and turned to lock up the pub.

Tonight as she walked towards her ute, however, she heard a strange noise and paused to listen. Seeing her stop, Bulldog came over and asked if she was okay. Bridie held up a hand. 'Do you hear that?'

Bulldog tilted his massive head and listened. 'Sounds like a cat.'

Bridie walked around her ute and towards the dark alley down the side of the pub, Bulldog close behind. When she gasped, the bouncer pushed her aside to see what she'd found. In the shadows a dark shape took form, and Bridie realised it was a *someone* not a *something* making the soft mewling cries.

Bulldog's gruff, 'Oi, come out here,' was met with a sob, and over his shoulder Bridie saw a small pale hand come up to shield what looked like a female face from their sight.

'Here, Bulldog. Let me try. She's scared.' Bridie moved around him and crept into the alley, close enough to speak in a gentle tone but far enough away to run if things turned nasty. 'It's okay. You're safe. Come on out of the dark and we can help you. Are you hurt?'

The woman moved her hand away from her face and Bridie felt as though someone had punched her in the stomach.

'*Phoebe?*'

Mascara had run down Phoebe's face and her eyes were unfocused and bleary. A half-full bottle of vodka lay on its side next to her and Bridie had a feeling that her night was about to get very messy.

'I wanna die, just leave me alone. I'm not worth it,' Phoebe said in a slurred voice that Bridie was trying to assess. Had she swallowed pills? Had she overdosed on something?

Bridie searched around quickly and saw a small bag with a narrow strap lying on the ground nearby. Digging through it, she couldn't find any empty bottles or anything else to suggest she'd been carrying drugs with her. There were no needles anywhere, and no rubbish of any kind nearby.

'Hey, isn't that—' Bulldog began.

'Bulldog, can you pick her up and bring her to the ute for me?' Bridie said when the girl seemed unable to walk in a straight line.

'You taking her up to the hospital?'

'I think she just needs to sleep it off, she reeks of grog.'

'You sure you can handle her?'

'Yeah, we'll be fine. I'll take her home and try to sober her up a bit.'

Bulldog carefully carried Phoebe to the ute, and Bridie realised just how small and delicate she really was. Somehow all that arrogance and bitterness she carried around made her seem bigger . . . tougher.

Bridie drove home and parked as close to her back door as possible. She eventually managed to half-carry, half-drag Phoebe into her spare bedroom. Until she was sure Phoebe was only drunk and had not taken any pills, she would have to sit by her bedside and watch over her.

It was a rough night and one that Bridie hoped never to repeat. Phoebe woke, confused and dazed, only to throw up violently all over herself. Bridie put her in the shower then changed the sheets and found her some clean pyjamas to get into. She put the dirty sheets and clothes in the wash, cleaned up the vomit, then tucked Phoebe back into bed.

She made herself a cup of tea and then stopped by the bed again, leaning close to check on Phoebe. The girl mumbled and Bridie jumped in surprise. 'Why are you doing this?' Phoebe moaned miserably.

'Doing what?'

'Being nice to me.'

Bridie sat down on the chair she'd pulled up earlier, perched gingerly on the edge. She didn't want to intrude on Phoebe's misery; they weren't exactly friends and she wasn't sure this would improve their relationship.

Knowing Phoebe, she'd probably think Bridie would use it against her.

'I couldn't just leave you in the alley.'

'Why not? No one cares if I live or die anyway,' Phoebe said, her voice still slurred, but with fatigue more than alcohol now.

'That's not true. Your family would miss you.'

'He can't stand to look at me,' she said as Bridie stood up and walked to the door. 'I didn't mean it . . .' she whispered.

Bridie couldn't make sense of her ramblings. 'Get some sleep, Phoebe.'

She leaned against the doorframe, not sure whether she should leave her alone, but she was exhausted after her shift. With one last look to make sure her unexpected guest had settled down, she headed to her own bed, shaking her head wearily. How had she ever thought her family was the only one that was screwed up?

჻

The bleep of the phone took a few minutes to penetrate the fog as she lay in bed halfway between sleep and consciousness.

Bridie searched the bedside table for anything resembling a phone. Where *was* the stinking thing?

She followed the bleating into the kitchen, remembering she'd forgotten to put it back in her room earlier. Just as she made a grab for it, it stopped ringing. With an annoyed growl, she put the phone down while she put on the jug. Now she was up she'd make a cuppa and take it back to bed.

Within a few minutes the phone rang again. Bridie answered on the second ring. 'Hello?'

'Bridie? Where were you? It rang out a minute ago.' It was so good to hear Shaun's voice, even as she registered how tired and strained he sounded.

'Looking for the phone.'

'Look, I was planning on coming into town today but everything's turned to shit out here. Dad's just come out of hospital—I can't go into it now, but I just wanted to let you know I won't be able to get in there.'

'What happened? Is he going to be okay?' she asked. She suspected the incident must be somehow related to Phoebe and the whole messy drama of last night.

He paused before answering and Bridie sensed there was more to it. 'Yeah,' he sighed. 'Old bastard's too stubborn to die just yet. Look, I'll fill you in later. The way we left things the other day . . . it's been eating me up inside. We need to talk. I wish I could just come by and see you, fix it somehow . . . I'm sorry, Bridie. I know this probably only adds to all the other things you're holding against me, but I honestly can't help it this time. I miss you,' he added softly.

Bridie felt the prick of tears and wiped her eyes. 'It's okay. You do what you have to do out there. I'll see you later.' She hung up slowly and stared at the phone.

'I take it that was my big brother?'

Bridie glanced over at the doorway. Phoebe looked like death warmed up. 'Yeah, he just called to say he wasn't coming in to town later. Your dad's out of hospital and Shaun said he's going to be okay.' Bridie searched for some response and thought she saw a slight drop of Phoebe's shoulders. Relief? Disappointment? 'Do you want anything? Tea? Dry biscuit?'

'A cup of tea would be great . . . thanks,' Phoebe added almost as an afterthought and sat herself down at the kitchen table. 'How come you didn't tell Shaun I was here?'

Bridie gave a shrug. 'I figured you might want some time alone before you faced him. You can call him back and let him know you're okay if you want. He sounded distracted. I bet they're worried about you.'

'Not likely. I can't go back there now. So, I guess I should thank you for last night.' Phoebe traced the handle of her teacup before lifting her gaze to meet Bridie's. 'I don't remember how much I told you last night. I vaguely remember you being in the room.'

'You didn't say anything—but even if you had, despite what you think of me, Phoebe, I am not, and never will be, a gossip.'

'I wasn't worried about that, actually.'

Bridie slid the container with the little round crackers towards Phoebe and gave a small nod. 'You should nibble on one of these. It'll help with the nausea.'

She watched as Phoebe took one. This was the first time Bridie had seen her without makeup; she seemed so tiny and breakable, it was a shock to think she was the same person who could hold her own against her big brother and a bully of a father. Phoebe's eyes were huge in her pale face. The pixie haircut made her look as though she were about twelve.

The warble of the magpies in the backyard drew her attention to the window and she saw the sun was now well and truly up. 'Let's go outside and drink our tea. You look like you could use a little sun.'

The women sat side by side in companionable silence. Bridie tipped back her head to soak up the early morning sunlight, loving its warmth on her face.

'He kicked me out,' Phoebe said eventually, and Bridie saw tears begin to well up once again. Her knees were drawn up and her thin arms were wrapped tightly around them, as though she was quite literally trying to hold herself together.

'What are you going to do now?' Bridie asked quietly.

Phoebe shrugged. 'I don't know. I don't want anything from that bastard, not any more.'

Bridie thought for a moment. 'Well, if you're prepared to work, I know you could get a few hours in the dining room at the Drovers.'

'Waitressing?'

Bridie lifted an eyebrow; from Phoebe's tone, you'd have thought she'd just suggested prostitution on the street corner. 'It's a job.'

Phoebe bit her bottom lip. 'I guess it can't be too hard carrying plates.'

Bridie forced herself to ignore Phoebe's careless insult, knowing that if she took the job she'd soon realise how hard waitressing really was.

'Well, you don't have to make any decisions right now. You can stay here for as long as you like, if you can handle sleeping in the single bed you were in last night.'

'Why are you doing this?'

'I didn't know you needed a reason to help someone.'

'Most people do.'

Bridie stood up and reached for Phoebe's empty cup. 'Maybe it's time to change things then.'

She took the cups inside to the sink, leaving Phoebe staring out at the paddock. Why *was* she doing this? She'd certainly had enough run-ins with prickly Phoebe Broderick to be justified in turning her back now. But Bridie had seen past the spoilt little rich girl exterior and caught a glimpse of the sad, lonely woman behind it. It would have felt like turning her back on a defenceless child, and that was something she'd never been able to do.

※

The sound of a horse race being called on the telly high up on the wall droned in the background, and the low murmur of voices lent a soothing note to the afternoon shift. Bridie loved this part of her day. There were none of the loud younger crowd trying to outdo each other, just the gentle small talk of older farmers.

She looked around at the scattering of men at tables and seated at the bar and smiled. She'd witnessed the close-knit nature of this community more than once in her lifetime. In times of trouble, she'd seen these people rally around each other, offering support and friendship. Through bushfires, drought, bank foreclosures and flood, the town had always helped its own pull through.

She'd miss that. She'd miss a lot of things when she left.

The thought suddenly saddened her.

The door into the bar opened and instantly she snapped out of her reverie.

'Hey, what happened?' she asked. 'Is everything okay?'

Shaun took off his hat and banged it against his thigh before taking a seat on the bar stool across from her. 'There was a fire in the shed—wiped out Dad's bloody prize rams. He almost killed himself trying to save them and ended up in hospital. Oh, and then my sheep mysteriously let themselves out of the yard and wiped out some of my crop,' he growled. 'It's over.'

Bridie felt a sharp hitch in her chest.

'Dad pulled the contract on the trial,' he explained. 'After harvest, it's back to his way once again.'

'What? But surely he can see what you've done has made some improvement already?'

'Nah. I'd have needed all five years to give him the proof on paper. It takes time for the crops to show their profitability, time for the soil to rejuvenate and improve,' he said, staring down bleakly at his interlocked hands.

Bridie bit her lip as she caught the disappointment on his face, wishing she knew what to say to make him feel better. 'So what are you going to do now?' she ventured uncertainly.

'I really don't know. I guess it's time to finally accept it's over. I can't go back to following bloody orders again—not like it has been.'

'Can you lease the land from someone else?' She didn't flinch from the cynical look he gave her, refusing to be deterred by his black mood. 'Surely there're properties around the district that you could lease, or better yet buy, to do your own thing?'

'I don't know what I'm going to do, Bridie, all right?' he snapped.

Bridie turned to walk away before he could see the hurt in her eyes. She was trying to help, and he was pushing her away . . . again.

She heard his muttered curse and stopped when he reached out to put his hand on her arm. 'Wait. Look, I'm sorry. I came here because I wanted to see you, not make you mad at me.'

Bridie let out a long sigh and felt the tension leave her shoulders. 'I get a break in about forty minutes.

If you're still around I can grab a coffee with you up at Marilyn's café.'

He gave a nod and she saw his eyes had lost a little of the misery they'd held before.

'While you're waiting, you might want to wander over and have a chat with old Jack.' She nodded her head towards the rough, stubble-faced farmer seated at a table on his own.

'Why's that?' Shaun frowned.

'Let's just say, I reckon the two of you might have more in common than you think.' Bridie moved away from Shaun and went down to the other end of the bar to collect some empty glasses. When she glanced up a few minutes later, she found Shaun and Jack engrossed in conversation. She began to hum along with a Dixie Chicks song, kicking herself for not having thought of getting those two together before now.

By the time her break had come around, the two men were still locked in discussion and Bridie didn't want to interrupt. She took her break out the back and left them to it. Later, Shaun came up to her just as she had finished wiping down the tables, picking her up and spinning her around, before kissing her in full view of the remaining patrons, all of whom cheered heartily.

When he let her go, Bridie stared at him in shock. 'Have you lost your mind?' she demanded, though failing to summon up the proper degree of outrage.

'You, Bridie Farrell, are amazing! I'm sorry I missed your break, but I'm going to make it up to you tonight after work. I'll meet you at your place, okay?'

'I don't finish until about nine,' she reminded him, still dazed by his excitement.

'No worries, I'll be there. I have to get moving—there's somewhere I need to be. I'll tell you all about it tonight.' He swooped down and kissed her once more, before leaving her to stare after him, still blinking like a startled owl.

༈

The house was almost in darkness when she walked inside after work. As her eyes adjusted, she noticed the dim glow of candlelight and she followed it into the kitchen. Bridie looked out the window and caught her breath. A small candlelit table was set up outside and pretty paper lanterns hung in the trees. More candles circled the table, making it look like something out of a fairytale. She moved to the back door.

Shaun stepped out of the shadows and walked across to her—he must have been watching her reaction.

'It's beautiful,' she whispered.

'No. You are.' He tugged her close and kissed her. When he lifted his head, the intensity of his gaze took her breath away. 'Marry me, Bridie.'

Bridie's heart kicked against her ribs.

Just then the front door banged, reminding Bridie that she hadn't got around to warning Shaun about . . .

'Phoebe?' Shaun's gaze switched between Bridie and his little sister in confusion and disbelief as she stood behind Bridie at the back door.

'I'm just going to my room,' Phoebe said quickly, turning to head down the hallway.

'*Your* room? What the hell are you talking about?' Shaun took the back steps two at a time, brushing past Bridie to stare down the hallway after his sister.

Bridie let out a small growl of irritation. Why did she always seem to be caught in the middle of some Broderick confrontation? 'Your father kicked her out of home. I told her she could stay here until she worked out what she wanted to do.'

'She's been *here* all this time?' he asked. 'Why didn't you tell me earlier?'

'I brought her home from . . . work,' she said carefully. Probably no need to reveal that she'd picked her up from the alleyway next to the pub. 'She'd had a little too much to drink and was pretty upset. I just figured she needed some time alone.'

'But she's been *here*?'

'It wasn't my place to tell you. I left it up to her to let you know where she was.'

'Dad told us she went back to the flat in Sydney.'

'Well, *clearly* she's not.'

Shaun let out a harsh sigh and rubbed the back of his neck. 'What was she wearing just now?'

'Her uniform. She's picked up a few shifts in the restaurant at the Drovers.'

'She's *working*?'

'Yes. Phoebe's living proof that there is life outside Jin-bloody-julu.'

'If I'd known she'd been wandering around in town I would have—'

'What? Come to kick me while I was down?' They both jumped when Phoebe's voice reached them from the dim hallway. She moved into the light, coming to a hesitant stop before her brother.

'Phoebe.' He paused, his hand dropping from his neck to hang wearily by his side. 'Are you all right?'

251

Her hollow laugh was full of suppressed pain. 'I'm just super. Although I bet there were a few chins wagging tonight when I served half the damn farming community. No doubt Dad will be pleased to hear about that. Go on, gloat. You may as well.'

'I don't want to gloat—what kind of bastard do you take me for?'

Bridie saw Phoebe's lower lip wobble a little.

'What are you going to do?' Shaun went on. 'You can't stay in Tooncanny. You know the old man is going to hit the roof when it gets back to him where you're working.'

Phoebe straightened her shoulders and lifted her head. 'He can rant all he likes—I'm done trying to please him. Right now, I'm just trying to work out a way to survive on my own, without his damn money.'

'You started the fire in the ram shed,' Shaun said, and Bridie noticed it wasn't a question. 'Why?'

'Because . . . he threw me off Jinjulu the night of your party . . . I thought he'd change his mind if I just let him cool off, but the next day he told me I had a week to make arrangements.'

'So you hit him where it hurt the most,' he said quietly.

A flash of pain flickered across Phoebe's face. 'I didn't mean to kill the sheep.' Her lip trembled and tears spilled from her eyelashes. 'Stupid damn things—they wouldn't leave their pens, and then the fire got out of control . . . It happened so fast. I ran to get help, but I couldn't find anyone, and then by the time I came back, you and Pete were pulling Dad out and I panicked. I didn't know he'd . . . I didn't mean to hurt him.'

'And you were punishing me, too, by letting the sheep out into the canola?'

Phoebe looked puzzled. 'I didn't go anywhere near your sheep.'

Shaun seemed to consider his sister for a few moments before giving a weary nod of his head.

'I suppose Dad's called the police in,' Phoebe said with a long sigh, clearly ready to accept her fate.

'No. I took care of it.'

Phoebe blinked uncertainly and glanced at Bridie for confirmation, but Bridie shrugged—she didn't know what he was talking about either.

'Why?'

'Because you're my sister. There isn't anything left of the shed, so no one will ever find out what happened. I'll help you in whatever way I can.'

'I don't deserve anyone's help,' she said miserably. 'Not after the way I've treated people.'

'Well, this is your chance to make things right. It's a new start, Phoebe. You can only go up from here.'

'What about you?' she asked.

Shaun looked across at Bridie and a tiny smile danced across his lips. 'I've got some big plans on the horizon too.'

Bridie swallowed nervously. She'd been so caught up in their conversation, she'd forgotten about his proposal.

'I've arrived right in the middle of something, haven't I?' Phoebe said with a wince as she took in the candles and the table set for two behind them through the back door. 'Sorry. I'll get out of your way.' She turned and disappeared with a flustered wave.

Silence settled between them then, and Bridie didn't know how to break it.

'Are you sure she can stay here? You don't mind?' he asked.

'I've already told her she's welcome to the spare room for as long as she needs it.'

Shaun seemed to be regarding her carefully, maybe unsure of how to push her for an answer to his proposal. The thought spurred her into action. 'Should we eat? I'm starving,' she said, making a move to see what he'd arranged for their dinner—anything to stall for time.

'Bridie.'

She froze and her eyes fluttered shut.

'You aren't going to say yes, are you?' he said.

A sick feeling settled in her stomach. What was wrong with her? She loved him—she knew she did. So why could she still not make herself say yes? What was holding her back? 'I just need . . .' she hesitated.

'What? For Christ's sake, Bridie, just tell me what it is you need from me,' he said roughly. She couldn't blame him for being frustrated by her reluctance. She knew it hurt him.

She shook her head helplessly. 'I don't know. Everything's happening too fast. I thought I had my life all worked out and then you came along and nothing's gone the way I planned.'

'I came along and messed everything up, you mean.'

'You didn't mess everything up. I just wasn't expecting you to come into my life. The timing really sucks.'

'Timing for what?'

'For me, Shaun. *Time for me*. For once, I just want to do something for me.'

'And marrying me isn't going to make you happy?'

'It's not about being happy. It's about finally, after all these years, not having to consider anyone else. Only, I *do*. I have to consider you—so once again I don't get to make a guilt-free choice, which is all I've ever wanted,' she said miserably.

'Well, excuse me for screwing up your life,' he snapped.

'I didn't mean it that way,' she protested.

'Make up your bloody mind, Bridie, because right now I'm not sure if I should celebrate or go and drown my sorrows. I've been living in limbo for days and it's driving me insane.'

'I know,' she said. 'But you surprised me with it on your birthday. Damn it, Shaun, I wasn't expecting that at all!'

'Not everything in your life has to be part of a five-year plan, Bridie. Do something spontaneous for a change. You say you've never had a chance to live your own life, well start now—stop planning everything and just start living.'

'That's easy for you to say—you've had your taste of freedom. You lived away from home, you went to uni. I took care of my mother until she died. Then I had a little brother to look after, who'd lost not only his mother but also his father in the space of a few months. How *dare* you preach to me about taking chances.'

'I'm sorry you had all that to deal with, Bridie, but stop using it as your excuse. You don't need to run away to find yourself. You are who you are. You're strong because of the things you've dealt with in your life. There isn't any great adventure out there waiting for you. This is it. You haven't been treading water waiting for Luke to finish school— you've been *living life*, just like everyone else on the planet. *This* is your life.'

Bridie shook her head, stung by his dismissal of the dreams she'd held so close to her heart for such a long time. 'This might be my *now*, but it isn't my future.'

He stared at her, his jaw clenched tightly. 'Then hurry up and figure out where your future is—and if I happen to be in it or not.'

He brushed past her, walking through the house and out to his ute without a backward glance.

Bridie wanted to call him back but she just couldn't find the strength. She heard his ute start up and drive away, her sadness deepening as the sound faded into silence.

Moving back to the kitchen, she sat at the table and dug out the envelope from her handbag she'd been carrying around for the last few weeks, too scared to open it. She wasn't sure why she had a sudden urge to read what was inside. The stamp on the letter was postmarked Wellington; the sender, Brian Farrell.

Just read the damn thing and be done with it, she told herself firmly.

She quickly picked at the sealed flap and slid a finger underneath. Taking a slow, deep breath, she unfolded the letter carefully and began to read.

After reading it through a second time, she knew what she had to do.

Twenty

Endless stretches of paddock passed by as she drove the long lonely road from Tooncanny to Wellington.

Ever since leaving early that morning she'd been calling herself all kinds of stupid. She knew her father wasn't going to tell her anything that would change the past, but since Luke had left, and with the turmoil of Shaun's marriage proposal, she'd done things she would never have thought she'd do in a hundred years.

The three hours it took to make the trip went surprisingly fast—almost too fast. As she left her trusty ute in the car park she found herself battling an attack of nerves.

Let's just get this over with, she told herself firmly. *Go in, listen to whatever it is he wants to tell you, and then leave. That's all you have to do.*

Bridie felt uncomfortable just walking into the prison. A young woman ahead of her held the hand of a small boy while balancing a toddler on her other hip. Bridie felt for her. She couldn't have been more than eighteen or nineteen, and she had dark circles beneath her eyes. Bridie overheard her tell the guard she was here to visit her boyfriend. It was such a depressing place, even for a visitor. She couldn't begin to imagine what it must be like to be an inmate.

She'd called and booked a visit, and now she had to go through this intimidating procedure just to get inside the visiting centre. After arriving at the main gatehouse she filled in a visitor's slip, then took a ticket and waited until her number was called.

She approached the counter and handed her slip to the large guard. He typed her information into the computer using two fingers. He was painfully slow and Bridie tried to control her agitation. 'You've been confirmed, Ms Farrell,' he said eventually. 'Please take a seat again.'

Bridie sat back down and waited until two officers came through the door, each leading a dog. The officers politely asked all the visitors to line up and explained that the drug-detection dogs were going to walk past them.

'Please do not touch the animals,' a stern-faced officer warned them as he began to walk down the line.

Apparently everyone in line was drug-free because the dogs were led back out of the room. Bridie then followed the line of visitors in past a metal detector, and *finally*, after all that, they were inside the visiting centre. She handed over the slip of paper she'd been given by the processing officer, then waited while they called her father into the

room. How people did this each week was beyond her—
she felt as though *she* were the prisoner.

As the door opened she caught her first glimpse of
Brian Farrell in over seven years. She was grateful for
the fact that she was already seated; she doubted her legs
would have been able to hold her upright had she been
standing.

He looked older. Much older than she'd been expecting.
His hair had gone grey; she tried to recall if it had been
turning grey the last time she'd seen him, but she couldn't
remember. So much of that time had been a blur of heartache and worry.

As he crossed the room his expression was so intense
that Bridie had to look away. She was quiet as he sat down
across from her; her throat felt as though it were suddenly
paralysed.

She let her eyes roam over his thick forearms, heavily
inked with tattoos. They looked intimidating, but she
remembered how, as a child, she'd sit on her father's lap
and trace the outlines of the pictures for hours.

'I'm glad you came, Bridie,' he said after a few minutes
of silence, his voice deep and gruff and all too familiar.

Bridie searched for something to say but came up blank.
What was there to say after all this time?

'I got a letter from Luke the other day,' he tried again.
'I can't believe he's old enough to have joined the army.'

Bridie looked down at her hands, linked tightly on the
table in front of her. 'He sounds happy on the phone,' she
volunteered.

'You did a real good job with him, Bridie. Your mum
would be real proud of you both.'

Bridie swallowed past a lump in her throat. 'I did what had to be done,' she shrugged.

The room made her feel so small and insignificant. The cold grey walls and disheartening atmosphere only added to her discomfort. This was a bad idea.

'I hear you have a bloke? Some rich farmer?'

She didn't want to talk about Shaun with her father. Knowing that she'd hurt Shaun made it hard for her to even think about him at the moment. And it annoyed her that Brian referred to Shaun in that way. Obviously having a man in her life wasn't interesting enough, it was the fact that he was from a well-off family that intrigued him. The bluntness of the question hit a nerve, making her lash out. 'Why would you want to hear about my life?'

'I'm your father,' he protested.

'You gave up all rights to know anything about me the day you made your choice to do something illegal.'

'I wanted a chance to explain it to you.'

'What's there to explain? You turned your back on your family.'

'It wasn't that black and white. Your uncles had got themselves in big trouble—they were young and stupid and had got all tangled up with the wrong kind of people. I couldn't let them go to that deal on their own. I know if anyone can understand that, Bridie, it's you. You'd do anything for Luke.'

'Not at the risk of losing my children,' she said.

'Look, it wasn't supposed to go all pear-shaped the way it did. It was going to be the last time. I'd promised your mother I was going straight and I meant it, but I was their elder brother, I couldn't let them just walk into that kind of trouble alone.'

She watched him clench his fists on the tabletop. 'Do I wish I'd done it differently? Hell yes!' he said, leaning forward in his seat. 'But I can't turn back the clock, and it doesn't solve anything to sit here and wish for the impossible.'

'If that's all you wanted to get off your chest,' she said, making to rise from her seat. She didn't come here to listen to excuses.

'Don't go,' he said in a thick voice. 'I just want to know you're doing okay.'

'And if I'm not, Dad?' she demanded, the stinging behind her eyes warning of approaching tears. 'What are you going to do about it, stuck in here? You can't do a damn thing, so why the hell do you even care?'

'Because I'm your father and, no matter what, I still love you,' he told her, his frustration a mirror image of her own.

'Well, you should have remembered that when you had to make your decision. You should have chosen me and Luke.' She drew a breath and it ended in a ragged sob.

'I'm sorry, Bridie, I'm really sorry,' he whispered, throwing his head back to stare at the ceiling in despair.

It took a minute to get herself under control, but she finally managed it. 'Like you said, there's nothing you can do about the past now. So let's just move on.'

'I really want you to do that, Bridie. I wanted to make sure you knew how bad I've felt knowing you were giving up your own dreams to do my job, raising Luke.'

'I would never have turned my back on him.' *Unlike you.* The words hung unspoken between them.

Brian met her hurt expression steadily, not flinching under the weight of her accusation. 'Your mother always wanted you to leave Tooncanny, get away from its small-town way of thinking. She even made me promise before she died that I wouldn't hold you back. If you're happy with this guy Luke told me about, then maybe it's all worked out. But if you have any doubts, I'd advise you to think long and hard before making a decision. In the long run it usually comes back to bite you on the arse.'

'It's a shame you didn't take your own advice.'

His dry chuckle held nothing but self-loathing.

Bridie searched her father's face. There was so much of Luke in his rugged features, despite the toll taken by years of brawls and drinking. His eyes were clear and alert; he seemed to have acquired a calm she hadn't anticipated.

'You look just like your mother,' he said quietly. He'd obviously been studying her as carefully as she'd been studying him. 'I miss that woman.'

Didn't they all?

'Don't live with regrets, Bridie. They'll eat you up in the end. I've seen in here how regret can twist a person. I live with the choices I made. I spent a long time angry at myself for wasting so much of my life, for throwing away my kids and wife. I don't want you to spend your life thinking about what might have been.'

'What if this is what was supposed to happen? What if this is it?' she asked, then wished she hadn't. She didn't want to sound so defenceless in this place, in front of this man.

'A spiritual person will tell you that no matter what you do, you'll end up where you're supposed to be.'

'And what would you say?'

'I'd say there's no such thing as fate. There are just choices. Good or bad—you make them and then you have to live with them.'

'Simple as that?' she asked with a raised eyebrow.

'Simple as that.'

Simple had never sounded so complicated.

༄

Much later that evening Bridie picked up the picture of her mother as a carefree teenager posing on a beach in Surfers Paradise. It had been taken before her life had changed direction. Before she found herself in a life she hadn't imagined. Bridie stared at it long into the night.

Early the next morning she packed her bags, dropped an envelope into the letterbox at the post office and pointed her ute towards the faint shadows of colour that were beginning to emerge on the horizon. This time she didn't look back at the *Welcome to Tooncanny* sign. She stared straight ahead through the tears and the anguish. From now on that's what she'd do. Look ahead and not back.

༄

After walking out on Bridie, Shaun had gone back to Jinjulu but spent the night drinking with Pete in his small cottage. He couldn't face seeing his father. His evening had been a roller-coaster of emotions and he was exhausted. How had it gone so wrong? After he'd spoken to Jack he'd been on top of the world; he'd been in such a good mood that he'd felt confident his plan to surprise Bridie with a romantic dinner would sway her to say yes to marrying him. The last person he'd expected to see had been his sister. The confrontation had ruined the romantic proposal he had planned and then the whole night had taken a nosedive from there.

'So what are you going to do?' Pete asked after handing Shaun another can of beer and taking a seat beside him on the small verandah.

'Well, I can't stay here, not now. I guess I'll take Jack up on his offer.'

'You sure you want to leave Jinjulu? Your old man's gonna be pissed off—big time.'

'I've been putting up with his crap for too long. Nothing I do is going to change his mind.' Shaun took a swig from his can. Damned if Bridie hadn't been right. He'd stayed and put up with his father for Jared's sake—in some weird way he'd thought staying and trying to make a go of it here would assuage some of the guilt he felt over his part in Jared's death . . . But he couldn't live like this any more.

The next morning, feeling like hell after a night drinking away his sorrows, he put his hat on and walked out Pete's front door. It was time to face his parents; the sooner that was done, the sooner he could start looking ahead.

He found Douglas and Constance in the dining room eating breakfast.

'I've got a list of jobs I need doing today,' his father said by way of a greeting. 'You're going to have to get a move on since you've decided to take your bloody time coming home.'

Shaun stared at his father and wondered if maybe there was something wrong with him. He was acting as though yesterday hadn't even happened.

'I'm through here, Dad. I'm moving out.'

'You're what?' Douglas looked up, scowling at Shaun.

'You reneged on our deal—remember?'

'So, what, you're sulking now?'

'No, I'm leaving. I'm not doing this any more, Dad. You can't treat people the way you do and expect them to keep coming back for more. I'm buying my own place.'

'Shaun—' His mother moved to stand up from her seat, and Shaun looked over at her with a sad shake of his head.

'You're both so busy making each other miserable that you don't give a damn about anyone else. You invited Alisha out here, Mum, even though you knew I wasn't interested in her. You messed with her life, and with Bridie's. People are getting hurt. You both need to wake up to yourselves.'

'I was trying to help.'

'You were trying to get your own way, Mum. You might be able to manipulate Dad like that, but not me, not any more. Oh, and by the way, Phoebe said to say hi. She's doing fine. She's not in Sydney, mind you, which was a bit of a surprise.'

'What do you mean, not in Sydney?' Constance asked, her eyes narrowing at her husband.

'She's still in Tooncanny. He threw her out too.'

Shaun saw his father's expression harden as his wife stared at him in outrage. 'You told me she was back at the flat,' she accused.

'She needs to appreciate what she's been given and see what it's like to live in the real world. She'll be back—they both will,' Douglas added, throwing Shaun an angry glare.

'I'm not going to stand by and let this happen again.' Daisy had burst into the room, startling them all. 'You will not let that girl fall into the same trap Jared did.'

'What trap?' Shaun asked, surprised by Daisy's fierce expression.

'Depression. I've been watching her like a hawk since she got back from that fancy school, waiting for one of you to do something about it . . . but I swear if anything happens to that girl, I'll make sure everyone knows just who is responsible.'

'Daisy!' Constance snapped.

'I think it's time you both came clean. Shaun deserves to know the truth—God knows, you made him suffer enough all these years. I will not stand by and let you destroy another child. I love these children as though they were my own. You two never deserved to have them.'

'Maybe you need to remember who you are, woman,' Douglas retorted.

'Oh, I know who I am. I know exactly who I am. Look at you, so smug and arrogant . . . You want to know why he finds it so hard to hand over any of the power?' Daisy asked, turning to Shaun. 'Because he still believes everyone is talking about him behind his back—isn't that right, Douglas? You remember how the whole district knew that your father had never wanted you to run the place. You're still hurting because your father *humiliated* you in front of everyone when he made it clear you were never going to run Jinjulu as well as he could.'

'How dare you!' Douglas roared.

'How dare *you*!' Daisy countered, and Shaun had never seen her as angry as she was right now. 'God blessed you with three beautiful children and look what you've done to them! I will never forgive either of you for what you've done—never!'

'Daisy, what are you talking about?' Shaun asked.

'Daisy, no,' Constance said quickly, almost fearfully.

'You've stood by and done nothing for Phoebe, even though she's been crying out for one of you to help her.'

'Oh, for God's sake, stop being so hysterical,' Douglas said.

'Tell Shaun about the letter Jared left,' Daisy said calmly.

'What letter?' Shaun asked.

'Jared and your father fought earlier that day—the day that he died. Phoebe came to me, upset because she'd been hiding beneath the desk in the office and heard it. She told me Jared was going to leave because he couldn't stand being stuck in the middle of his father and you any more. She said Jared had sounded strange and she'd been scared. I went to the office to find out what had happened, but no one was there. I found a note ripped up—it was on the floor by the bin.'

'What do you mean, a note?' Shaun asked.

Daisy reached for his hand. 'Love, it was a suicide note.'

'No,' Shaun said, shaking his head and moving away from Daisy's touch. 'No. That's not . . .' He stared at Daisy in disbelief. 'No. He wouldn't have done that . . . I'd have known,' he added lamely. Wouldn't he? Surely if his brother had been suicidal he'd have picked up some kind of sign? He desperately searched his mind for something that might have given him a clue. Sure, Jared had been a bit quiet over that last year or so, and yeah, he was copping a lot of abuse from Dad, but weren't they all? *Maybe not as much as Jared was.* Dad had always been harder on Jared. Where Shaun could shrug off his father's criticisms, Jared had taken them to heart; he'd been more of a worrier. But suicide?

Shaun turned to his father. 'Is this true? Was there a note?'

267

'Don't you raise your voice at me, boy!'

Shaun stared at the man who had fathered him and felt . . . nothing. Even now, confronted with the truth, Douglas wouldn't admit he'd been wrong. 'You found a note and you still didn't go out and look for him?' Shaun stared at his father in disbelief. 'How the hell did you not see something was wrong?'

'How was I supposed to know he was serious?' Douglas grunted.

Shaun gaped at his father.

'I didn't raise a bunch of crybabies,' Douglas spat. 'If Jared had a problem he should have manned up and talked to me about it, not written me a letter.'

'Oh yeah, 'cause you're just so damn approachable.' Shaun looked across at his mother, who was crying silently, and suddenly it hit him—it all made sense. This was the missing piece of the puzzle. 'You *knew* all this time?'

'Darling . . .'

'You knew and you never said anything?'

'I didn't find out until later,' she protested weakly. 'Not until after he was found and Daisy showed it to me.'

'After *I found him*!' Shaun yelled, his voice breaking. 'You two deserve each other. Jesus, I hope you'll be happy living here all alone.'

'Where do you think you're going?' his father demanded.

Shaun ignored him, heading for the door.

'You won't walk out on Jinjulu,' Douglas scoffed.

Shaun didn't even break stride. 'Watch me.'

His mother stood in the doorway of his bedroom crying as he threw clothes into a duffle bag. He couldn't look at her. She and Douglas had lied to and manipulated their children. They might each have had different reasons but the end result was the same—they were only doing what benefited themselves. Constance had used the truth to punish her husband, holding the knowledge over his head like a sword. His father had simply swept it aside, as if Jared was no longer of any consequence.

Even now his father still wouldn't admit that he'd been wrong. He'd called his son's bluff instead of accepting that Jared was finding the pressure too much to handle. Douglas Broderick was a prime example of why people out here found it so difficult to come forward and ask for help when they weren't coping. Who wanted to be looked down upon as being weak just because they needed help?

Shaun felt a cocktail of emotions: rage at his father's callousness in not reaching out to help his son; grief over his brother's death, which might have been preventable; and guilt—he'd always feel guilt. Maybe this changed things slightly, but the fact would always remain that if he'd stayed at home instead of going to that party he'd have been able to stop Jared doing what he'd done.

Maybe he'd have just done it another time, or maybe that note would have shaken up his mother at least and she would have got him some help. There was no way to know for sure now, and that fact alone saddened him beyond words.

Twenty-one

The soothing wash of the waves on the sand erased the stress of a busy day at work and revitalised her flagging energy levels.

It was the middle of school holidays and Surfers seemed to be knee deep in tourists. She'd been here almost a month.

For the first few days after arriving in town, she'd stayed in a small, ugly motel room. Conscious of her limited savings, she'd begun desperately searching the rentals section of the newspaper. Rent was astronomical. Visions of living within walking distance of the beach vanished after only a few minutes of scanning the real estate pages. But after only a week she'd secured a job at a busy beachside bistro and bar, impressing her new boss with her willingness to start immediately. She'd just stopped in to drop off a résumé, but they'd been short-staffed and clearly not coping with a sudden influx of hungry customers. Donning an apron, she'd jumped in and lent a hand, winning instant approval from the husband and wife team who, she later learned, had taken over the business that very day.

On the third day in her new job, Bridie had taken her break with Ben, another young bartender. He told her that he'd been sharing his beachfront apartment with his mate and his mate's girlfriend until they'd decided they wanted their own space and left him in a bit of a tight spot trying to cover the rent. The place had turned out to be perfect; it was small but clean, and, best of all, it was near the beach.

The first few days after leaving Tooncanny had been the worst. She'd turned off her phone and refused to check the messages. She knew Shaun would have hated getting her goodbye in a letter, but it was the only way she could do it. There was no way she'd have had the strength to walk away from him in person. She knew he would never understand why she had to leave. How could she explain it to him when she couldn't find the words to explain it to herself? It was just something she needed to do. The thought of waking up a few years down the track and regretting that she'd turned down her one shot at freedom terrified her.

She would *not* end up like her mother, no matter how much she'd adored Beth. She would always remember the sadness in Beth's eyes as she talked about not taking that apprenticeship when she'd had the chance, where she *could have* ended up . . . Bridie didn't want to live with regrets like that.

She could have asked Shaun to give her time to figure it out, she supposed, but she knew that giving him false hope would only drag out his pain. No, she did what had to be done, she told herself firmly. Convincing her heart of that, though, wasn't so easy.

The screech of a seagull overhead startled her from her thoughts. Ahead she saw two men, their surfboards on the sand nearby, pulling on wetsuits. She recognised Ben immediately and was trying to decide whether she should stop and say hello or keep walking, when he glanced up and waved her over.

'Tye, this is my new housemate, Bridie,' Ben said to his companion.

'Hello, Bridie, I've been hearing all about you,' Tye said, and Bridie liked the deep, gravelly tone of his voice. The frankness with which his eyes roamed over her body should have annoyed her, but somehow the way he did it made it feel like a compliment. A flicker of awareness sparked deep inside her and she took a step away from him, confused by the unexpected reaction.

He was gorgeous, all bronzed, toned muscle. She'd have to be blind or lying if she didn't acknowledge that much. She found herself staring at his washboard abs; felt like touching them to see if they were real. She instinctively tucked her fingers into her palms to stop herself.

She lifted her gaze, realising he'd asked her something, and felt a blush creep up her neck. 'Sorry?'

A slow sexy grin spread across his face as his eyes held hers. 'I asked if you surf.'

'Oh. No. I've never tried it.'

'You should, I think you'd like it,' he said, bending down and picking up his board. 'Let me know when you want a lesson.'

'Maybe.' She wasn't sure she would cope too well out there beyond the wave breaks. The threat of sharks was a little too daunting for a country girl like her.

'See ya round,' Tye said, sending her one last lingering look before he turned away to jog down to the water.

'See ya, Bridie,' Ben called, following his mate out into the waves.

She stood on the beach and watched them for a few minutes before walking back to the apartment. That brief moment of attraction had unsettled her more than she cared to admit. Where the hell had that come from? She pushed away the niggling sensation of guilt. She hadn't come all this way just to fall at the feet of the first bronzed surfer she met. This wasn't about romance. It was about finding herself and her future.

She missed Shaun.

Bridie blinked back sudden tears. She missed the smell of wet sheep and diesel. A sad smile touched her lips at the thought. 'You're living your dream,' she reminded herself softly. 'You had to do it.'

～

Shaun took off his hat and wiped his forehead with his sleeve as he stared out with a sense of pride over the newly cultivated paddock. It was his first crop. He'd moved onto Jack's property two months ago.

Leaving Jinjulu had been hard, very hard, but at the same time it had felt liberating, like starting a whole new chapter in his life.

The sun was sinking low in the sky as his gaze wandered further, taking in the patchwork of cultivated paddocks he'd been busy planting over the last few weeks. He'd done this countless times before, but this time it *meant* something. This time it was *his*. The last couple of months he'd worked himself into the ground in order to forget Bridie—or rather to stop himself running all the way to the damn Gold Coast after her—and now all that hard work was paying off. He could see progress.

With a whistle he called Mick back to the ute. Time to call it a day and head back to the house. Jack's house, but soon to be *his*. As the house came into view, Shaun's mood changed. It was stupid, but ever since he'd asked Bridie to marry him, he'd been picturing what it would be like to come home after a hard day's work to find her waiting for him. In his head he saw her waiting on the front verandah, a smile on her face as she greeted him with a knee-buckling kiss and dragged him inside for a shower. As the warmth of his fantasy drained away, he gave a sarcastic grunt. The empty house that stood before him was dark and lonely . . . a perfect description of how he felt himself these days.

He heated up leftovers, then sat at the small kitchen table to eat. The clock in the lounge room ticked loudly, keeping him company. He could watch the evening news but it only depressed him; he had enough of his own problems to deal with without adding the rest of the world's troubles to his burden.

Sitting back after he'd finished his meal he took a long swig of his beer and shut his eyes.

Christ, he was tired.

He dragged himself to his feet to wash the dishes before making his way to the bedroom. He knew he should go and have a shower but instead he sat down on the edge of the bed and looked across at his bedside table and the folded letter that lay there. Almost against his will, he reached for it and unfolded the grubby paper. He didn't need to read it—it was burned onto his brain by now—but reading it allowed him to feel some kind of connection to Bridie, and at the end of the day, lying in this quiet house, he needed to feel her close.

Daisy had delivered the letter to him the day after he walked off Jinjulu. She'd brought along some bags of groceries, then stayed and cooked up enough food to feed an army. She'd filled his freezer and had been coming over once a week to wash and cook for him ever since. He'd told her he could fend for himself, but he liked having her around so he didn't push it. More than once he'd asked her to move in here but she wouldn't hear of it. 'Jinjulu is my home,' she'd said gently. 'I can't imagine leaving it now.' He hadn't really worked out how he felt about her part in the cover-up over Jared's death. He guessed that, as he'd left so soon after Jared's funeral, it wasn't as though he was there for her to tell. And she did risk losing her home and her job by telling him. But still, he wished he'd known. He wished he'd picked up on the signs of his brother's depression. He wished a lot of things.

As soon as he'd realised the letter Daisy gave him was from Bridie he'd known it wasn't good news. He'd been trying to call her but kept being diverted to her message bank. He'd waited until Daisy had left before taking the letter out onto the front verandah and sitting down to read it.

Shaun,

I know this is taking the coward's way out, but it's the only way I can think of to get through to you. You haven't taken my leaving seriously and I just don't have the strength to fight you on this any more. I can't ask you to wait around until I figure this out—that's not fair—but I have to do this, for my peace of mind. My dream has always been to leave Tooncanny, to see what else is out there . . . If I don't do this now, I never will.

I'm sorry I'm leaving without a goodbye, but I'm not sure I'd be strong enough to leave if you asked me again to stay. I do love you, Shaun. I know it mustn't seem like it right now, but I do. It hurts more than you know to leave, but I have to. It wouldn't be fair to stay and someday blame you for my regrets.

You're going to do great things—I believe in you. Just take the plunge and make it happen.

Bridie

He let his tired eyes skim the pages for the hundredth time until they fluttered closed and he fell asleep, dreaming of Bridie and what might have been.

⌇

Another beautiful day, Bridie thought as she walked out of the bar on her lunch break. She loved coming to work. When she wasn't run off her feet, she could soak up the view of the glorious sun-kissed beach and enjoy the holiday atmosphere of the tourists strolling along the esplanade.

She'd been trying to find the exact spot where her mother had been standing when that photograph was taken, but she hadn't had much luck—Surfers Paradise had changed a lot since the seventies. It was also hard to reconcile the downtrodden woman her mother had become with the bright-eyed teenager who'd had dreams of living here and making a bright future for herself.

Bridie had grown up hearing her mother's stories of coming here with her own parents for holidays. She'd described the place in detail, although Bridie suspected her mother wouldn't recognise it today. She'd always promised to bring Bridie and Luke up here for a holiday, but there'd never been enough money; then, when she got sick, they'd run out of time.

Her phone rang and Bridie shook off her thoughts to answer it.

'Hi, stranger.'

'Phoebe. Hi. How's everything going?' Sometimes it didn't seem quite real that she and Phoebe now exchanged weekly phone calls. Who would have thought they'd become BFFs after their less-than-civil encounters in the past? Phoebe was renting her house and Bridie was thankful that she was there to take care of the place.

'Same old, same old. Nothing ever happens in Tooncanny. What's been happening with you?'

'Work, work and more work.'

'You know, you could have been doing that here. I thought you moved to get a bit of excitement in your life?'

'You still have to work so you can afford to have some excitement, you know.'

'Tell me about it. Working sucks.'

Bridie couldn't bring herself to judge Phoebe for her childish, spoilt attitude. She actually felt a little sorry for her. To go from never having to worry about money and doing pretty much what you wanted to suddenly having nothing was a huge leap.

'Have you spoken with your mother yet?' Bridie asked.

Phoebe had rung her shortly after finding out about the suicide note. Just how twisted Douglas and Constance were shouldn't have surprised Bridie any more, but it had. Her heart ached for Shaun and how terrible he must be feeling. She'd called him, more than once actually, but each time she'd hung up before the call had connected. She was scared he would hang up on her, and she wouldn't have blamed him—she'd broken up with him in a letter and left town without any real warning, but that didn't mean she'd stopped loving him.

She would never understand why Constance had withheld the knowledge of her son's suicide; she knew that Constance loved her children in her own way and Jared's death would have been a terrible blow. She hoped for Phoebe's sake that mother and daughter could reconcile at some point; she knew how painful it was to miss your mother.

'I just can't yet,' Phoebe said when Bridie brought it up. 'It's too soon. Maybe one day. I hear Dad's as hard-headed as ever. He keeps telling everyone Shaun'll give up and come back to Jinjulu—I don't think he can quite believe he had the guts to walk away.'

'How's Shaun? Have you seen him lately?'

'Why?'

'What do you mean, why?'

'What do you care? You walked out on him, remember.'

'Phoebe, don't start,' Bridie groaned.

'What? I'm just reminding you that you've got a new life now. You don't have to worry about the old one any more.'

'I still worry about him.'

'Then you should come back and see for yourself.'

'Phoebe . . .' God, she could be frustrating. They'd had this argument more than once. Since the Broderick family meltdown, Shaun and Phoebe had grown a lot closer. It was nice to see some good coming out of the whole ugly mess, but this protective-kid-sister thing was becoming a pain.

'He's been working hard,' Phoebe said finally.

Well, that didn't tell her much. He always worked hard.

'Alf and Bulldog keep telling me to make sure I say hi to you. They miss you too. So have you got the coast out of your system yet? When are you coming back?'

'I've only been gone two months. Anyway, you shouldn't be too eager for me to come back—it'd put an end to your peace and quiet and you'd be kicked out of the big bedroom. How on earth would you fit all your clothes in the spare room?'

Phoebe gave a small grunt of agreement and mercifully changed the topic, filling Bridie in on the latest gossip from the Drovers. These conversations were both bitter and sweet. She loved hearing about everyone, but it always left her feeling terribly homesick.

Bridie crumpled the wrapper from her lunch into a ball and stood up, preparing to head back to work. Only three more hours and she could go home and get changed into her swimmers. Turning from the bin, she glanced up and felt her heart slam against her chest as she caught sight of a man in an akubra walking towards her.

It took a few moments to get herself under control as he walked on by, his wide-eyed gaze taking in the scantily clad girls and miles of pristine beach.

Just another country boy on a holiday to the Gold Coast, she thought as she shook off her startled reaction to the hat, such a familiar sight back in Tooncanny but so out of place here.

No time to analyse the brief flare of hope that hat had sparked in her. She had work to do. Work was what she needed to keep her mind from straying into territory she wasn't ready to deal with at the moment.

༄

Bridie had the next morning off, which meant she had a chance to go down to the beach for an early walk. The blanket of smooth white sand felt cold beneath her feet, and even at this early hour there were already footprints marring its surface. The moment lost some of its magic when she looked up and noticed just how many other people were out and about. The visions she'd had of early morning walks along the beach had never involved a crowd of overtanned, overweight retirees with minuscule bathing suits and yappy dogs.

She decided to let go of her disappointment and focus instead on the beauty of the morning and how lucky she was to be able to wake up to this every day. As usual, there was an abundance of surfers out claiming their waves, looking free and graceful as they glided across the water. As one of the surfers came into shore she saw with a confusing leap of excitement that it was Tye.

He emerged from the water like some Greek god, shaking his golden mane. He was . . . beautiful. He spotted her and made his way over.

Before meeting this man, she'd never have considered a man to be beautiful; she certainly would never have thought she could be *attracted* to a man who could be described as beautiful. But here he was, grinning down at her with eyes that sparkled and promised all sorts of devilish delights.

'You going to give this a try then?' he asked, nodding at his long board.

'Me? Oh, I don't know.' Bridie stared at the board warily.

'Come on, live a little,' he taunted gently.

This is what you wanted, Bridie! To live! So do something about it! Getting to her feet, she wiped her sandy hands on her long beach shirt, before dragging it over her head and dropping it onto the sand.

'So we'll go through a few of the basics here, and then we'll take her out for a paddle, okay?'

She wished her voice had sounded a little more confident as she agreed, but paddling out into the ocean on a narrow fibreglass board was not what she considered a sane thing to be doing.

Tye drilled her in the basics of lying on the board and getting to her feet, making her do it over and over until he was satisfied.

'Ready to take her out?'

'You know, I don't really think I'm experienced enough to be out in the—'

He bent down and placed a gentle kiss on her lips, silencing her protests.

'—water,' she finished with a whisper of breath.

He led her out into the small rolling waves and she gasped at the shock of cold water on her ankles. He stopped when the water reached thigh height and held the board for her while she slid onto it, lying on her belly.

With her attention fixed firmly on the open ocean before her, she didn't realise he intended to come *with* her on the board until she felt his rubbery wetsuit across her calves. As she turned to look over her shoulder, he winked and gave her a wicked grin. 'Don't mind me, I'm just coming along to make sure you don't break my board. Turn around and start paddling,' he instructed when she blinked at him uncertainly.

Thinking it was safer to look straight ahead and not worry about the sexy surfer pressed against her in a very distracting manner, she did as he ordered and began to paddle. They broke through the first of the waves, but as they got further out the waves became bigger; she gasped as one broke over her, forcing her to hold her breath and squeeze her eyes shut.

'Okay, now we're going to turn around, and when I tell you to, start paddling, okay?' he called.

She managed to nod, but from the corner of her eye she caught a glimpse of the next wave rolling in and began to panic.

'Paddle!' he yelled, and there was no time to argue; out of sheer terror she began paddling for all she was worth. She felt the board rise with the swell and suddenly they were being catapulted across the water on the crest of a huge wave.

It registered, somewhere in her terrified mind, that it was actually . . . fun.

'Next lesson we'll try getting you up on your feet,' he told her as they waded from the water and back onto the beach.

'I don't know, I think I should quit while I'm ahead. I survived this far, I'd hate to push my luck,' she laughed.

'You don't seem like a quitter to me, Bridie,' he said seriously.

They sat down on the sand in companionable silence for a few minutes before Bridie asked, 'So what do you do? I only ever see you down here surfing.'

'As little as possible,' he shrugged.

She took a longer look at him and tried to work out his age. He was older than her; in fact, when she looked closer, he was not nearly as young as she'd first assumed. She judged him to be in his early thirties.

'That must be nice,' she murmured. She couldn't help but compare his laidback attitude to that of the hardworking farming community she'd been born and raised in. Those dusty, thirsty men who came into the pub after a long day working—she could just imagine what they'd have to say about Mr Tanned and Sexy here.

He grinned at her. 'It's just a lifestyle choice. Anyone can make it if they want to—it's not a big deal.'

She wondered how he paid rent and bought food on this *lifestyle*.

'I better go and get ready for work,' she said finally, unable to think of anything to talk to him about. A pang of loneliness hit her as she remembered how easy it had been to talk to Shaun. God, she missed him.

'See ya round,' Tye said, getting up and walking away with his board.

Finally, she felt as though she could exhale and relax. She always felt on edge when she was around Tye. She couldn't read him; he was a different species to the men she was used to, and she wasn't sure whether that was thrilling or exhausting.

꒛

As she walked home after her shift, Bridie heard her phone ringing. She began searching through her bag, swerving to avoid kids on skateboards and tourists walking hand in hand around her.

'What on earth were you doing?' Phoebe asked after Bridie's slightly harried hello.

'Finding the phone.'

'Took you long enough.'

Bridie bit back a snappy reply, but it took some effort. She'd had a particularly long day and was really not in the mood to be accommodating. 'How are you?'

'I'm great . . . Better than great even.'

'Why? What's happened?'

'I'm moving to Perth.'

'What? How? When?'

'Calm down. You think you're the only one who can spread their wings and fly outta here?'

Bridie heard the amusement in her friend's voice and some of her initial shock dissipated. 'Spill . . . I want details.'

'Well, I got a call from Pete the other day. Did I mention he left Jinjulu after Shaun did? We've been kinda seeing each other, and when we realised it was getting serious he decided to leave Jinjulu—even though I thought it was quite funny that the leading hand was sneaking around with the boss's daughter! He got a job in Western Australia and the other day he called and asked me to move over there to join him. He sounded so happy and kept talking about how there was so much work everywhere in WA, so I got off the phone and applied for a heap of jobs . . . and I got one! I'm going to work for a while, save some money and then go to uni and get serious about my fine arts degree.'

'Oh wow, Phoebe. I'm so happy for you.' Bridie was in shock. Phoebe and Pete? She hadn't seen that coming at all. Man, she left town and the whole place underwent a shake-up!

'Yeah. I'm pretty excited.' The line went quiet for a moment and Bridie thought they might have been cut off.

'I just wanted to say thank you, Bridie. I don't deserve a friend like you but I'm so grateful for everything you've done for me,' Phoebe blurted out.

Bridie was caught off guard for a minute and she blinked away the sting of tears. 'You're a good person, Phoebe. You deserve to be happy.'

'So do you . . . Which is why I think you should come back to Tooncanny. You don't belong up there. You should be back here with my big brother. I know you think you're happy, but you're not. Neither of you are.'

Bridie gave a surprised chuckle at the sudden insight Phoebe had developed, and searched for some kind of argument.

Phoebe went on, 'Look, I'm the last person who should be giving anyone grief about the choices they've made, but one thing I do know is that there comes a time when you have to acknowledge you've been hurting yourself long enough and then do something about it.'

Bridie was floored. Phoebe might be right, but how did you know if you'd given something new a decent chance? Yes, she got homesick, and yes, she was lonely, but surely these things eventually went away?

But what if they don't? What if this is as good as it gets? a little voice asked.

How did you know when enough was enough? And why did even contemplating going back feel like giving up?

⌒

'Hey, Bridie! Wait up.'

Bridie turned to see Tye jogging along the beach towards her, surfboard under his arm and sun-bleached hair blowing in the breeze.

'I was hoping to see you down here today.' He was bare-chested, the top of his wetsuit undone and hanging down around his waist.

'Hey, Tye. How was your day?'

'Great. The waves were awesome.'

Bridie shook her head and sent him a mystified smile. 'How can you be so laidback about not working?'

'The way I see it, I have plenty of time to work, but you're only young once,' he grinned. 'Did Ben tell you there's a party on tonight? Are you coming?'

She was distracted by the bulge of his bicep as he shifted his surfboard from one arm to the other. The tribal tattoo around his arm quivered and his stomach muscles flexed for a moment. She tried not to stare. 'I don't know. Ben didn't mention it.'

'Well, I'm inviting you.'

'I don't even know the people. Won't it be a bit weird if I just turn up to a party like that?'

His chuckle was deep and rough. 'That's the beauty of these parties. You never know who's going to turn up. Everyone's welcome.'

There was still so much about this place she had to get used to. 'I suppose I could go. It's the first Saturday night I've had off since I've been here.'

Well, Bridie, here's your chance to find out if things can get better here or not. Maybe it's time to take the plunge with a new guy.

'Then I'll see you there,' he said, looking at her a little longer than was merely friendly.

She had a funny tingle in her belly at the thought of him finding her attractive. She sure hadn't been feeling attractive, working long hours and dealing with a constant stream of tourists all day long; she'd felt frazzled and worn out. But she was getting used to the pace of work now. Only the other day she'd paused in front of the bathroom mirror to inspect her reflection. She noticed she had a tan from all her long walks along the beach, and it seemed to make her eyes bluer somehow. She'd spent part of her first paycheque on a trip to the hairdresser and her hair was now layered in a feathery cut that gently framed her face.

Tye turned to walk away and Bridie couldn't help but admire his muscular physique as he jogged down the beach.

'Hey, wait! I don't know where the party is,' she called after him.

'Ask Ben!' he called back, before launching himself into the water and paddling his board out over the shallow breaking waves.

Great. What if Ben didn't want her to go? That could be awkward. She rinsed off her feet under the tap at the side of the apartment building and slipped on her shoes as she walked inside.

When Ben got home, Bridie asked him about the party. 'Tye invited me. Is that okay?'

'Yeah, it's fine. I would have asked you to come if I thought you were into that kind of thing, but hey,' he said, shrugging, 'you're welcome to tag along with me.'

They chatted about work for most of the trip there. It still gave her a thrill to see all the bright lights and busy streets. Ben pulled up outside a weathered old beach house at the end of a cul-de-sac. Bridie climbed out of the car, following him shyly.

He greeted people as they made their way inside, seeming to know everyone. Women in bikinis wandered around, drinks in hand, and men in board shorts sprawled on lounges and deckchairs. She lost Ben almost immediately and found herself standing alone. She could smell the tang of marijuana floating through the air. This was not the kind of party she'd had in mind when she'd accepted the invitation. Feeling awkward and out of place, she made her way out the back, hoping to find a nice quiet spot to hide in while she worked up the courage to mingle with a crowd of complete strangers.

'You made it.'

The deep voice surprised her, and she breathed out as she realised it was Tye walking towards her. Her heart lurched when she saw that he was again bare-chested, his low-slung board shorts emphasising the narrowness of his hips and the broadness of his shoulders.

'I didn't think you'd show up,' he said, coming to a stop in front of her.

He was so close that Bridie could smell the fresh scent of sea and man. He slowly reached up and tucked a strand of hair behind her ear, tracing the side of her cheek with his finger. 'I was afraid to get my hopes up.'

Bridie stared into his half-closed eyes. 'Do you want to go for a walk?' she asked, hoping she didn't sound as nervous as she felt.

'Sure.' He took her hand and they headed through the low shrubs that covered the sandy backyard and down onto the beach. The moonlight was breathtaking as it skimmed the white sand and glistened across the inky ocean, but it wasn't home.

What was she doing here? Really?

'I've been trying to work you out and I keep coming up blank,' she said.

He gave a low chuckle and squeezed her hand. 'Why waste your time trying to work out everyone you meet? Why not just accept people for who they are?'

'Because I'm curious. You never answered me earlier when I asked you what you do when you're not surfing—which I might add seems to be all you do.'

'It really bugs you that much?' he said, pulling her to a halt to look down at her.

'It doesn't bug me.' She rolled her eyes at his cocked eyebrow and gave a small huff. 'Okay, it does bug me . . . a bit.'

'I used to have a high-pressure job in the banking sector. I made some money on the stock market, so now I hire a financial adviser to handle it all while I spend the day surfing.'

'So you don't do anything now except surf?'

'Nope.'

The concept seemed . . . wrong. Where she came from people worked hard; they partied hard as well, but they worked hard first. She wasn't sure how to take this strange concept of all play and no work. Still, it wasn't her place to say anything—maybe his old job really had taken a lot out of him and he just needed to take a break from the world for a while. 'How long since you left your old job?'

'About eight years ago.'

No one went on an eight-year break from work at his age, no matter how stressful their job may have been. It didn't sit right with her.

'Maybe we should head back,' she said.

'Are you always this judgemental, Bridie Farrell?' he asked.

'I'm not judging you,' she said a tad defensively. Was she? With a little sigh of defeat, she realised she was doing the one thing she'd fought against her entire life back in Tooncanny. 'I'm sorry. You have the right to live however you want. I apologise if I gave you the impression I was judging you.'

Bridie turned away and preceded him back towards the house. The wind was beginning to pick up and it wasn't as mellow as it had been when they'd first come down. As they neared the house, Tye tugged on her hand, turning her towards him.

'Wait a minute. There's something I've been thinking about doing all day,' he murmured. His head lowered and she felt the warmth of his breath against her skin as he brushed his lips across her own.

As far as kisses went, it was great. Tye obviously knew what he was doing, but it lacked the knee-buckling effect of Shaun's kisses.

He wasn't Shaun.

This wasn't what she wanted.

Pulling out of his embrace, Bridie gave an apologetic smile. 'I've got to go.' It was time to go home.

Home.

The thought made her stop and catch her breath. Where was home now? It sure as hell wasn't Ben's apartment.

She missed the clean fresh smell of the paddocks in the morning. She missed her cows and their comforting presence.

She missed Shaun.

Bridie pulled out her mobile, scrolling down until she came to Shaun's name. Her thumb hovered over the call button. God, what she'd give to hear his voice right now. Tipping her head back, she searched the silvery clouds above for the courage to call him. She didn't find it.

Lying in bed later, trying to sleep, she couldn't shake the empty feeling inside. *This* had been her dream? *This* was what she'd held on to for so many years? All she felt right now was out of place, lost and very, very alone.

෨

A few days later she was surprised by a phone call from her father. 'I'm getting out, Bridie,' he said quietly.

'When? How? Oh my God,' Bridie murmured as the implications set in.

He'd applied for parole but hadn't told her—she thought perhaps it was because he hadn't really expected it to be granted. When his voice cracked as he told her that he was being released, Bridie broke down and cried right along with him.

Time away from Tooncanny and long walks on the beach had given her perspective on a lot of things in her life. She'd realised that she'd been so bitter for so many years that it had coloured her way of thinking. Childhood hurts had festered in the stagnant familiarity of Tooncanny. Maybe she'd needed to see things from an adult's perspective.

Since leaving Tooncanny she'd started writing to her father regularly. He wrote long letters back and each time she opened and read them as soon as they arrived. Through the letters they were making a fresh start, slowly rebuilding the father–daughter relationship they'd lost along the way.

'Where will you go?' she asked after she'd composed herself.

'Your uncle Tom'll put me up for a bit.'

'No,' she said, then hurried to add, 'I mean, there's no need to be cooped up over there. My house is empty now that Phoebe's gone.'

'Are you offering your house just to keep me out of trouble, Bridie?'

She should have guessed he'd see through her. She might have been making progress with her dad, but she still didn't trust the rest of the Farrells.

'Bridie, I'm an old man, I'm not some kid who needs you to worry about him falling in with a bad crowd. Stop trying to be my mother and just be my daughter. They're still my family. I can't turn my back on them.'

In the end, though, he agreed to stay in her house when she told him she was worried about it being empty. She didn't feel the least bit guilty about using emotional blackmail if it got a positive outcome. If her father believed he was doing her a favour by staying in her house, then she'd milk it for all it was worth. If it also kept him from living with his wayward brother, then all the better.

'I wish I could be there when he gets out,' Luke said when he called the next day, disappointment palpable in his voice.

'Well, it's pretty unlikely they'd give you leave for something like that. Dad understands.'

'Yeah, but I still wanted to be there.'

He sounded tired, as usual. It wasn't as bad as when he'd been going through basic training, but he was kept busy now that his specialty training in the infantry had started. There was, however, a new maturity and an underlying pride in his voice that still sometimes caught her off guard. Her little brother had gone and grown up on her.

She wasn't sure where her offer to come out and help her father get settled in came from. It was out of her mouth before she knew what she was saying. She just couldn't bear the thought of her dad coming out of prison, after seven long years, to an empty house. She wanted to be there for him. It was strange how things worked out. A few months ago she would never have imagined they'd be at this point.

⁓

The beach was miserable, with grey clouds hovering along the horizon. A cold wind whipped at her clothes and Bridie wrapped her arms tightly around her middle as she stared out over the choppy sea.

The water seemed to be reflecting her turmoil. This was exactly how she felt—wild, churned-up and unsettled.

As she turned away, she saw a familiar figure sitting on the beach, his arms linked loosely around his knees as he stared out over the angry ocean.

She hesitated, slowing her steps, debating whether she should keep walking or stop and acknowledge him. Tye glanced up as she neared and for a moment she felt that familiar kick of attraction.

'Hey,' she said.

'Hey.'

'Not going out today?' She nodded out at the waves crashing against the sand.

'I will later. There's supposed to be a big swell coming in.'

'Really? And that's what you're waiting to go out in?'

'Storms bring in the best waves,' he said.

She eyed the water doubtfully. She really was out of her depth here. She wasn't in tune with the ocean. It was all very nice on calm flat days, but on days like today it unsettled her. Give her the open plains any day.

'Wanna hook up later?' he said.

'I think I'll pass. I've got to go away for a few days.' She waved goodbye and turned away. As she climbed the steps to the footpath, the first drops of rain hit and she breathed in the sweet smell of rain and salt air. Something was brewing on the horizon, and for the first time since leaving Tooncanny she knew she was ready for it.

Twenty-two

The late afternoon sun was blinding as she came over the final rise in the road before the *Welcome to Tooncanny* sign. She should have realised that leaving at the time she had would mean she'd be driving into the sun, but she'd been in so much of a hurry to get here she hadn't thought through that bit.

The windscreen was smeared with dust and bugs, and the glare of the orange and red sunset made her squint as she tried to keep an eye on the side of the road, watching for kangaroos.

She pulled into the driveway of her house and instantly warmth flowed through her. It reminded her of snuggling up in her mother's old dressing-gown when she was home sick from school—somehow it just made everything feel better.

She lugged in her small suitcase and the box of groceries she'd brought with her. There wasn't much to unpack; she wasn't planning to stay long, just a few days. Her dad would be released in three days' time and she wanted to be there to pick him up.

Through the back window she caught a glimpse of the cattle out grazing, but they weren't her old favourites—these were black Angus, not her fat little Herefords. It seemed everything had moved on without her. Had she? Was she any different to the woman she'd been before?

She made a slow inspection of the house, opening the doors, pausing outside Luke's bedroom as memories of their years together flooded her mind. Opening the windows, she let the gentle evening breeze blow through and clear out the stuffy closed-up smell. She inhaled deeply and caught the smell of wood smoke in the air. It was a stark reminder that winter was fast approaching.

༄

The town was almost deserted when she pulled up in front of the Drovers the next day. She went in to say hello to Alf and Bulldog and was surprised when they pointed to the flyers pinned up on the noticeboard in the foyer.

It was showtime in Tooncanny.

For a moment she could almost smell the aroma of waffles and hot chips.

The thought flashed through her mind that it wouldn't hurt to take a drive past the showground, for old time's sake, but she quickly dismissed it. It could hurt—a lot.

༄

Bridie stepped back off the bottom rung of the show ring at the end of the men's camp-drafting finals.

He looked as breathtaking as she'd remembered, moving with fluid grace in the saddle. Her gaze followed him as he dismounted and waited for the judges to total their scores. She drunk him in as he calmly exchanged chitchat with his fellow competitors. It was so good to see him again. She watched as his strong hands rubbed his horse's neck affectionately, and she wondered whether it was possible to be jealous of a horse.

The announcer read out the final scores; Shaun was announced as the winner and Bridie joined in as a cheer went up from the crowd.

Slowly she made her way towards the rows of horse floats and caravans parked where the majority of the participants were camped for the show weekend. Shaun was easy to spot in his red shirt and black hat; he stood head and shoulders above everyone around him.

For a minute, she hung back and watched as he rubbed down the horse's massive sweat-stained neck. She briefly considered turning and walking away. What if he didn't want to see her again? Who could blame him? She wasn't sure why she was doing this herself.

It hadn't been part of her original plan, but then she'd seen the canvas signs advertising the Tooncanny District Agriculture Show and a yearning so powerful had grabbed hold of her that she'd found herself driving out to the showground before she'd even realised she'd made up her mind to go.

A year.

Had it only been a year since that night they'd watched the sun set together? It felt more like a decade. She'd changed . . . moved on; had he? She finally felt as though her life was her own, and yet since driving through the deserted main street yesterday, it was as though her past was trying to smother her new-found freedom. Nostalgia was playing dirty, tugging at her heartstrings and trying to confuse her with the sensation of belonging.

With her thoughts still in turmoil she looked up to realise he was now standing very still next to the horse, staring at her as though he'd seen a ghost.

With a deep breath she pushed away her nerves and walked towards him. Even from this distance she could smell horse and leather and man, and she felt a little light-headed.

'Surprise,' she murmured faintly. He didn't reply; in fact he hardly moved at all. 'Congratulations,' Bridie said. 'I caught the last bit of your ride. Looks like those judges finally got it right.'

He blinked and raised his hand to smooth the soft hair on the horse's neck. 'What are you doing here?'

His abrupt question struck her squarely in the chest. He wasn't going to bother with polite conversation. He was going straight for the jugular.

'I'm back in town for a few days. My dad's getting released and he'll be staying at my place for a while until he sorts himself out. I came back to clean the place up a bit before he gets here.'

'So you're not back for good?' He kept his voice neutral, not giving anything away, and try as she might she couldn't quite decipher the look in his eyes. Did he care? Was he relieved? Maybe he had a girlfriend and thought her return would mess up his new relationship.

'Just a few days.'

He gave a curt nod of his head. 'I have to get this guy cooled down and put away.'

'Oh. Right. Sorry, I didn't mean to interrupt. I just thought I'd come over and say hello,' she stammered, backing away. At least one question had been answered for her. He was obviously *not* all that excited about her return. 'Nice to see you again. I'll, umm . . . see you around.' Turning on her heel, she hurried away before she could make a bigger fool of herself. This had been a bad idea, a *very* bad idea.

'Bridie! Hold up a second.'

She stopped and turned reluctantly. Was it really necessary to drag out her humiliation?

'Just give me a sec—it won't take long to finish up here.'

What could she say to that? After all, she was the one who had initiated the meeting; the least she could do was hang around and wait for him. 'Sure, go ahead.'

He led the big horse away to the other side of the float and Bridie leaned on the tailgate of his ute to wait, noticing as she did so that there was a rolled-up sleeping bag, some blankets, an esky and a box of groceries in the tray.

A shiver ran through her as the breeze picked up, and she pulled her long cardigan around her tightly. She wasn't sure if the action was to ward off the chill in the air or the chill of Shaun's cool reaction.

༚

Shaun rested his head against the side of the horse float and closed his eyes. He let out a low growl. She was back. *Just like that.*

How many times over the last few months had he driven himself crazy thinking she would turn up out of the blue and surprise him one day? So many that he'd wished he could just hate her and move on. Then tonight here she was.

It was Bridie—but it *wasn't* Bridie.

There was something different about her. A confidence, an inner glow that he hadn't seen before. She was still beautiful, maybe even more so than he remembered, but she wasn't Bridie Farrell from Tooncanny, middle of nowhere, any more.

When he'd asked if she was back for good he'd held his breath. Could he do this again? Was he going to be able to walk back out there, catch up like old friends and then wave her off . . . *again*? He seriously doubted it. He should have just let her go when she all but ran away from him a few minutes ago, but he couldn't. God help him, he *needed* to see her.

He rounded the corner and saw her sitting on the back of his ute. He took a deep breath before heading across to her. 'Have you had dinner yet?'

She jumped at the sound of his voice and he saw her nervously wipe her hands on the thighs of her jeans before shaking her head.

'Me neither. Wanna grab something?'

She slid lightly to the ground and he forced his eyes away from the tight fit of her jeans around the gentle swell of her backside.

'Sure.'

He noticed that she'd done something to her hair as well. It was still thick and wavy and dark, but it seemed . . . stylish. He had a wild urge to run his fingers through it and mess it up. He itched to see it just the way it looked after they'd made love, her hair as out of control as she could make him feel just by smiling at him.

But those days were long gone.

Dead as his dreams.

჈

Bridie wished she could breathe properly. She'd lost the ability to do that the minute he'd called out and asked her to wait for him.

He wasn't happy, blind Freddy could see that. His brow was creased in a frown and his strong jaw was clenched. He had a five o'clock shadow, and when he swept off his hat as he crossed the rough ground that separated them she saw that his hair had been cut into a short, almost military-style haircut. He looked tough, angry, like the rumble of an approaching thunderstorm. He came to a stop in front of her and she swallowed. She felt tears threatening and forced herself to straighten her spine and get a grip.

'So how have you been?' she asked.

'Fine.'

Okay . . . 'So you and Jack made a deal? I heard you'd gone out on your own,' she tried again.

'We've gone into business together. It's looking promising,' he said, unable to keep the hint of pride from his voice.

'That's really great.' Her smile wavered slightly. 'Jack always was a decent bloke. I'm glad you could help each other out.'

The smell of onions and beer greeted them. Despite the nerves in her stomach, she was starving. They ordered steak sandwiches, and as Shaun passed her one, she wondered

301

if he was remembering last year. So much had happened between them since then.

Looking across at him, she saw the hard edge to his jaw and the stern, almost bitter expression. *She'd* done this to him. Robbed him of his old carefree attitude, turned him into this angry stranger.

They sat down quietly on the grandstand seats.

'So you finally made it to the Gold Coast then?' he said, breaking the silence between them.

She nodded. 'I work in a restaurant right on the beach-front.'

'Bit different to the Drovers.'

Like chalk and cheese, she thought sadly. *Like you and me.*

'So you like it?'

'It's everything I expected it to be,' she answered slowly. And it was. It was bright lights and busy streets, people and traffic and golden beaches.

Conversation came to a standstill again and they ate in silence for a while. She turned slightly and caught him watching her, but he dropped his gaze quickly and reached for his can of beer.

'How's your brother doing?' he said.

A smile lit up her eyes and Shaun felt his breath catch slightly. 'He's down in Victoria, at Puckapunyal.'

'So he did it, huh?'

'He sure did.' The pride in her voice was unmistakable and a lump formed in his throat at the sound. 'You should have seen him marching out. He looked so handsome in his uniform.' It'd been hard to believe it was the same sulky teenager who'd given her such a hard time. 'There's talk of him getting ready to go overseas soon.'

'Yeah?'

'He's over the moon,' she said, shaking her head.

'I guess it's what they train to do,' he said with a shrug. 'Phoebe's over in WA now.'

'Yeah, I know. She sounds happy. I'm glad.'

'I forgot you two keep in touch.'

Bridie thought he sounded a little put out by that. She couldn't blame him; she'd hate to know that Luke was in touch with Shaun and hadn't passed on any news to her. She shifted uncomfortably, taking a sip of her beer. 'How about you? What's going to happen with Jinjulu and your father?'

His eyes narrowed. 'Who knows,' he said, then added with a sigh, 'He'll come around in his own good time. If he doesn't, I really don't care. I thought I would, but I don't. I miss Jinjulu, but you were right—working my own place and making my own decisions has put everything back into perspective. I'm finally doing what I was born to do.'

'How does it work with Jack?'

'He's happy to be a silent partner. I bought out half his mortgage upfront and will have the rest paid off over the next few years. I get to run things on my own terms. He's living with his daughter now and getting to enjoy his retirement and grandkids without having a huge mortgage hanging over his head. Everyone's happy.' He glanced across at her. 'So you and your old man patched things up then?'

'We're working on it. It'll take a while. He's been away for a long time.'

'Time doesn't matter if you love someone. How long they've been gone doesn't make any difference,' he said almost bitterly. 'Look, I have to get back. It was good to see you again, Bridie,' he said gruffly.

'Yeah . . . you too,' she forced out.

'See ya later.' He took the steps of the grandstand two at a time, as though running away from his past. Which, of course, he was. He was running from her.

The hurt that sliced through her was like a physical pain, making her draw up her legs to hug her arms around her knees.

౨

Shaun kicked the tyre of his ute. It was an updated version of his pride and joy, replaced by his insurance company and gleaming under the moth-ridden lights around the main arena.

He'd been so close to falling to his bloody knees and begging her to come back to him, to forget the stupid notion of returning to the Gold Coast and stay here with him. He'd had to leave so he wouldn't make a fool of himself—again.

How pathetic was he? He'd already been rejected once, his proposal thrown back in his face when she left without giving him a chance to figure out an alternative. Damn it, he'd have gone with her if she'd given him half a bloody chance. He was angry that she'd taken it upon herself to decide what she considered was best for him.

Was he really so weak he could just shrug off the fact that she'd left, ripped his heart out, and beg her to come back?

Yes.

The knowledge that he would probably forgive her anything was not something that sat right with him. He had his pride, after all. No man, beast or force of nature could make him sink to his knees and cry like a baby . . . nothing except Bridie Farrell. She held his heart, and what was left of his pathetic self-respect, in the palm of her hand, and he was helpless to do a damn thing about it.

༂

The whole next day Bridie scrubbed and cleaned until the house shone.

The place had been empty for a few weeks now and Bridie wondered if, deep down, she'd refused to consider putting it on the market because she wanted to hold on to a piece of her past. She'd told herself it was a safety net; if the worst happened and she lost her job at the restaurant and couldn't find anything else, she felt safe knowing she still had a place to live, back here.

She left early the next morning to drive to Wellington. Her stomach was a knot of nerves. She could only imagine how her father would be feeling today as he waited for her to arrive. His last few hours behind bars. What would it be like for him as he contemplated his upcoming freedom?

She waited out the front of the prison for him. The moment she saw him appear, all her intentions to remain cool, calm and collected vanished and she was once again that little girl who'd loved sitting on her daddy's lap, tracing his colourful tattoos.

'Dad,' she whispered as she threw her arms around his neck and held him tight.

She wasn't sure how long they stood there, but eventually she leaned back far enough to smile and get a decent look at him. Cupping her face, he gently wiped away her tears with his thumbs and shook his head in disbelief. 'I imagined this day for so long, but this is so much better than anything I dreamed of. It's a new start, Bridie.'

And it was. For both of them.

～

When there was nothing left to do, she packed her overnight case and stood by the front door, giving the little house she'd loved a final once-over before walking towards her ute.

'Remember, the list with the neighbours' phone numbers, bin nights and emergency numbers is on the fridge,' she reminded her father as he stood by the door to say goodbye.

'I know, you told me that already,' he sighed, but she suspected he didn't mind that she was mothering him a little. 'Drive safe, and call me when you get there.' He gave her one last hug before she slid in behind the steering wheel.

'I know, you told me that already,' she mimicked with a grin.

'I love you, Bridie,' he told her, bending down to look at her through the open car window.

Her smile faltered at his words and she felt her eyes burn with tears. 'I love you too, Dad,' she whispered, before squeezing his hand. 'I'll call you tonight,' she said, then reversed quickly out of the driveway before she lost her battle to stay strong.

A quick glance in the rear-view mirror as she passed the *Welcome to Tooncanny* sign brought a lump of emotion to her throat. Tears welled and spilled onto her cheeks. For God's sake! She'd left before. She could do it again.

When it became too hard to see through her tears, she pulled over to the side of the road and let the great hulking sobs shake her body.

After the sobs had subsided, Bridie lifted her head and stared through the windscreen at the road stretching ahead, then looked into the mirror at the road that led back to Tooncanny. With a strength she didn't realise she had, she wiped her eyes, straightened her shoulders and took a deep breath before pulling the ute back onto the road.

૪

The house was old and weather-beaten, a hardy farmer's house that had weathered more than one storm and still stood strong and resilient against the harshness of the environment.

Bridie pulled the ute to a stop and waited. He was standing by the fence watching her. He hadn't moved so much as a muscle as she'd slowly driven up the driveway. Bridie fought an attack of nerves as she pushed open the door and climbed out of the ute.

Behind him, horses stood lazily in the stockyards and she sent them a brief glance before joining him at the rails. Resting her elbows on the fourth rung, she kept her eyes on the dusty yards and the horses as they flicked flies with their long dark tails.

'You on your way then?' he asked, his voice sounding like sandpaper on timber.

'I was,' she said, still keeping her eyes firmly on the horses.

'Was?'

'I got as far as the Tooncanny limits and turned around.'

A silence fell between them, thick enough to reach out and touch. 'Why'd you do that?'

'I realised there was something missing,' she said, taking a breath and turning her body slightly so that she faced him.

'I thought that's why you left—to find what you were missing?'

'It was,' Bridie said quietly.

'And did you find it?'

'Yep,' she said. 'The minute I drove back to town and saw you.'

Shaun kept his face neutral, and Bridie couldn't tell what he was thinking. His horse, the same one he'd ridden at the show, made his way over to the fence and stuck his head over the rail. Bridie watched Shaun rub the big head affectionately. 'What about your dreams?' he asked.

'It finally dawned on me that they weren't mine. They were my mother's,' she said. Despite the heartache they'd caused, she couldn't regret them. The time away had opened her eyes to her life in Tooncanny. It had allowed her to let go of the anger she'd been carrying around inside for so long. She'd needed to leave to know that she wanted to come back—of her own free will.

'I liked my job and I love the ocean, but it's not home, and everything about the place just kept reminding me how much I missed you.'

'What happens if you realise Tooncanny is too small for you? I didn't handle a Dear John letter very well the first time, I'm not going to wait around for a second one.'

In his shoes, she knew she would have been hurt and angry too. 'You're right, I have no business walking back into your life. If you'd left me, I wouldn't be welcoming you back with open arms either.' Pushing away from the yards, she looked down at the dry clumps of grass at the bottom of the post. 'I just wanted to tell you I'm going back to Surfers, to work out my two weeks' notice, and then I'll be coming home.'

She had almost made it to the ute before he caught up with her, turning her back to face him and slipping a large hand around her wrist. 'I wouldn't have left you, Bridie— that's the difference.'

His face blurred as tears fell. 'I'm so sorry,' she said, reaching up to touch his rough cheek with her palm. 'I just couldn't deal with any more responsibilities. I didn't want to risk marrying you, only to look back and wonder if I'd chosen the easy way out, like my mum did.'

'We aren't your parents, Bridie. You can't compare us to them. You didn't give me a chance to put my case. You just left. You left me a piece of paper!'

'I know,' she groaned.

'A letter, Bridie. That's all you thought I was worth?'

'Of course not,' she whispered. 'Look, I was being selfish, okay? I'm sorry I hurt you, but just *once* I needed to put myself before someone else—just once! There was no way you were going to understand that. I had to leave and I had to do it without you trying to talk me out of it, because I knew I'd never go then.'

'I knew you always wanted to leave, but after Luke left, things changed between us and I thought you were happy. I thought you'd change your mind if we got married.'

'I *was* happy, and that scared me.'

Shaun ran a hand over his short hair as he stared at her

with a frown of bewilderment. 'Christ, you would have to be the most confusing, irrational bloody woman on the planet.'

'Yeah, I've been told that before.' She met his gaze steadily. 'Turns out, I went all the way up there to discover that the thing I wanted most was back here in Tooncanny.'

'Hate it when that happens,' he whispered.

She chuckled but it ended in a rough sob, and she leaned into his open arms gratefully. 'I'm so sorry I put you through that. I don't deserve a second chance, but I'm hoping you're silly enough to ignore common sense and give me one anyway.'

He gave a grunt, burying his face in her hair and holding her tightly to him. 'Lucky for you I seem to be a slow learner where you're concerned.'

She looked up and kissed him with everything she had in order to rid herself of all the pain, sorrow and heartache she'd held on to for so long, replacing it with a feeling so powerful and all-encompassing that she thought she might collapse under the weight of it.

Behind them, the sun was about to set, throwing its fiery reds and oranges across the trunks of the trees around them.

Bridie pulled back and looked at Shaun. 'There's just one more thing,' she said quietly.

'Am I going to like this?' he asked warily.

'I don't know,' she hedged. 'I can only move back here if you agree to one thing.'

'Only *one* thing?' he asked sarcastically.

'Well, it's a pretty big one thing actually.'

'Okay,' he sighed wearily. 'What is it?'

'You can't ask me to marry you again,' she said, and Shaun frowned. Before he could protest, she added quickly, 'Because I'm asking you, Shaun. I know you have no reason to believe me, but I promise I'll never leave you like that again and I'll spend the rest of my life making sure you know how happy you make me. So will you please marry me?'

Shaun stared at her silently and Bridie felt a moment of panic when he didn't answer. Hiding her disappointment, she dropped her gaze and stepped back. 'It's okay—it was expecting a lot for you to have forgiven me this soon, I knew that.'

'Haven't you been listening? I'm in love with you, you stubborn, infuriating bloody woman! I say we book two tickets to Hawaii right now and get it done within the week!'

Bridie let out a none-too-steady breath. 'I'm glad you mentioned that.' She dug in her pocket and pulled out a folded piece of paper that she handed to him.

Shaun opened it and laughed incredulously. 'You seriously booked two tickets to Hawaii?'

Driving back into Tooncanny, she'd known what she had to do. Bulldog had been surprised by her loud banging on the back door and the tear-stained face that had greeted him, but when she'd asked for a favour he'd let her into the office at the Drovers to use the computer without asking any questions. She'd known it was a risk—there was no guarantee Shaun would even want to speak to her again, let alone fly to Hawaii to marry her—but she was willing to put it all on the line for him as he'd done for her.

'Marry me, Shaun. Please.'

'No.' He shook his head firmly. 'You are not taking away every last ounce of my manhood! You. Marry. Me,' he said.

'Must we argue about everything?' she said with a roll of her eyes, but she couldn't hide the smile that lit up her face.

'We wouldn't argue if you just agreed with everything I said,' he pointed out calmly.

'Then you're in for a world of disappointment, because there's no way we're ever going to agree about anything.'

He drew her back into his arms and smiled. 'You may be right, but it sure will be fun making up after all the arguments.' He kissed her and for a moment she forgot everything except the feel of his lips against hers.

She pulled away eventually and looked up at him, tracing his strong jaw line lovingly. 'Yes, I'll marry you.'

'Well, it's about time,' he grinned, before lowering his head once more.

Tomorrow would be a brand-new day, the first of their new life together, full of endless possibilities, because, finally, she was home.

Acknowledgements

Thank you to Julia: without her, my books would only be half the story they've become. I'm so very lucky to have you.

My long-suffering family and friends, thanks for all you do. Without you, life would be considerably suckier!

Thank you Sophie for taking me on—what have you got yourself into?!

The amazing team at Allen & Unwin: Louise, Christa, Amy, Kylie, Patrizia, and everyone else at A&U who work so hard to bring my books to life.

To all the people I've emailed, rung, stalked and generally bugged over the last few years writing this book, a big thank you: namely, Catherine Finnegan, Neil Westcott, Frank and Paulla Brownhill, Toni Blakemore, David Ross, and Brenton Miller. Also to my fantastic Facebook and

Twitter friends: you guys are amazing, always ready to help me out whenever I send out a mayday! Thank you to my local community, and a big thank you to all the readers who have supported me on this journey. I'm so very humbled and delighted that you read my books.